KU-503-591

THE SHOPGIRL'S
FORBIDDEN LOVE

Jenni Fletcher

MILLS & BOON

First Published in Great Britain 2022
by Mills & Boon, an imprint of HarperCollins*Publishers* Ltd,
1 London Bridge Street, London, SE1 9GF

www.harpercollins.co.uk

HarperCollins*Publishers*
1st Floor, Watermarque Building,
Ringsend Road, Dublin 4, Ireland

The Shopgirl's Forbidden Love © 2022 Jenni Fletcher

ISBN: 978-0-263-30176-2

06/22

MIX
Paper from
responsible sources
FSC® C007454

This book is produced from independently certified FSC™ paper
to ensure responsible forest management.
For more information visit www.harpercollins.co.uk/green.

Printed and Bound in Spain using 100% Renewable Electricity
at CPI Black Print, Barcelona

For Mimi B and all the feisty girls

Chapter One

City of Bath—1799

'There's nobody about. Get over there and be quick about it!'

'No!' Fourteen-year-old Nancy MacQueen wrenched her arm out of her stepfather's grasp and stepped back around the iron railings at the end of the street. 'I'm not doing it.'

'What do you mean "no"?' Her stepfather's eyes narrowed. They were bloodshot, she noticed, with dark purple rims, as if he were still suffering the after-effects of the night before halfway through the next afternoon, which was undoubtedly the case. She sincerely hoped he had a raging headache to go with it.

'I mean that it's wrong.' She lifted her chin imperiously, summoning up six years' worth of resentment and contempt to peer down her nose at him.

'It's your ma's birthday. Don't you want to get her something she likes?'

'Of course I do, but I'm not a thief.'

'It's only one orange. You know how much she likes 'em.'

'Then why can't you just go into the shop and buy one like a decent person?'

'And why can't you stop arguing for once?' Her stepfather pushed his face closer, enveloping her in a cloud of alcohol fumes so powerful she almost gagged. 'I've never known a girl with a tongue as sharp as yours before. You'll never find a husband that way.'

'Good!' she spat back, standing her ground though the stench alone was beginning to make her feel light-headed. 'Because I don't want one!'

'Then you'd better find some other way to take care of yourself 'cos you'll be out on your ear the way you're carrying on.'

'I can manage on my own!'

'I'd like to see you try.'

'I will.' She shoved her own face forward despite the smell. 'I'm going to make something of my life, you'll see, and I won't need a man to do it!'

'Well, until then, you can do what you're told.

Now hurry up before somebody comes out.' Her stepfather's mouth twisted into a sneer. 'Unless you want to spoil today for your ma?'

'My being in gaol might spoil it, too. I could be transported for stealing.'

'Better you 'an me.' A pair of hands descended upon her shoulders, spinning her round and shoving her out past the railings again. 'An' don't look so nervous. You're a fast runner, ain't you?'

Nancy muttered an oath before dragging her feet reluctantly down the street. She didn't know this area of Bath very well. It was halfway up one of the many hills, where the middle classes lived, as opposed to the aristocracy at the top and everyone else, the people like *her*, at the bottom. If she was caught stealing and had to make a run for it, then she could always dive off into one of the side streets, but she had no idea where she might end up.

Which meant that the sensible thing to do would be to run away now and let her stepfather rant about it later, but for once he was telling the truth. Oranges really were her mother's favourite treat. Getting one for her birthday would put a rare smile on her face—and how much was an orange really? A couple of pennies at most. If only *she'd* had a few pennies then she would gladly have bought one herself, but her mother took both of their earnings and handed the money straight over to her worthless stepfather for him to squander, usually on the same day, and apparently ale was more important to him than a birthday present.

She paused briefly to throw a ferocious glare over her shoulder. The nerve of the man to suggest that she might ever want a husband! As if *he* were such a wonderful example! As if he'd ever been more than a stone around her mother's neck, dragging her down. The pair of them together were enough to put anyone off marriage for life. No, she was perfectly capable of taking care of herself, thank you very much.

None of which reflections were going to help with her current predicament... She tensed, aware of her heartbeat accelerating as she approached her target. The pavement outside Redbourne's General Store was an extension of the shop itself. Most of the merchandise was kept inside, but there were a few crates of fruit and vegetables standing out on the street, one of which contained, as luck would have it, a pile of surprisingly fresh-looking oranges. It wouldn't be too hard to scoop one up for her mother. In fact, it wouldn't be hard at all. Frankly, it seemed almost too easy. Just one, mind, and just this once.

If she was going to steal, then she wouldn't be greedy about it. She would be like Robin Hood, taking from the rich, or in this case, middle class, to give to the downtrodden poor, a group that definitely included her mother. And to assuage her conscience, she wouldn't let as much as a drop of orange juice pass her own lips…

A surreptitious glance through the shop window revealed three members of staff, all male and all busy serving a scattering of customers. None of them appeared to have noticed her yet, although they would soon if she lingered. She certainly looked suspicious enough with her head covered in a large woollen cap, but she had no choice about that. A single glimpse of her conspicuous ruby-coloured hair would be all that was necessary to identify her to a magistrate.

She threw one last resentful look back at her stepfather and then leaned over, pretending to examine the quality of a sack of potatoes as she took a single step sideways and lowered a hand. *Closer… Closer… Almost there…* Her fingers brushed against the rough skin of an orange and then closed around it. *Ha!* A rush of triumph mingled with guilt as she stood upright again. Unfortunately, with her head bowed, she didn't notice a customer come striding down the shop steps at the same moment, jostling past and knocking her off balance.

'Oof!' She toppled straight on top of the crate of oranges, knocking half of the contents on to the ground.

'Watch where you're standing!' a man's voice snapped as if *she'd* been the one at fault. Whoever he was, he was tall and elegantly dressed, like a butler or some other kind of upper servant, and obviously thought himself worth several hundred of her, presenting a clear view of his back as he strode off down the street without as much as pausing to help her up.

Nancy opened her mouth to shout something scathing and then bit her tongue, realising that, as horrible as the man was, he'd just presented her with a perfect opportunity. The oranges were scattered about her feet like round, brightly coloured autumn leaves. Who was to say how far one might have rolled on its own? Impulsively, she stretched a foot out, kicking one along the pavement in the direction of her stepfather before clambering back to her feet, thrusting her shoulders back and stalking off indignantly after it. Let the Redbourne's staff think that she was too affronted to shop there! If she had any money, then it would be the truth!

She was half a dozen steps away, about to

bend down and retrieve her ill-gotten citrusy gains, when she heard another voice.

'Excuse me, miss?'

'Ye-es?' She stiffened and turned around slowly, taking care to keep herself between the orange and the owner of said voice. To her surprise, he was young, about her own age or maybe a little older, with a thatch of rich chestnut curls and matching brown eyes fringed with black lashes in a face that was pleasant-looking rather than overtly handsome. It was also a kind face, she noticed with some relief, like that of a friendly and eager-to-please puppy, a spaniel maybe, so much that she was tempted to reach out and pat him on the head.

'Are you injured?' His brow creased with concern as he saw her expression tense. 'I saw what happened through the window.'

'No.' She lifted a hand to her head, self-consciously tugging her cap lower. 'No harm done.'

'He should have stopped to help you.'

She couldn't resist rolling her eyes in agreement. Yes, the man should have, but she would never have expected it. She was young and obviously not remotely genteel. Her shapeless and tattered clothes, which might once have had some semblance of colour but were now simply a washed-out grey, marked her out as a person of little consequence. The man probably wouldn't have cared if he'd driven over her with a carriage. He might even have done it deliberately—and then a second time to really emphasise the point. She'd been a momentary inconvenience to him, that was all. A nobody.

'Were you looking for something in particular?' The boy gestured back at the shop. 'I'd like to make some kind of amends, if you'll allow me. Call it an apology on his behalf.'

'A what?'

'An apology,' he repeated. 'For our customer's bad manners.'

'You don't… I mean…' Nancy gaped at him, momentarily lost for words. Her first thought was that the offer was some kind of joke, but the boy looked and sounded completely sincere. She didn't remember the last time anyone had apologised to her, if anyone *ever* had, or shown such consideration for her welfare either. It felt strange…good, as if she'd drunk something warm on a cold day and her insides were tingling. Glowing even, as if she'd just swallowed sunshine… She blinked a few times, wondering if she'd actually hit her head on the pavement when she'd fallen and was hallucinating. Surely anyone this nice *had* to be a figment of her imagination? Especially a man!

'Who *are* you?' she finally managed to ask.

'James Redbourne. Jem to my friends.' His smile was disarmingly sincere. 'This is my father's store.'

'Oh.' She felt her cheeks flush an incriminating shade of red, horribly aware of the orange lying on the ground behind her. His father's orange! She'd had low points in her life before—quite a lot of them, to be honest—but this had to be one of the lowest. She was trying to steal from his family's shop and he was being nice! Suddenly she wished he would leave so that she could run away and cover her face in shame. If he'd go, then she would make a vow never to even *think* about stealing ever again, no matter whose birthday it was. As for Robin Hood, he could go back to Sherwood Forest and stay there. 'Thank you, but I was just looking. There's nothing I need.'

'But I insist.' To make matters a hundred times worse, the boy reached for one of the oranges left in the crate and held it out to her.

'No, I can't.' She staggered backwards, appalled at the prospect of simply being given the very item she was trying to steal. Regrettably, the movement caused the heel of her boot to connect with the fruit behind her, which dutifully rolled out from her skirts and into view.

She was aware of the exact second the boy

noticed it, his eyes dropping briefly to the pavement and then lifting back to hers with a look of enquiry.

'Jem!' An older man emerged from the shop before either of them could say anything else, his resemblance to the other marking him out as James Redbourne Senior. 'What are you doing?'

Instinctively, Nancy rocked forward on to the balls of her feet, bracing herself to run, but something about the boy's expression held her still. He didn't look like a person who was about to denounce her and then haul her off to gaol. He didn't even look angry. He looked...*something* else, something she wasn't sure she recognised and yet made her feel doubly mortified.

'I'm just making sure the young lady's all right, Father.' He half turned his head, though his eyes never left hers.

Young lady? If her jaw hadn't actually been attached, she thought it might have fallen off in surprise. An apology was shocking enough, but *lady*?

'What's that you're holding?' The older man came closer. She could see by the dismissive way his eyes skimmed over her that he was questioning his son's choice of words, too.

'An apology gift, only I dropped one of them.' The boy reached down, picking the other, incriminating orange up off the ground and then holding both out towards her. 'Here you are, miss, and please don't be put off shopping here again. We'd be more than happy to see you.'

Nancy swallowed hard. She could practically taste her shame, like bile in her throat. She was a thief and this boy knew it and that *something* expression on his face wasn't anger, but pity. *Pity!* She would almost have preferred gaol. She'd let herself be bullied by her stepfather into lowering herself to his paltry level, and this boy, this James Redbourne—Jem to his friends—had been there to witness it. And to top it all off, he pitied her enough to let her go with no questions asked. Humiliation and self-loathing scorched through her. Well, never again! Never again would she allow herself to be bullied or pitied or at the mercy of any man, not for any reason, no matter how *nice* he seemed! The sooner she escaped from her mother and stepfather's house and forged an independent and honest and *man-free* life for herself, the better!

'No, thank you.' She thrust her chin into the air. He might not be angry with her, but she was suddenly, blood-boilingly livid with him. How dare he pity her! How dare he let her go! How dare he be *nice*! 'I don't want anything from you.'

Then she swung about, abandoning the oranges

and stalking away up the street with her head held high, aware of Jem Redbourne's eyes boring into her shoulder blades the whole time.

Chapter Two

One year later, 1800

Bath had to be one of the most beautiful cities in the world, Jem thought wistfully, straddling the bough of a towering sycamore tree in the centre of Sydney Gardens and resting his head against the trunk. The distinctive honey-coloured stone of its buildings took on a silvery hue in the pale winter light, especially when there was a faint dusting of snow on the ground like today, an effect that made the air itself seem to shimmer with millions of tiny, translucent crystals. He'd never lived anywhere else, but he'd visited both Bristol and London on business with his father and neither of them had remotely compared.

'So what do you think of my idea?' His best friend Sebastian Fortini clambered on to a neighbouring branch.

'Honestly, I thought you were joking.' Jem looked across in surprise. 'Why would you want to join the navy? You've never even seen the sea.'

'I've rowed on the river. I'm pretty good at it, too.'

'That's like comparing apples and oranges. You're always close to the shore on a river and you don't get seasick.'

'I won't get sick at sea either, I know it.' Sebastian's face took on a dreamy yet determined expression. 'It's where I'm meant to be, I can feel it in my bones.'

'What does your father say?'

'*He's* not the problem. He knows what it's like to want adventure. My mother's another matter. She says I'm too young to go anywhere yet.'

Jem heaved a sigh, watching a cloud of breath emerge from his lips and spiral upwards into the air. 'At least you have one parent on your side.'

'Still taking over the family business, then?' Sebastian pulled out a pocketknife and started carving his initials into the tree trunk.

'Yes, although I don't mind that, to be honest. I like the shop. I'd like it even more if my father actually trusted me instead of ignoring all of my ideas. It would just be nice to have a choice about any of it. My parents have my whole life mapped out for me.'

'You'd better watch out or they'll be picking a wife for you next.' Sebastian smirked. 'You need to provide the next generation of Redbournes to inherit.'

'Don't joke,' Jem groaned. He'd just celebrated his sixteenth birthday and wouldn't have put it past his mother to be looking for a bride already...and he knew exactly what kind of woman she'd choose, too. Someone modest and calm and obedient whom *she* would get on with, never mind him. And while modest and calm and obedient were all very well, they didn't strike him as particularly exciting. Nothing about his future seemed very exciting. A small part of him wondered whether he ought to run off and join the navy, too, but a bigger part knew he could never do that to his parents.

If Sebastian left, which was surely just a matter of time now he'd got the idea into his head, then the Fortinis would still have Anna to help in their biscuit shop, whereas he was an only child and all of his parents' ambitions were focused squarely and entirely on him—a fact they referred to every couple of days in case he was ever in danger of forgetting. Still, where he lived and worked was one thing. Whom he married, *if* he married, was another and he was determined to make that particular choice for himself, no matter how much his mother *knew best*.

'You know, it might not be such a bad idea,' Sebastian commented, snapping his knife shut.

'What?'

'Letting your parents choose a wife for you. You're far too romantic.'

'I am not.'

'You are! You probably believe in love at first sight.'

'There's nothing wrong with romance.'

'Not within reason, but you'll never catch me losing my head over anyone. There's no such thing as the perfect woman.' Sebastian shook his head sagely. 'There are just women. Some are more suited to you than others, but that's all.'

'That doesn't mean I should marry the first *suitable* one my parents choose.'

'No, but you also don't want to spend your life pining for some ideal.'

'I'll take my chances. Speaking of my parents…' Jem swung his legs back over the bough '… I ought to be getting back to the shop. Are you coming or would you rather stay up here and freeze?'

'I'll freeze. This is good practice for the crow's nest. I need to get accustomed to all the elements.'

'Enjoy your practice, then.' Jem slid his way down the trunk. 'Just don't run off to sea without saying goodbye, will you?'

'As long as you don't get married without telling me.' Sebastian grinned. 'If anyone's going to be your best man, then it ought to be yours truly. Best friend's privilege and all that.'

'That's not funny.' Jem jumped the last few feet to the ground, waved and then headed towards the northern edge of the park where a low-hanging branch allowed him to vault over the fence without being spotted by any of the wardens. It was a matter of pride that in seven years of roaming the park together, neither he nor Sebastian had ever been caught. Chased, yes—countless times—but caught, never.

With a shiver, he tugged his jacket collar up around his neck and started off homewards, wending his way along the crescents and circles of Bath. Apart from a few brief interludes, the sun had been trapped behind pewter-coloured clouds for most of the day and the temperature had barely risen above a few degrees, leaving treacherous patches of ice on the more shadowy areas of pavement, like invisible skating rinks lying in wait for unsuspecting pedestrians.

He'd just rounded a corner when he noticed the cloaked figure of a girl up ahead, slipping and sliding her way along one such patch of ice. She was obviously carrying something in front of her because instead of putting her arms out for balance, she was wobbling wildly from side to side, scrambling for purchase on the perilous flagstones. As he approached, her feet finally came out from under her, sending her flying backwards through the air.

'Look out!' He sprang forward, stretching his arms out and catching her neatly around the waist. Unfortunately, the impetus of her fall, combined with the slipperiness of the ice beneath his boots, undermined his attempt at a rescue as he lost his own footing and they both tumbled downwards together.

'Oof!' He bit back an oath as she landed heavily in his lap. Which wouldn't have been so bad if she hadn't also been twisting around at the same moment, presumably to see who had just grabbed her waist, which meant that her elbow, rather than splaying harmlessly out to the side, connected sharply with an extremely sensitive area of his body. Arguably *the* most sensitive area of his body. It certainly felt like it at that moment.

It took several seconds before he was able to get his breath back and then several more as her futile attempts to scramble back to her feet caused both her and the elbow to slip again, jabbing him in the exact same sensitive area. This time, he couldn't hold back a heartfelt and embarrassingly high-pitched yelp of pain. Once more and his parents' hopes for a new generation of Redbournes were going to be thwarted from the outset.

'Sorry!' The girl finally succeeded in rolling herself over, bracing her hands on the pavement on either side of his shoulders and staring down into his face. *'You!'*

Jem looked up, eyes watering, to find himself confronted with a pair of fierce blue eyes set in a pale, freckled face, all surrounded by a mass of wild red curls. Not copper red either, but *red* red. Ruby red. Scarlet red. Spectacular, stunning, flaming fire red, barely restrained beneath a threadbare brown bonnet.

His entire body actually convulsed with surprise. The hair was new, but the face was not. After more than a year, he still remembered the first time he'd seen it, which was honestly surprising since he hadn't been able to see a great deal of it even then. As he recalled, her forehead and eyebrows had been completely hidden and the rest of her features overshadowed by a large cap; an item which, considering her hair and what she'd been doing, suddenly made a great deal more sense.

'Me,' he acknowledged, pleased both to see her again and to find that she remembered him, too. 'And you.'

'What do you think you were doing, pulling at me like that?' She sounded angry. *That* was familiar as well.

'I was trying to stop you from falling over.' He made a face. 'Obviously I wasn't very successful.'

'No, you weren't!' Her eyes darted from him to the bundle she'd been carrying. It had come undone, strewing a collection of vegetables—onions and turnips and carrots—all over the cobbles. 'And those are paid for.' Her voice had a strongly defensive edge.

'I never said that they weren't.' He wriggled to one side, attempting to extricate himself from beneath her body. She wasn't heavy, but two elbows in the groin was more than enough for one day and she struck him as somewhat volatile. Besides, as much as he enjoyed having a pretty redhead straddle him in the middle of the street in broad daylight, he really didn't want any word of it getting back to his mother.

'Good.' The girl clambered sideways, too, gathering the vegetables back into a piece of muslin cloth and tying the corners into a knot before attempting to get back to her feet. Her face was almost as red as her hair, though he suspected that had as much to do with the cold as with embarrassment. Her clothes looked far too thin for such a wintry day. Her cloak was threadbare in places, her throat was exposed and she wasn't wearing any gloves.

'Wait a moment.' He pushed himself up carefully, holding a hand out in case either of them needed to make a grab for the other again. 'We should cross the road. The other pavement looks safer.'

The girl glanced at the opposite side and then at his outstretched hand dubiously. 'I can manage on my own.'

'But we'll be safer together. Four legs are more stable than two.'

'In that case, maybe we should just crawl and make it eight.' She threw him a pointed look, but accepted his hand anyway, shuffling and wobbling alongside him until they reached safer territory.

'Thank you.' She nodded grudgingly, releasing his hand the moment they were across. 'And sorry about elbowing you in the—' She waved a hand in the vague direction of his trousers. 'You know.'

'It didn't hurt that much,' he lied. 'Don't worry about it.'

'Right…well…' Her gaze slid off down the street. 'I should—'

'So what brings you to this area of town?' he interrupted before she could make her excuses and leave. Despite the elbow-jabbing, he felt strangely reluctant to let her go so soon.

'How do you know I'm not from this part of town?' She sounded defensive again.

'Because I live on the next street and I know everyone around here. It comes from working in a shop and I haven't seen you since…' He bit his tongue, wanting to kick himself for the words. Mentioning their first meeting didn't seem like a particularly good idea at that moment.

'Mmm.' Her jaw tightened. 'I live in the Avon Street district, if you must know. I've just been looking for a job around here.'

He resisted the urge to lift his eyebrows. Avon Street was notorious for its criminal element, which actually made it fitting for a woman he'd first met when she'd been attempting to steal from his family's store. He could practically hear his father's voice in his head ordering him to spin on his heel and walk away from her, but as it turned out, he wasn't as obedient as he'd always supposed. Something about her made it impossible for him to walk away.

Even aside from all that glorious hair, she wasn't like any girl he'd ever met before. Most girls were *too* nice to him. They simpered and smiled and batted their lashes as if they had motes of dust permanently trapped in their eyes. This girl wasn't remotely nice. She didn't seem to care that he was James Redbourne Junior of Redbourne's General Store. It was refreshing. It was real. And just because she'd tried to steal from him once didn't mean that she was still a thief. It would be wrong to judge her simply by where she lived…

'So what kind of work are you looking for?' He smiled encouragingly. 'I'd be happy to ask around and see if any positions are available.'

'Why?' Her eyebrows snapped together. 'Why would you do that?'

'To be helpful.'

'Oh…' She drew her brows even tighter, apparently surprised and suspicious at the same time. 'No, thank you. I don't need any help.'

'Well, if you change your mind, you know where to find me.' He lifted his shoulders and glanced up at the sky. Snow was falling again, filling the air with tiny flakes like sugar. For a moment, the whole scene struck him as exquisitely beautiful and significant in a way that he couldn't explain. The snow, the city, *her*. Most of all, her. 'Hopefully, this means we'll be seeing a bit more of each other in future?'

'Perhaps.' From the tone of her voice, she wasn't particularly thrilled by the prospect.

'I could carry those for you now, if you like?' He gestured towards the bundle of vegetables. 'They look heavy.'

'They're not.'

'I'd still be happy to walk you home,' he persisted. 'In case there's any more ice. I make a pretty good cushion for falling on.'

'You do, but I can manage.' She pursed her lips in a way that didn't brook any further argument, though it was hard to take her seriously when a flake of snow had just landed on the very tip of her nose. 'What?' Her voice sharpened as she saw his expression change. 'Are you laughing at me?'

'No!' He shook his head, wrenching his lips back into a straight line. 'It's just…you have snow on your nose.'

'Where?' She lifted a hand and rubbed it vigorously over her face.

'It wasn't a criticism.' He shook his head quickly, horrified to see that, without gloves, the tips of her fingers looked almost blue. 'It looked sweet.'

'Sweet?' She sounded appalled.

'That wasn't a criticism either. Here.' He wrenched his own gloves off and offered them to her. 'Take these as an apology.'

'I don't need your gloves.'

'I know. I just thought—'

'I'm perfectly capable of looking after myself.'

'I'm sure that you are, but I—'

'I left mine at home, that's all.'

'Right. I didn't mean to offend you.' He put the gloves back on again, aware that he was saying all the wrong things. 'I'm Jem, by the way.'

'I know.' She lifted her eyebrows condescendingly. 'You told me the last time.'

'In that case, maybe you could tell me your name, too? Now that we're sort of acquainted.' He smiled in the way that he'd seen Sebastian smile at girls. Slightly lopsidedly and with just a hint of flirtatiousness. Personally, he'd never met anyone he'd particularly wanted to flirt with before, but for once—for *her*—he wanted to try.

'I could.' She gave him a look that was somehow colder than the ice they'd just fallen on. 'But I'm not going to. Thank you for your help, Mr Redbourne. Now goodbye.'

And that, Jem reflected as she stalked away,

was that. When it came to talking to girls, he apparently had a lot still to learn. Maybe he ought to let his parents choose a wife for him, after all.

Chapter Three

Another year later, 1801

'There's absolutely no point in me going!' Nancy flung a handful of cutlery on to the kitchen table, braced her hands over the edge and scowled at her mother.

'He'll be hungry.'

'He'll be drunk.'

'He will not.'

'He will and you know it!'

'Nancy Margaret MacQueen.' Her mother's face reddened. 'You go and fetch your stepfather home right this moment. As long as you live under my roof, you'll do as I say.'

'Well, at least that won't be for much longer!' Nancy tossed her head, raising her voice defiantly. 'I've got a new job. A good one, too. I'm going to be a kitchen maid in one of the big houses on the Circus.'

'What?' Her mother's expression froze. 'What about helping me with the washing?'

'I can't, not any more. You'll just have to find somebody else.'

She tossed her head a second time, trying to shake off a sharp pang of guilt. This wasn't how she'd wanted to break the news about her leaving home, but as usual, her temper had got the better of her. Half of her felt wretched about abandoning her mother, especially knowing that it would be impossible for her to cope with the workload alone, but the other half was afraid that if she didn't escape soon then she'd end up being dragged down alongside her, doing the same miserable, back-breaking work all day, every day just to support a bone idle, feckless waste-of-space man.

Leaving home wasn't only about gaining her independence any more. It was self-preservation. She'd put it off for long enough, almost leaving several times and then changing her mind at the last moment, but it was time. She was sixteen years old and sick of steam and starch and lye soap, of rubbing her hands raw to wash other people's clothing, of touching finery she had no hope of ever wearing herself. She wanted more from life and she'd never get it until she left this place behind her. Only as it turned out, leaving her mother wasn't quite so easy.

'You know you could come with me.' She reached out impulsively, clasping her mother's hands tightly between hers. 'You could get a job in one of the houses, too. You don't *have* to stay with him if you're not happy.'

'What do you mean? Leave your stepfather?' Her mother looked first horrified and then angry. 'How could you say such a thing? You're always trying to turn me against him and cause problems—and now this! Whatever will he think about you leaving?'

'I don't care what he thinks!' For a moment Nancy wished she hadn't already thrown the cutlery down so that she could hurl it against the wall. She might have known her mother would only look at her leaving in terms of how it would affect *him*. 'He's got nothing to do with me!'

'You've never given him a chance!'

'And you've given him too many. Every time he comes home smelling of ale and other women, you just—'

'Stop it!' Her mother clamped her hands over her ears. 'Stop saying such things! I don't know what I did to deserve such an ungrateful, cruel daughter, but it must have been something terrible. You've been nothing but a—'

'All right, all right, I'll go and find him!' Nancy tore her apron off. 'If it means so much to you, I'll go!'

'Well, you needn't act like it's some great occasion.' Her mother shifted her hands to her hips. 'All I'm asking is for you to go down to the Golden Lion and tell your stepfather his supper's on the table.'

Asking her to go into a room full of drunken men, more like, Nancy thought bitterly, just to be told that he didn't want to come home, not that her mother would ever accept that. No doubt she'd find some way to blame *her* for his non-appearance and then sit up all night waiting for him. Her infatuation would have been pathetic if it hadn't also been so tragic.

'Just bear in mind that I can't drag him away if he says he's not hungry.' She threw her mother a warning look. Much as she'd like to drag him. By the roots of his hair preferably. Through a patch of nettles and then over some hot coals. With spikes.

'Good girl. You know you're almost pretty when you're not scowling.'

Nancy clamped her brows together deliberately. Her many shortcomings and the various ways in which she might correct them were her mother's favourite subject. She was too bad-tempered apparently, not to mention too red-haired, too freckled, too sharp-tongued and too opinionated. Too much of so many things. Well, the way she looked was the way she looked and as for the rest, whose fault were they? How was it possible *not* to be argumentative and bad-tempered when she'd grown up in a home like theirs? She was lucky not to have frown lines already.

She didn't bother with a bonnet, simply flinging a tattered green shawl over her shoulders before making her way through the almost deserted, darkening streets towards her stepfather's favourite tavern. Fortunately, it was easy enough to find him, ensconced in a dingy corner, playing cards with a group of men she vaguely recognised from other similar expeditions.

'Ahem.' She cleared her throat loudly as she approached the table. Experience had taught her that it was best to say her piece as quickly as possible, preferably without stopping. A moving target was harder to grope and she had no confidence in her stepfather doing anything to protect her honour. He'd be far more likely to sell it. 'Supper's on the table, Ma says.'

'Does she?' Her stepfather didn't lift his gaze

from his cards. 'Well, it'll 'ave to wait. I'm on to a winning streak 'ere.'

'Then you should get out while you're ahead. Everyone knows that.'

'Oi!' A man she'd never seen before squawked like an enraged cockerel, revealing a mouth devoid of any visible teeth. 'Who are you and why you tryin' to stop the game?'

'This is Nancy, my stepdaughter.'

'Never!' Toothless leapt to his feet and grasped one of her curls between his fingers. 'She don't get this hair from you.'

'Of course, I don't.' Nancy knocked his hand away. '*Stepdaughter*, he said.'

'She just struck me! Did you see that? Littl' harpy!'

'And I'll do it harder next time.'

'Oh, yeah?'

'Try it and see!'

'All right, then…' Toothless lifted his hand again, only to find his wrist caught in mid-air and not by her.

'Is this person bothering you?'

Nancy jerked her head around, struck with a strange tingle of awareness, as if she already knew who it was, even if it couldn't be, not here, not again…and yet it was. She'd only seen those brown puppy-dog eyes twice, the last time just over a year ago, but she had a feeling she would have recognised them anywhere, even if the look in them now was different from anything she'd ever seen there before. They—*he*—looked furious. *James Redbourne. Jem to his friends.* That detail had stuck in her mind from their first meeting. But what was he doing there now?

'What's it to you?' Toothless answered before she could find her voice again.

'I don't like to see ladies being bothered.'

'Ladies?' Her stepfather finally saw fit to intervene. 'You're 'avin' a laugh. Ain't nothin' ladylike about this one. What's it to do with you anyway?' He turned his gaze accusingly towards her. 'Do you know 'im?'

'Don't be daft.' Nancy glared back. 'I only came to deliver a message and that's done so now I'm going. Come or stay as you like. I don't care.'

'Fiery, ain't she?' Toothless leered. 'Bet she'd be a wild one under the sheets.'

'How dare you!' Nancy drew her arm back, resolving to dislodge any remaining teeth he might have, but Jem Redbourne's fist got there first, sending Toothless sprawling backwards across the table, scattering cards, coins and other players in every direction.

It was like a boulder being tossed into a pond, Nancy thought, impressed, as a combination of shouts and jeers erupted around them, though she didn't wait to see where the ripples would end. Instead she grabbed hold of her protector's jacket and hauled him behind her, barrelling a path through a crowd of laughing and interested onlookers towards the door.

'Run!' she shrieked as they charged out of the tavern together, pursued by angry shouts and a few, thankfully sluggish, footsteps, hurtling down to the bottom of the street before veering sideways into an alley.

'Are you mad?' She dragged him out of sight and into the shadows with her. 'What the hell did you do that for?'

'I wasn't going to stand by and let you be insulted!' His expression was still angry, as if he wanted to go back and punch somebody else.

'Why not? What does it have to do with you?' She lifted her hands to his chest and shoved, suddenly aware that in the heat of the moment, she'd pulled him right up against her, close enough for her to feel the thud of his pulse through his shirt. It felt strong and heavy and for some reason she couldn't fathom, it made hers pound harder in response. 'It might have escaped your attention, but there were half a dozen of them and only one of you.'

'Two of us.' A dark-haired man came sprinting around the corner after them. 'That was a first. I've never seen you lose your temper before, Jem, but give me some warning next time. I'd just paid for our ale.' He shook his head mournfully. 'Such a waste.'

'Who are you?' Nancy demanded, looking him up and down.

'Sebastian Fortini, soon to be Midshipman Fortini. A pleasure to meet you.' The man winked and then peered back around the edge of the alley. 'It's usually me who gets us into these sorts of scrapes, but it looks like we're safe. They were probably too drunk to run after us.'

'Or arguing over spilled coins.' Nancy rolled her eyes before turning her attention back to Jem, poking her forefinger against a surprisingly firm and immovable chest. 'That was a stupid thing to do.'

'That man was threatening you. He'd already grabbed your hair.'

'I was safe enough. The other one was my stepfather.'

'And he let his companion talk to you like that?'

'I didn't say he was a *good* stepfather.' She poked again. His chest really was incredibly firm. 'That's not the point anyway. You had no business interfering in my affairs. *Again.* I told you before, I'm perfectly capable of taking care of myself. There was no call for you to sweep in and help me.'

'Then I apologise.' He folded his arms. *'Again.'*

'Um…if I could just interrupt this exchange of pleasantries for a moment?' Future Midshipman Fortini cleared his throat, though neither of them turned their heads, continuing to glare at each other instead. 'Ah…maybe not. In that case, I'm off to the Red Dragon before I die of thirst. See you later, Jem. Good evening, Miss—?'

'Just Miss to you.'

'Good evening then, Just Miss. It's been a delight.'

'You should go with him.' Nancy narrowed her eyes at Jem as his friend departed. 'We've said all there is to say.'

'Maybe, but I can't just leave you here alone, not at this time of the evening.'

'Why? What do you want? Because if you think that I owe you something for tonight—'

'I don't think that.' If she wasn't mistaken, he actually blushed. 'But it's dark and I need to make sure you get home safely.'

'Oh, for pity's sake!' She let out a strangled cry of frustration. 'I don't need an escort! Do you know how many times I've been sent to fetch my stepfather from places like this? More than I can count. So I don't need you or any other man coming to my rescue. Which you would have learned for yourself if you hadn't interfered.'

'Look...' he sounded equally frustrated '... I'm sorry if I *interfered* when you didn't want me to, but I can't just let you go off on your own in the dark. I'll walk ten feet behind you if you want. You don't have to acknowledge me or talk to me, but I need to do the right thing.'

'The right—?' She shook her head in disbelief. 'Are you *always* this ridiculously honourable?'

'There's nothing ridiculous about honour.'

She clamped her hands over her forehead, enraged, indignant and impressed all at the same time. He seemed too good to be true, as if honour was really important to him, as if he were the very antithesis of her stepfather, a kind and decent and genuinely good man, as if he were determined to challenge all of her ideas about the opposite sex and prove that such paragons actually existed.

He was acting like some old-fashioned knight in shining armour with a sword and a shield and maybe a unicorn to sweep her up on. Which was a surprisingly appealing image, except that it painted her as a damsel in distress and there was no way on earth that she was going to submit to that description. She didn't need a man to rescue her, especially one who'd seen her at arguably the most shameful moment of her life!

Still, there was something undeniably touching about the noble look on his face, something that made it hard to stay angry at him. He still looked just as pleasant as he had when they'd first met and yet his features had changed, too, turning from a boy's into a man's.

The brow was wider, the jaw firmer, the cheekbones more defined. In fact, now that she let herself notice—something she'd absolutely refused to do when they'd met in the snow—she realised that at some point over the past couple of years he'd gone from being reasonably good-looking to *extremely* handsome, with the most gorgeous eyes she'd ever seen. Eyes that were the exact same colour as his hair, she'd observed back in the tavern, chestnut with flecks of amber...

She felt a tingle run down her spine as she gazed up into their swirling depths and found them staring back just as intently, as if he were thinking flattering things about her, too, as if she were a person who mattered, as if she were *someone*. The breath snagged in her throat abruptly and before she could think better of it— before she could think at all—her fingers were bunching themselves in the fabric of his shirt and she was tugging him down towards her, simultaneously lifting her mouth to meet his.

It was supposed to be brief. It was supposed to be just a peck. Honestly, she'd intended to kiss him and then push him away again at once, but once their lips touched, that plan didn't seem quite so straightforward any more. In fact, it seemed downright impossible to let go. She'd never kissed any man before and the sudden spark that ignited in her abdomen took her completely by surprise, even more so when, instead of petering out, it flared and then spread, coursing through her bloodstream until her entire body was enveloped with heat.

Instead of moving away, she found herself leaning closer, too, her fingers claiming more and more of his shirt as he gave a low murmur of surprise and then swept his arms around her waist, splaying his fingers across her lower back and pinning her against him.

He'd grown since the last time they'd met, she realised, arching her body backwards, so that now he was half a head taller than she was. Broader, too, not to mention muscular and brawny and other things she didn't know the words for. He even smelled good. Musky with a faint hint of pine needles. She breathed the scent in, completely swept up in the moment, as if the kiss had unleashed a whole new range of feelings inside her. The whole experience was heady and intoxicating and so hot that she felt in genuine danger of being scorched.

That thought gave her the strength to push him away.

'Nancy MacQueen,' she announced as he gazed down at her, panting slightly, his expression stunned. 'Now stop being so nice and leave—me—alone.'

Then she was off, darting around the corner and away down the street before he had a chance to recover from the shock.

To her chagrin, it took her a couple of hours to cool down.

Chapter Four

One more year later, 1802

'What do *you* want?' Nancy stood on the back doorstep of her employer's residence, rubbing her hands on a dishcloth somewhat more vigorously than necessary.

'What kind of greeting is that?' Her stepfather scraped his foot casually along a boot cleaner.

'The only one you deserve. Whatever it is you want this time, the answer's no.'

'Hold on a minute.' Her stepfather held his hands up, looking so wounded that anyone who didn't know him might actually have been convinced. 'I haven't asked for anything.'

'But you're about to.'

'You're right.' He had the nerve to laugh. 'But it's not for me. It's for your ma. She needs help with the rent.'

'I gave her some money last week.'

'Not enough.' He looked speculatively up at the house. 'It's a nice place you've found to live here. Who'd have thought it, a daughter of mine working in a house like this?'

'Stepdaughter.' Nancy threw a swift look over her shoulder, checking to see whether Mrs Hawkins, the housekeeper, was listening. 'What happened to the money I gave her?'

'All gone. She's lost a lot of work since you walked out. Couldn't keep up with it all on her own, not at 'er age.' He gave her a sly look. 'She hardly earns enough to make ends meet these days.'

Nancy fought to keep her expression neutral. She'd suspected that this would happen, but she'd still hoped her mother would find somebody to replace her, unlikely as that had seemed given that nobody else would simply hand over their half of the wages. It was the reason she always gave her a few extra coins when she visited, but apparently they weren't enough. The arrival of her stepfather on her employer's doorstep was a new and unwelcome development.

'Maybe *you* should help with the washing?' She lifted her chin, refusing to let him see how guilty she felt.

'Me?' He sounded offended. 'That's women's work.'

'At least it's work. When was the last time you did any?'

'That's none of your business.'

'But I thought I was your *daughter*.' She made her voice deliberately mocking. 'Can't a *daughter* offer some advice?'

'No. She can give her mother some more of what she earns.'

Nancy gritted her teeth. Tempted as she was to keep arguing, experience told her it would be like shouting at a wall and if she wasn't careful, Mrs Hawkins would be along soon to scold her for time-wasting. 'How much does she need?'

'Well…' Her stepfather's eyes glinted avariciously. 'The truth is, there's barely enough money to feed the both of us.'

'*You* don't look very hungry.'

'Any leftovers you've got in that kitchen still wouldn't go amiss.' He craned his neck, looking past her hopefully.

'Don't even think about it.'

'Come on, there must be something.'

'No.' She lifted an arm, blocking the doorway in case he got any ideas.

'All right then, but your ma still needs your help. She's *your* ma, after all.'

'And *your* wife.'

'I have other things to pay for. You wouldn't want her to starve, would you?'

'You're contemptible.' Nancy shot him a fearsome glare and then relented. 'Fine. I'll meet you at the top of Milsom Street tomorrow morning at ten o'clock.'

'Tomorrow?' His features contorted with annoyance. 'Why not now?'

'Because in case you hadn't noticed, I'm working! It's tomorrow or not at all.'

'Tomorrow, then.' He rammed his cap back on his head. 'Ten o'clock. Don't be late.'

'Don't be drunk.' Nancy threw him one last disdainful look before slamming the door in his face. Ten o'clock indeed! If he really thought she had any intention of meeting him in the street to hand over her hard-earned wages, then he was deluded as well as selfish. She'd help her mother, but she'd do it in person. At ten o'clock precisely when her stepfather wouldn't be at home, if she could persuade Mrs Hawkins to let her go for an hour.

She shook her head as she made her way back to the bowl of half-peeled potatoes in the kitchen. Giving her mother the money directly probably wouldn't make much of a difference. Honestly, she had little hope of her holding on to it for any longer than it took her stepfather to get home, but at least this way there was a chance she'd do the sensible thing and hide some away. Under the floorboards, behind the loose brick by the fireplace, inside a mattress, anywhere that *he* wouldn't find it. Besides, the thought of him waiting around pointlessly on Milsom Street gave her some private satisfaction. With any luck, it would rain.

The sky was frustratingly cloudless as Nancy made her way through the Avon Street district at a quarter past ten the next morning, rubbing the insides of her wrists across her cheeks as she tried to pull her jagged emotions back together. Her mother had practically ripped the money out of her hands and then rounded on her for the way she'd deceived her stepfather. It had been a wicked thing to do, apparently, as well as ungrateful in some unspecified way, especially since the whole situation was all *her* fault for abandoning them in the first place.

Nancy had listened to the accusations in silence for a few minutes and then left at the point the comments had turned personal. Usually she argued back, but today she felt too weary. Weary of the whole situation, of feeling so perpetually angry and frustrated, not just with her mother and stepfather, but at herself for not being able to make a clean break when she'd left home. At the rate she was handing over her wages, she might as well have stayed washing clothes.

Now she trudged onwards, occasionally pressing a hand to her chest as she tried to soothe the bruised heart underneath. Meetings with her mother always left her feeling like this, as if she were dragging a large boulder behind her, one that seemed to get bigger and heavier every time they met. She knew that it would drag her backwards given half a chance, but no matter how big it became or how frayed the cord that connected them, she couldn't seem to let go. Her mother was the only family she had left. And if she hadn't felt lonely and depressed before, that thought made her feel thoroughly miserable.

The sound of laughter on the street ahead startled her out of her thoughts. She'd been staring so intently at the pavement that she hadn't paid much attention to the route she'd been taking back to the Circus, simply walking in an uphill direction, but now she realised that her footsteps had led her almost directly to Redbourne's General Store, a place she'd deliberately avoided for the past three years, ever since the day of her disgrace.

She stopped and stood absolutely still for a

few seconds, staring at the scene ahead while trying to decide whether to turn around and take a different route or to keep going. The laughter was coming from a thin, elderly man standing on the pavement beside a rickety-looking handcart, chatting happily to another, younger man who was busy lifting boxes of produce into the cart for him—a man who, at that precise moment, struck her as the most utterly gorgeous specimen of masculinity she'd ever set eyes upon.

Jem Redbourne.

Her pulse kicked and then accelerated wildly. She'd thought that he'd grown the last time she'd seen him, but now he was even bigger. Not remotely like a puppy any more—more like a bear. Taller and broader and decidedly more muscular, as if he'd spent the entire year since they'd last met lifting barrels. And the last time they'd met had been on a spring evening when he'd punched a man to protect her honour and she'd kissed him in an alleyway…

Had it really been a whole year? She swallowed, her throat turning dry at the memory. She'd convinced herself afterwards that the kiss had only been a means of distracting him so that she could run away, but in all honesty, her thoughts hadn't been anywhere near that coherent. She'd acted on impulse, kissing him simply because she'd *wanted* to kiss him, and for a few insane seconds, she'd actually enjoyed it, too—her one and only, entirely out of character, never-to-be-repeated kiss. Watching him now, she could vividly recall the feeling of his lips, soft and smooth and warm against hers, as well as the bristles on his jaw, scratching lightly against her chin before she'd pulled away, even the scent of him...pine needles. The memory was just as intense as if it had happened yesterday, heating her blood all over again.

She wondered if he remembered it, too.

A sigh pushed its way past her lips before she could stop it. He was smiling as he talked to the old man. *Of course* he was smiling. He was being his usual too-good-to-be-true self. Because he *had* to be too good to be true, didn't he? Nobody could be that nice and decent, could they? Not for no reason. And yet he *seemed* to be genuine, the kind of man who wouldn't send you off to gaol for stealing an orange, who would run to catch you when you slipped on ice, who would stand up for you when some drunken fool made a grab for your hair. And if he really *was* that genuinely nice, then maybe he was also the kind of person who would listen to someone who needed to talk, especially when that someone had nobody else they could talk to. The other staff she lived with were pleasant enough, but there was nobody she could truly call a friend, nobody she could open her heart to, especially about a subject as personal as her mother. Whereas Jem… well, he wasn't a friend, either, and yet she had the strangest feeling that if she could talk to anyone, it was him.

She curled her fingers into her palms, considering. It would be the first time in her life that she'd ever asked a man for anything, but Jem had kind eyes. She'd always thought that. And they'd kissed. Surely that counted for something? Could she—should she—talk to him?

No sooner had the thought entered her head than the old man pulled his cart away, rolling off down the street at the same moment as Jem Redbourne turned his head and looked straight at her.

Jem lifted a hand to tip his cap, momentarily forgetting that he wasn't wearing one and tapping his forehead instead, thrown into confusion by the sight of the woman standing a few yards away. For a disorientated moment he was back in a dark alleyway a year before, with her small but determined hands grasping his shirt and her beautiful, bow-shaped, incredibly argumentative lips pressed against his. Their kiss had been a few heady seconds of bliss before she'd run away into the darkness, but he remembered every detail: the soapy scent of her skin, the lush warmth of her mouth, the faint taste of honey, not to mention the sudden rush of blood to his head that seemed to have had some kind of stunning effect on his senses because by the time he'd come back to himself, there had been no sign of her, though he'd walked the streets for almost an hour afterwards, searching. It had been his first kiss, one that had somehow spoiled him for any others because the few he'd had since hadn't felt remotely the same. Not even close.

Unfortunately, while the experience had been deeply memorable for him, it had clearly meant nothing to her. Less than nothing if the speed with which she'd run away had been anything to judge by. It had just been a ploy, a way to stun him for a few seconds to give her a chance to escape, which had worked. He hadn't set eyes on her again until today and today he wasn't sure whether to feel pleased, excited or alarmed.

'Good morning, Miss MacQueen.' He remembered how to speak at last, adopting what he hoped was a nonchalant expression, one that faded the moment he took a couple of steps closer. Aside from the fact that she wasn't moving, the skin across her forehead was taut and her blue eyes held a dejected, uncertain look. *Definitely* not an expression he'd ever seen on her face before. 'Are you unwell?'

'No.' She blinked several times in rapid succession. 'Why?'

'You look upset.'

She opened her mouth as if she were about to deny it and then changed her mind. 'I've just been to visit my mother. She tends to have that effect.'

'I'm sorry to hear that.' He reached for an empty crate, turning it over and pushing it towards her. 'Perhaps you'd like to sit down and rest for a few moments? It's a fair walk from Avon Street.'

'I can't.' To his surprise, she sounded genuinely regretful. 'If anyone were to see me, I'd lose my position.'

'Ah.' He nodded. That was probably true, especially if she were seen talking to a man. 'You found a job around here then?'

'Yes, on the Circus. I've been a kitchen maid in one of the houses for almost a year now.'

'A year?' He lifted an eyebrow. 'In that case, I'm surprised we haven't bumped into each other before.'

'Mmm.' She dropped her gaze evasively. 'I don't usually buy the food.'

They lapsed into silence as she stared down at the pavement, looking so downhearted and hopeless that it was all he could do not to reach out and wrap an arm around her. Not that she'd likely appreciate it. Judging by past experience, he'd be lucky if she didn't rip it off. Still, he felt that he ought to do something…

'You know…' he spoke slowly, braced for her to snap at him '…you can rest inside if you want? The shop's empty.'

She lifted her head again, her eyes flickering with an expression he couldn't interpret. On the plus side, it wasn't outright hostility.

'I don't want to inconvenience you.'

'You wouldn't be. I'd like to sit down myself. It's been a busy morning.'

'What about your father?'

'He's not here. I'm the only one working today.'

'Oh.' She glanced up and down the street. 'All right, but just for a few minutes.'

'As long as you want.' He inclined his head, holding the door open for her to precede him into the store, amazed that she was actually accepting his offer. 'Here.' He found two stools and placed one on either side of the counter. 'Take a seat.'

'Thank you.' She gave a tight smile. 'Sometimes I wish Bath wasn't quite so hilly.'

'I know what you mean, especially when I'm making deliveries on foot.'

'I can imagine. It must be exhausting.' Her gaze drifted nervously back to the door.

'I'll let you know if I see anyone coming.'

'What?' She jerked her head back around. 'Oh. It's just... I like my job and they treat me well. I'd hate to lose it.'

'I'm sure that won't happen, but if anyone you know comes in, you can pretend to be shopping.' He picked up a tea caddy and placed it between them. 'There. How's that?'

'Very convincing.' She smiled again. 'Just as long as you don't expect me to pay for it.'

'Understood.'

'You know, I've never been inside here before.' She looked up at the shelves with wide eyes. 'It's nice.'

'Thank you.' He stretched an arm out along the counter. It felt odd to be sitting so close to her, this girl he'd once kissed, who he'd met only three times before and about whom he knew almost nothing, but whose face he'd never been able to forget. Sadness aside, her circumstances seemed to have improved since the last time they'd met. Her clothes weren't so ragged and her skin had a healthier glow. As for her hair, that was just as gloriously bright and curly as ever. He wondered how old she was. A little younger than him, probably. Sixteen or seventeen maybe…

'Seventeen.'

'I'm sorry?'

She gave him a curious look. 'You just asked me how old I was.'

'Out loud?' He bit his tongue. 'I mean, yes, of course I did.'

'Although some days I feel like forty.' She sighed. 'Today, for example.'

'You don't look it.'

'You don't have to lie.'

'I'm not. You look nice. Pretty.' He ran a finger around the inside of his collar. He'd thought his ability to talk to girls had improved somewhat over the past couple of years, but apparently not with her.

'Thank you.'

'You're welcome.' He cleared his throat awkwardly. 'You know, if you want to talk about whatever's upset you, I'm a good listener.'

'I know.' She blinked. 'I mean, you've always seemed like you would be.'

'I would never repeat anything you told me either.'

'I doubt anyone else would be interested.'

'But *I* am.'

Her blue eyes widened as if she wasn't sure what to make of that.

'If you think it would help, that is,' he added quickly. 'I don't want to pry.'

There was a long silence while she chewed on her bottom lip, her expression wavering as if she were having some kind of internal argument with herself, before the words burst forth in a torrent. 'It's my mother. She's so infuriating!'

'In what way?'

'Every way!' She shuffled on her stool. 'She and I used to be close. As close as any mother and daughter could be. My father died when I was six and for the next two years, it was just the two of us. We did everything together. She was so strong and independent and I thought that nothing would ever come between us. *Then* she met the man who became my stepfather.' She screwed her mouth up, a pained expression crossing her face.

'He seemed nice at first, charming even, but once he'd moved in and had his feet under the table, everything changed, including my mother. It was like she was obsessed with him. She still is, even though he doesn't make her happy. He doesn't even work any more. He just drinks and expects her to keep him in ale and card money and the worst of it is that she tolerates it!

'I don't understand how she can let him treat her so badly, how she can make such a fool of herself over a man, but if I say anything, *I'm* the one in the wrong. And then she says that I never gave him a chance, but I did! Some days, I find it hard to believe she's still my mother. All he does is drag her down and down and she lets him.' She paused for breath. 'It makes visiting her a trial.'

'I'm sorry.' Jem knitted his brows, slowly absorbing everything she'd just told him, willing no customers to walk in and disturb them. He felt as though he were seeing a completely new, communicative side of her, but he suspected that anything as abrupt as the doorbell ringing might jolt her back to her normal abrasive self. 'That does sound difficult.'

'I know I should stop arguing and just go along with whatever she says, but I can't. It would be like giving up on her.' Nancy slumped forward across the counter, her gaze inward-looking. 'So I don't know what to do.'

'Forgive me for asking, but does your stepfather ever hurt her?'

'No. He's lazy and selfish, but he's not violent, if that's what you mean. He just uses her.'

'Maybe she loves him?'

'That's not love.' Her voice hardened. 'Love

means kindness and respect and taking care of each other, doesn't it?'

'I think so, yes, but not everyone is the same.' He paused sympathetically. 'What was your real father like?'

'Honestly, I don't remember much about him, just a voice and a smile. My stepfather *never* smiles, not properly. Nor does my mother any more. I don't remember the last time her lips even twitched. Not around me anyway. All we do now is argue. She thinks that I judge her, which I do. A lot.' Her eyes flashed. 'But I can't help how I feel.'

'I know.'

'And I shouldn't have to apologise for it either.'

'I agree.'

'So you see, there's nothing to be done. That's why I got a job as a maid and left home. I had to. I couldn't live that way any more, working from dawn until dusk and then handing all of my wages over to a man I despised as if I owed him anything. I want to make something of my life.'

She lifted her chin and then dropped it abruptly again. 'But my stepfather says that I've abandoned her and he's right. I *know* I did the right thing by leaving, but I still feel like a terrible daughter. And I can't see any way to make things better either except for giving her money, which is never enough. Sometimes I think I ought to stop seeing her entirely, but I can't do that. I love her.'

'Then you're not a terrible daughter.' Jem leaned forward, laying his arms across the counter beside hers. 'Sometimes you have to put yourself first, especially when somebody else is holding you back. You're not bad. You're brave.'

'Brave?' She sounded sceptical.

'Yes. It takes courage to leave a situation like that, to assert yourself and be your own person. There have been lots of times when I've wished I had that kind of courage.'

'*You?* Something tells me that your parents and mine don't have a huge amount in common.'

'Maybe not, but that doesn't mean mine are always easy to deal with.' He was the one who glanced towards the door this time, making sure that nobody had crept in and was listening. 'I don't mean to complain. I know that our situations are different and I know that I'm lucky. One day this whole business will be mine, but in the meantime, it's like I'm still a child. Sometimes I think that my father still sees me as a ten-year-old boy, but there are so many things I'd like to do with the place. Actually, not with *this* place.

'I want us to move into bigger premises. I want to store a bigger range of produce, to take on more staff, too. I want a chance to prove myself, to make something of my life that isn't just continuing my father's legacy. To build my *own* legacy. I have so many ideas, but…'

'Your parents won't let you?' she said when his voice trailed away.

'My father won't even listen.' He smiled ruefully.

'Then why don't you be brave, too? Set up your own shop.' Her eyes flickered mischievously. 'A rival one.'

'I can just imagine my father's face.'

'It would force him to take you seriously. He wouldn't be able to hold you back then.'

'That's true, but I couldn't do that to my father. He'd be devastated.' He drew in a deep breath and then let it out again in a sigh. 'Or maybe I'm making excuses and I'm just not as brave as you.'

'I doubt that. Have you spoken to your father about how you feel?'

'I've tried.' He nodded, wondering how they'd got on to this subject. He was supposed to be listening to her problems, not telling her his, only now that he'd started talking, he wanted to keep going. It was a long time since he'd talked properly to anyone, about anything other than ledgers and shopkeeping, that was, ever since Sebastian had finally left to join the navy. Now he realised how much he missed having somebody to talk to. 'It just never seems to be a good time, especially at the moment.'

'Why especially?'

He grimaced. 'My mother collapsed a few months ago. Upstairs in my father's office.' He lifted his eyes to the ceiling. 'It was her heart.'

'I'm sorry to hear that. How is she now?'

'Better. She'll never be quite the same, I think. She can't do as much and she needs more rest, but she puts on a brave face.' He clenched his jaw. 'Only sometimes I wish that she wouldn't. It might force my father to come to terms with what's happened, but he refuses to accept anything's changed. Maybe that's why he won't listen to me. It's like he thinks that if everything else stays the same as it was before, then it means nothing's happened and there's no danger of her collapsing again. Which there is, but I can't talk to him about that either.' He spread his hands out. 'So you see, it's not a good time for talking about my own ambitions.'

'No, I suppose not. You're a good son.'

'Or a cowardly one.'

She tipped her head sideways with the air of

an inquisitive robin. 'Would you say that they've been good parents?'

'The best.' He was slightly offended by the question. 'I couldn't have asked for better ones.'

'And you still feel close to them?'

'Yes. Very.'

'Then that's the difference between me and you. My mother and I used to be close, but now all we ever do is argue and insult each other. It makes it a lot easier for me to be brave, if that's what I'm really being. So don't call yourself cowardly. You don't deserve it.'

'Then I won't.' He held on to her gaze. 'On condition that you don't call yourself a bad daughter either.'

'All right.' She laughed. 'You have an agreement.'

He almost fell off his stool, taken aback by the sound of her laughter. It was the first time that he'd ever seen her smile properly and the sight was as warm and vibrant as her hair, with added dimples. Three of them, on either side of her mouth, one on the left, two on the right. He found his gaze drawn inexorably to her lips. For once, they weren't set into an angry line. Instead they looked plump and full and tempting. As he watched, her tongue darted out, licking along the seam, causing an instantaneous reaction in the lower half of his body.

'You know, you really have made me feel better.' Obviously, she wasn't a mind-reader because she was still smiling.

'I'm glad I could help.' He was suddenly, extremely glad to be sitting down.

'I appreciate it.' She reached a hand out and placed her fingers gently on his wrist. 'Truly.'

He stiffened at the contact, aware of his body temperature soaring and his pulse thrumming, far too loudly, in his head. He didn't seem to be able to move either, as if her fingers were actually pinning him down. Even his expression felt strangely immobile, as if he were frozen in the moment while the world shifted around him.

For a few seconds, he simply stared at her while she stared back at him, unable to blink or to breathe, wondering if time had actually just stopped and they were each going to remain exactly as they were, trapped in the moment for ever—which didn't seem so bad, to be honest, although he'd prefer it if she kissed him again—before she pulled her hand away abruptly, jumping up from her seat with a start as if she hadn't known what her own fingers had been doing.

'In any case, I won't be a kitchen maid for much longer if I don't get back to work soon.'

She was already walking briskly towards the door. 'The housekeeper was kind to let me go for an hour, but we'll be preparing luncheon soon.'

'I hope that things improve with your mother,' he called after her, still unable to get up from behind the counter.

She looked back as she reached for the door handle, though she seemed to have trouble meeting his eyes. 'So do I and I hope that your mother recovers, too. *And* that you talk to your father.'

'I will.' He inclined his head. 'Some day. I promise.'

'Good.' She opened the door, although she didn't go through it, her expression turning sombre. 'Do you remember the first day we met? Out on the pavement here?'

'I do.'

'I was trying to steal from you.' She looked directly at him again. 'But you already knew that, didn't you?'

'Yes.' There didn't seem much point in denying it.

'I was going to take an orange for my mother, as a gift for her birthday, but that's no excuse. I've never done anything like it again.'

'You didn't do it the first time. You wouldn't take that orange even when I tried to give it to you.'

'I couldn't. I haven't touched one since. I don't

even like the colour any more.' She pulled her shoulders back. 'I'm not a thief. I wanted you to know that.'

'I do.' He decided it was finally safe to get up and go after her. 'I wouldn't have held an orange against you anyway.'

Instead of smiling as he'd hoped, her face took on a puzzled expression. 'Are you really this nice?'

He stopped halfway across the shop floor. 'What do you mean?'

'I've just never met anyone so nice before, especially a man. It's hard to believe that you're real.'

'You say that like I ought to be in a circus.'

'Maybe you should. In my experience, men are only nice when they want something in return.'

'I told you before, I'm not like that.' He took another step closer, moving slowly and deliberately, approaching her as if she were a wild cat. 'But I enjoyed our talk. Maybe we could do it again some time? As friends, I mean.'

She didn't answer at once, her gaze roaming over his face for a few seconds before a shutter descended over her eyes. 'No. Thank you for listening to me, but, no. We're not friends and this…' She waved a hand between them. 'This can never happen again.'

Jem opened his mouth to make some reply, but she was already out of the door and gone.

Again.

Chapter Five

Four years later, May 1806

'Then the Baroness called me into her private sitting room to see her!' Nancy announced, inhaling the spicy aroma of cinnamon as she pushed a rolling pin industriously back and forth across the kitchen table. 'I thought that I'd done something wrong and she was about to dismiss me.'

'She can be quite intimidating.' Henrietta, her friend, co-worker and fellow resident of Belles Biscuit Shop, hoisted a bag of flour on to the table. Despite the heat and activity of the kitchen, she still looked as perfect as a heroine in some oil painting. Helen of Troy, maybe. Or Guinevere. If she hadn't also been so lovely and soft-hearted, it would have been quite easy to re-sent her, Nancy thought affectionately. 'So what happened next?'

'She said that a little bird had told her I preferred working here instead of as her kitchen maid and that she ought to be quite offended.'

'That sounds like her. What did you say in reply?'

'Nothing. I was still trying to think of an answer when she said she applauded my good judgement and that I ought to move my belongings over straight away.'

'Then it's all worked out for the best.' Henrietta laughed as she tipped the flour into a bowl set on some scales. 'I think I'd be scared to have her as my grandmother-in-law, but Anna seems very fond of her.'

'I'm very grateful to her—to both of them. I *do* prefer working here. I feel like I've finally found the place I belong. And I love baking.'

'Well, that's perfect because I love you being here, too.' Henrietta tipped the contents of her bowl into another, larger one. 'I'm still nervous about managing the place for Anna now that she's moving to Derbyshire. It helps to have a friend working alongside me.'

Nancy beamed, feeling a warm glow at the words. Belles Biscuit Shop was more than a place of business. It was a real home, with real friends, too. She'd never had any of those before and it was a wonderful feeling. At long last, she felt that she was making a success of her life. Even her relationship with her mother wasn't quite so fraught these days, or at least they'd both lost the will to argue, which meant that the biggest problem she had now was her yellow shop gown.

She shuddered as she glanced at it hanging on the back of the kitchen door, ready for when they opened the shop. The style was pretty enough, but she absolutely loathed the colour. Yellow was all very well for a blonde with a perfect complexion like Henrietta, but it was downright impossible for a person with red hair. One of these days, she would make a formal request to Anna for a change. Just about any other shade would do. Anything but yellow—and maybe orange.

'I think you're going to be a wonderful manager,' she reassured Henrietta, nudging her thoughts firmly away from anything citrusy. 'And I'm happy to help with whatever you need.'

'Thank you.' Henrietta smiled one of the perfect smiles that had half the male population of Bath drooling after her. 'In that case, we need two dozen more lemons, if you wouldn't mind popping to Redbourne's later?'

Anything but that... There was a heavy clatter as Nancy dropped her rolling pin on to the floor, narrowly missing her toes. She'd managed to avoid setting foot inside the new, bigger and better Redbourne's Store on Great Pulteney Street so far, although she'd seen Jem at a distance on several occasions. His shop appeared to attract a disproportionate number of female customers, she'd noticed, but she'd been determined never to become one.

'Oops.' She bent down to retrieve her rolling pin, struggling to think of an excuse. 'I could, but are you sure that Redbourne's are the best value?'

'Oh, yes, Mr Redbourne is very fair and he's given us an even better deal since his father retired. I'm so glad he's moved to this side of the river.' Henrietta began stirring her biscuit mixture, oblivious to the inner turmoil her words were causing. 'It's much more convenient.'

'What about Mr Etton next door?'

'He doesn't stock lemons and you know he's been grumpy ever since Anna turned down his proposal. Besides, Mr Redbourne is one of the few shop-owners who actually employs women so we ought to support him for that.'

'Mmm.' Nancy bit down on her bottom lip, unable to dispute that particular point. None the less, she found herself revising her earlier opinion about the shop dress. As it turned out, that wasn't her biggest problem, after all. Jem

Redbourne was. It was all just so typical! She'd finally found her dream job and dream home—conveniently, all in one setting—and *he* had to move in around the corner! If they hadn't both moved at almost exactly the same time, she might have suspected he'd done it solely to annoy her!

'Nancy?' Henrietta was looking at her strangely, she realised. 'Are you all right? You look like you want to pummel that dough.'

'Oh… I'm fine.' She lowered her head, unable to contort her features into anything resembling a smile. She didn't want to see Jem Redbourne again. The last time they'd spoken she'd been feeling low and depressed enough to let down her guard and open her heart and tell him things that she'd never told anyone else. And he'd done the same. She'd actually had the impression that he'd wanted to talk to her as much as she'd wanted to talk to him, as if they'd both fulfilled some need in the other. It had felt like a true meeting of minds. For half an hour on a spring morning, they'd been completely in tune, completely compatible, completely…her heart clenched at the thought…*perfect* for each other.

Which was why it had been such a huge mistake.

The blunt truth about that day was that she'd

liked him. After their conversation, it had been impossible to deny it. More than that, she'd felt herself drawn to him. Even apart from the size of his shoulders and arm muscles, there had been a moment when she'd touched his wrist and her heart had first leapt and then softened and she'd felt a connection that she'd never imagined was possible, not with anyone. And then there had been another moment when the urge to kiss him again had been so strong that she'd had to leap out of her chair and practically run to the door to stop herself.

All of which combined had meant that she'd had no choice but to never go anywhere near his shop again and, on the few occasions when they'd met on the street afterwards, to avoid eye contact and any kind of acknowledgement that they'd ever met, let alone touched lips. Because she hadn't wanted to like him or to feel a connection. That way led to madness, or at least to ending up like her mother. Men dragged women down, she'd learned that the hard way, even if he'd *seemed* like an exception.

She shook her head, mocking herself for her own past foolishness. In the end, she'd known it didn't matter whether he was an exception or not. That was as true now as it had been four years ago. Because the even blunter truth was that he was James Redbourne of Redbourne's General Store and he could do far better than a woman like her. He *would* do far better.

He might not be a gentleman, but they still weren't remotely in the same social class and it wasn't as if she was a beauty or had anything else to offer. She was a nobody, no matter how much he might have made her feel like a somebody, and he'd probably forgotten her by now anyway. Which was just fine with her. She was perfectly happy as she was. She'd achieved what she'd wanted in life: her independence, not to mention a wonderful new home, a wonderful new job and wonderful new friends. The last thing she needed was a man disturbing her equilibrium.

Even if he already had.

Damn it.

'So do you mind going for lemons later?' Henrietta was starting to look worried.

'Of course not.' Nancy dragged a smile on to her face at last. 'I'd be happy to.'

'Wonderful. In that case, let's get these finished and I'll start work on the window display.'

Lemons… If it had been any thinner, Nancy thought she might have snapped her rolling pin in half… At least it wasn't oranges, but lemons were almost as bad. Well, she'd go to Redbourne's Store later and if he still remembered her after all this time—which was a big if—she'd make it crystal clear that there would be no more conversations and *absolutely* no connections. She didn't want to like Jem Redbourne any more than she already did. Which meant that she was going to have to be ruder to him than ever.

She was going to have to be horrible.

Perfect. Jem stood in the middle of the shop floor and turned slowly around in a circle. Even several months after moving into his new premises, he still enjoyed the experience of just standing, arms folded, looking around at the gleaming mahogany counters, polished oak floors and neatly ordered shelves. It gave him a deep and profound sense of satisfaction. Since his father's retirement, the business was finally his. Still his father's legacy, of course, but in a whole new location, under *his* control and with *his* rules. He was finally his own man. And it was about time.

'You're doing it again.' Owen, one of his assistants, chuckled as he rubbed a polishing cloth over one of the counters. At sixty-eight years old, his days of lifting boxes and climbing ladders were over, but he'd worked at Redbourne's for almost thirty years and Jem hadn't had the heart to make him retire until he wanted to.

'I know.' Jem grinned sheepishly. 'I can't help it. It's just how I always imagined the new place would look.'

'You've done a wonderful job.' Agnes, Owen's sprightly sixty-one-year-old wife, poked her head out from the storeroom at the back of the shop. 'Your parents are very proud. They said so when they visited last month.'

Jem smiled without answering. It was true that they'd said so, although he'd known that his father had been biting his tongue over a few of the changes, too. If only he'd been so tactful on other subjects. Unfortunately, neither he nor his mother had held back from reminding him, several times, that there was still one thing missing for him to be truly settled. He'd been tempted to stuff wax into his ears, refusing to get drawn into that particular discussion again.

He would, as he'd already told them on numerous occasions, get married when and to whom he chose, no matter how many 'suitable' young ladies they persisted in introducing him to. It was just a relief they'd moved out to the country or he had a feeling they would be bringing prospective brides for his inspection every day.

'Why don't the two of you take a break now the morning rush has passed?' he offered. 'I can hold the fort for a while.'

'Are you certain?' Agnes glanced at the door as if she expected a crowd of eager shoppers to burst through at any moment.

'Absolutely. Go and take a walk in the sunshine. It's a lovely day.' He jerked his head towards Owen. 'Make him buy you something nice.'

'I'd be so lucky.' Agnes laughed as she took hold of her husband's arm. 'But if you insist.'

'You ought to increase my wages for this,' Owen grumbled good-naturedly on his way past.

Jem laughed, waiting until they were out of the door before leaning against the counter and tipping his head back to admire the stuccoed ceiling rose he'd insisted upon. Most people probably didn't notice that particular detail—his father thought it was a waste of money, he knew—but it looked beautiful to him. It was only about five seconds, however, before the bell above the door jingled, forcing him upright again.

He turned and felt an immediate jolt, as if all the hairs on the back of his neck had just stood to attention at once. For a moment, everything looked so perfect, he wondered if he was actually dreaming. He'd caught only occasional glimpses of Miss MacQueen since the day, four years before, when they'd talked in the old shop, when she'd told him so convincingly that she didn't want to be friends, and yet a part of him had always held out the hope that, if he just waited long enough, she might eventually change her mind and reappear in his life.

And here she was, looking just as he remembered—no, even prettier—with the glorious mass of her red hair rolled into a messy bun on top of her head. All of a sudden, his parents' words about marriage began to make sense. Not that she was likely the kind of woman they had in mind, but still…maybe it wasn't *such* a terrible idea?

'Mr Redbourne.' Her voice was clipped.

'Jem.' He corrected her with a smile, too pleased to see her to object to her tone.

'Like I said, *Mr* Redbourne.'

'It's a pleasure to see you again.'

Her blue gaze flickered with surprise. 'Is it?'

'Yes.' Something about the conversation felt very familiar. 'What do you think of the new place?'

'It looks good.' She threw a cursory glance around. 'You finally spoke to your father, then?'

'Yes. I told him I wanted more responsibility, otherwise it was time for me to stand on my own two feet and start a business of my own. It didn't go very well.'

'Then how did you manage this?'

'Fortunately, my mother agreed with me. She told him it was time to retire and move to the country.'

'Ah. How is she?'

'Better. And your mother?'

'The same.' She made a face. 'Although we don't argue as much.'

'That sounds like progress.'

'Mmm. Anyway, I'm here for lemons. Two dozen, if you have them?'

'I do.' He reached into a box, selecting twenty-four of the best-looking fruit and placing them on to the counter. 'So…how have you been?'

'Very well. How much will that be?'

He rubbed a hand over his jaw, unable at that moment to do even the most basic mathematical sum. He remembered selling two dozen lemons the week before to another young woman, Miss Henrietta Gardiner, from Belles Biscuit Shop just around the corner on Swainswick Crescent. Which could be a coincidence. Or maybe…?

'You don't happen to work at Belles, do you?'

She tensed visibly, staring hard at his face for several seconds as if she were considering whether or not to answer, before nodding briskly. 'Yes.'

'Then we're neighbours?' He smiled. 'In that case, there's no charge.'

'What? No.' She looked from him to the lemons and back again. 'I want to pay.'

'But I won't accept.'

'I refuse to be indebted.'

'You won't be. They're for Belles, aren't they?'

'That's not the point. Don't be so...'

'Ridiculously honourable?' He lifted an eyebrow and her eyes flashed so brightly that for a moment he actually thought he saw tiny lightning bolts streaking across them, but at least that proved she knew what he was talking about. Which meant that she remembered that evening in the alleyway, too... That was something.

'Exactly.' She pursed her lips.

'I suppose I can't help it.'

'*Try!*' She reached into her purse, grabbed a handful of coins and tossed them on to the counter before sweeping the lemons into her basket. 'We may be neighbours, Mr Redbourne, but we will *never* be friends. Good day!'

November

'Good morning, Miss Carr. Is Sebastian about?' Jem tipped his hat to a departing customer before closing the door of Belles firmly behind him. His best friend had left the navy and returned to Bath a couple of weeks before and, although he was officially staying with Jem, was now spending most of his time at Swainswick Crescent with Henrietta and her nephews. Which meant that whenever Jem wanted to find him, like now, his best bet was the biscuit shop.

'I'm afraid you've just missed him.' The new shopgirl, Belinda, was up on a ladder, stacking tins behind the counter. 'He and Henrietta have taken the boys to the park. She's hoping that if they wear themselves out with exercise today then they might not mind being cooped up in a stagecoach on the journey to Derbyshire tomorrow.'

'It's certainly worth a try.' Jem glanced past the counter, through the narrow hallway that led to the kitchen. There seemed to be even more banging and clattering than usual.

'Nancy's been teaching me how to bake,' Belinda explained, sounding faintly embarrassed. 'Only I keep making silly mistakes and ruining the biscuits. Right now she's trying to make the last batch look presentable so that we can sell them cheaply outside the Pump Rooms later. I'm lucky she's so patient.'

'Nancy?' It took a supreme effort of will to keep his eyebrows in place.

'Yes.' Belinda nodded her head vigorously. 'I know what you're thinking, but she is with me. Truly. She's very kind.'

'I'm sure she is.' Jem smiled politely, unable to shake the feeling that there was something odd about Miss Carr, or, if not odd, then definitely out of place. As pleasant as she was, she obviously didn't know the first thing about baking—or shopkeeping for that matter. Judging by her hands, she hadn't worked a day before in her life, which made it particularly surprising that Henrietta had hired her—doubly so that the short-tempered Nancy tolerated her. Not that it was any of his business, of course, but there was definitely some mystery there.

'All done.' The allegedly kind and patient woman in question came marching through from the kitchen at that moment, wiping her hands on her apron and coming to an abrupt halt at the sight of him. 'What do *you* want?'

Jem held his hands up in a gesture of peace. After several months of being neighbours, he'd grown accustomed to her rudeness. She'd never tried to initiate another conversation with him and he was starting to think that he was a glutton for punishment for even *wanting* to see, let alone talk to her. It was almost impossible to believe she was the same woman who'd opened her heart to him that one morning almost five years ago now—that he'd opened his heart to, as well. Just like their one, even longer-ago kiss, it obviously hadn't meant that she liked him.

Quite the opposite, in fact, if her subsequent behaviour was any indication. She actively and intensely *disliked* him. She thought that he was 'nice', a description he suspected was another way of saying dull. His only consolation was that she seemed to dislike every other man, too. According to Sebastian, she'd even thrown a pile of books at *his* head.

Still, he wished that she would at least *try* to be civil, especially today. He and Sebastian had spent the previous evening scouring Bath's taverns for Henrietta's absent brother and his head was still feeling woolly. As it turned out, men didn't like to answer questions if you weren't drinking with them and buying another round, too. On top of which, he'd had a letter from his father that morning and its contents were lying heavy on his mind.

'I was looking for Sebastian.'

'He's not here.' She folded her arms pointedly.

'So I've just discovered, but that wasn't the only reason I came. Here.' He put a box of marbles and pack of cards on to the table. 'Henrietta said the boys don't have many toys. I thought these might keep them occupied on the journey.'

'Oh.' Apparently she didn't have a retort for that. 'Very well, I'll give them to her.'

'*And* I'd like a box of cinnamon Belles, too. It's Agnes's birthday and they're her favourites.'

'Size?'

'One of the big tins.' He hardened his voice. 'If it's not too much trouble?'

Her blue eyes widened, registering surprise at his tone. If he wasn't mistaken, which he probably was, there was even a faint hint of regret in them, too, before she blinked and it was gone.

'Belinda will see to it, won't you?' She glanced at her companion, who immediately nodded. 'I have more important things to be doing.'

Jem sighed as Nancy tossed her head and stormed back down the hallway, earning himself a sympathetic look from Belinda. It was hopeless. Nancy was never going to mellow towards him. If anything, her manner only seemed to get worse and he was sick to his back teeth of being insulted and glared at.

Maybe it was time to give up on her and move on. And maybe it was better this way. His mother probably wouldn't approve of a woman like Nancy and, thanks to the contents of his father's letter, making her happy had just become more important than ever... If only he could get those red curls out of his head, his life would be a hundred times easier. Unfortunately, after seven years, their attraction was just as powerful as ever.

Chapter Six

Four months later, March 1807

The party to celebrate the opening of Henrietta's Tea Shop on Great Pulteney Street was a triumphant success, not least because it gave the assembled guests a chance to toast the newlyweds, Henrietta and Sebastian, after their surprise elopement to Gretna Green. Everyone was enjoying themselves so much that most people didn't even notice when Henrietta herself, along with Belinda and Nancy, crept away to discuss the other strange events of the evening in private.

Jem, having noticed them huddled together in a corner, had offered the use of his office in Redbourne's next door and then escorted them there like a gentleman. Because he *was* a gentleman, Nancy thought with irritation, if not by birth then by temperament. It was one of the things she found most attractive and infuriating about him.

So now here she was, perched on the edge of his desk, listening as Belinda told Henrietta the truth about her identity. Even knowing what was coming—she'd learned her friend's secret a short while before—it was still strange for Nancy to hear the story again. Even stranger to believe that she'd been working and living alongside a real-life duchess for the past few months, so it was no wonder that Henrietta was looking so amazed. Stunned, really.

There had been so many changes to absorb recently, both personal and professional. Henrietta had got married, left Belles and then set up her own business with Sebastian all within the space of a few short months, and her mind was obviously spinning. It was going to take her a while to catch up and this wasn't the best evening to try. It wouldn't be long before the revellers next door noticed their absence. Unfortunately, thanks to the arrival of a certain duke, circumstances meant that it was now or never for Belinda's confession.

'He might be stiff-necked and severe and about as warm as an ice sculpture, but I believe that he's honourable,' Belinda, whose real name was Beatrix, explained about the husband whose sudden reappearance in her life had thrown their lives into fresh chaos. 'He's not pretending to care about me. He admits he only married me for my money. Now all he wants is six weeks to persuade me to stay married. He won't succeed, but it's my only hope of a divorce.'

'Ahem.' They were interrupted by a discreet cough from the doorway. 'Sebastian's asking for you, Henrietta.'

'What did you just hear?' Nancy sprang off the desk, glaring accusingly as Jem advanced into the room.

'Probably a little more than I should have.' He sounded apologetic. 'I'm sorry. I did knock.'

'It's all right. I trust you.' Beatrix got to her feet, too. 'It's time to get back to the party anyway.'

'How are we supposed to celebrate now?' Nancy demanded, folding her arms around her midriff. She was behaving petulantly, she knew, but her temper was shorter than ever at the thought of Beatrix leaving Belles, even if it was only for six weeks, especially with some unwelcome, unwanted, insensitive *husband*. 'I'm going to stay here for a few minutes.' She shot Jem an aggrieved look. 'If you don't mind?'

'Of course not. Whatever you need.'

'I'll be back before you know it.' Beatrix

squeezed her arm as she went out, heading back to the party. 'I'll see you in a few minutes?'

Nancy jerked her head without answering, simply watching as they all trooped out.

'Well…' Jem was the last to go. 'I'll leave you in peace.'

'Wait!' she called out impulsively. Now that it came to it, she found she didn't want to be completely alone. 'Stay for a few minutes? If you don't mind.'

'If that's what you want.' He turned back, although he didn't come any closer, the look of shock on his face almost comical. After the way that she'd treated him for the past eight years, alternately angry and confiding—to be fair, mostly angry—she supposed it was hardly surprising, though it caused her a sharp stab of guilt, too. Maybe it was time to relent and accept his offer of friendship, after all. Now that Henrietta and Sebastian were married it would be hard to avoid his company in the future. And no matter what anyone thought, she didn't enjoy being horrible.

'So…' She sat down in the sumptuous green leather armchair in front of his desk. 'How much did you really hear?'

'That Belinda wants a divorce.' He gave his

head a bemused shake. 'I didn't even know she was married.'

'She is, but she's not Belinda. Her real name is Beatrix and she's a duchess.'

'A duchess?' He let out a low whistle. 'Honestly, that's a little hard to believe.'

'I know. It sounds ridiculous, but it's the truth. She ran away from her husband on their wedding day, but now they've come to some bizarre arrangement in order for her to get a divorce so she's leaving with him in the morning. It's only for six weeks unless...'

'Unless?'

'It doesn't matter. It won't happen.'

'So, in the meantime, you're running Belles by yourself? That's a lot to cope with alone.'

'I can manage. I'm not afraid of hard work.' She clenched her jaw as she looked around. 'Thank you for letting me stay. This is cosy.'

'I spend half of my life in here so I thought I should make it comfortable.' He went to sit behind the desk, reaching into a drawer and pulling out a glass and bottle. 'Care for one?'

'No, thank you. I don't drink.'

'Never?'

'Only on special occasions. You remember my stepfather? Some people put you off certain habits.'

'Ah.' He looked thoughtfully at the bottle before putting it back in the drawer again. 'I suppose so.'

'You don't have to do that. I didn't mean it that way.'

'I know, but like you said, I've met your stepfather.'

Nancy gave him a measured look across the desk. It was exasperating how he seemed to become more attractive every time they met. Today, there was a new air of confidence and self-assurance about him—which was partly due to their surroundings, she realised. This office was *his* domain. He'd designed it, he owned it and he belonged there. For some reason, it made the air around them feel unusually heavy, like the atmosphere before a storm, popping and crackling with tension. It made her breath quicken, too, the same way it had in the alley just before she'd kissed him all those years ago. Despite her best efforts, she'd never forgotten that feeling.

'I've been horrible to you, haven't I?' She pushed herself up and went to stand on his side of the desk, leaning back against the hard, mahogany surface. 'Actually, don't answer that. I know I have been, but it was never *just* you. I'm horrible to all men. I always have been, at least ever since my stepfather first appeared. I never wanted anything to do with any of you. As far as I can tell, men drag women down and turn them into fools. The best thing a woman can be in life is independent.'

'Not all men are the same.'

'I know.' She peered at him from beneath her lashes. 'You're different. I think I knew that from the first day we met, although I told myself otherwise. You were kind without wanting anything in return, but you felt sorry for me, too. I saw it in your eyes that day. I was already furious at myself for having been so foolish and weak, for letting my stepfather bully me into doing something I knew was wrong, and the fact that you saw it and pitied me…it made me furious. I wanted independence, not pity. You saw me at one of the lowest points of my life and every time I saw you afterwards, it reminded me of that day. It made me feel angry and ashamed all over again.'

'Nice to know I have that effect on women.'

'It's hardly *all* women. And you were always so kind to me in return, like you were trying to prove that there were nice men in the world. I suppose I was extra horrible to you because I didn't want to believe it.' She lifted an eyebrow accusingly. 'But you know, you could have *tried* being rude back.'

'No, I couldn't.'

'No.' She sighed, letting her gaze sweep over his face. 'I don't suppose you could. I'm sorry that I've been so horrible. You didn't deserve it.'

'Do you think you can ever get over it? Feeling angry and ashamed every time you see me, I mean? Because the truth is, I like you, Nancy. I always have.' He made a face. 'Although not so much recently.'

'I suppose I can't blame you for that.'

'But what I'm trying to say is, I *really* like you. So if there's a chance that you might be able to put those feelings aside and maybe come to like me, too, then…' He pushed his chair back, turning it slightly so that his knees brushed against her skirts. 'I'd like to court you, if you'll let me?'

'You want to court me?' She gasped the words in amazement, fighting a strange tightness in her chest. 'After the way I've behaved towards you?'

'Yes.' He lifted his eyes to the ceiling. 'I don't entirely understand it either.'

She gave a startled laugh, her mind starting to race almost as fast as her heartbeat. It seemed bizarre, inconceivable, that he might seriously like her. No matter how nice he'd been in the past or what connection they'd shared, she'd never let herself really believe it had meant anything more than good manners and a passing fancy. 'I don't know what to say…'

'Say that you'll come with me for a walk one day.' His eyes seemed to turn very dark suddenly, holding on to hers in a way that made it impossible to look away. 'Say that you won't tell me to leave you alone after five minutes and then refuse to talk to me for another three years. Say that you'll give me a chance to prove myself. *Trust me.*' He reached a hand out, catching one of hers and toying gently with her fingers. 'I would never drag you down or turn you into a fool, Nancy, I promise.'

She caught her breath, staring down at his hand. It was a trustworthy hand, she found herself thinking, the fingers long and strong and tapered. Before she knew what she was doing, she'd slid her own through the gaps, twining them together. Because she believed him. Because she already trusted him. Because he wasn't like her stepfather and if she let him court her then she wouldn't have to worry about turning into her mother, and yet…and yet…

'But you own a shop and I'm just a shopgirl!' she burst out finally. 'And even that's a huge step up for me. You should court somebody of your own class.'

'That doesn't matter to me.'

'You don't know where I've come from. Have you ever *been* to Avon Street?'

'Once, and I don't care.'

'Your family would be horrified.'

A shadow, brief but unmistakable, crossed his face. 'They'd come around.'

'But I'm not—' She stopped mid-sentence. *Not good enough.* Those were the words on the very tip of her tongue, but she didn't really believe them, did she? No, she believed that everyone was the equal of their neighbour and that neighbourhood extended all the way from Avon Street to Mayfair. Anna and Henrietta and Beatrix had all proven that. It didn't matter where she came from. She was honest, all except for that one time, hard-working and… Well, she couldn't think of any more positive qualities at that moment, but she was just as good as anyone else. Even if a voice at the back of her mind, a voice that was actually two voices, a combination of her mother and stepfather's, whispered the opposite—that she was a nobody from nowhere who'd only recently learned to read and write. *Too argumentative, too strange-looking, too stubborn…* How could she repay Jem's good nature by inflicting somebody like *herself* on him? How long would it be before he came to regret his offer? She knew first-hand what happened when relationships went wrong. Being dragged down by a man would be bad enough, but what if she was the one doing the dragging? How much worse would she feel then?

'Why did you kiss me that night in the alley?' His voice penetrated her thoughts. 'Was it only to stop me from escorting you home?'

'Partly.' She drew her tongue along her lips, remembering. 'And partly because I wanted to see what it would be like. You just seemed so good and honourable. I'd never met anyone like you before. You were almost too perfect. You still are. Whereas I'm...'

'What?' His brows contracted when she paused.

'This!' She lifted her hands above her head and then swept them downwards. 'Angry and loud and *red*! I'm a long way from perfect.'

'Maybe in your eyes. Not in mine.'

'Really?' She inhaled sharply, a heady mix of emotions swelling inside her as he tugged on her hand, drawing her down into his lap.

'Really.' He looked earnest and honest and devastatingly handsome. 'I wish you could see yourself through my eyes. You're beautiful and spirited and your hair is the most stunning colour I've ever seen. Personally, I love red. It's been my favourite colour for the past eight years.

Nancy…' his gaze intensified '…do you believe in love at first sight?'

'What?' For just about the first time in her life, she had no idea what to say.

'I know, it sounds crazy, but after that first time I saw you, it was like I couldn't forget you. You've been in my head ever since.'

'That's not love.'

'Maybe not, but it's something, and just because something sounds unlikely doesn't mean that it's not true.'

He let go of her hand then to lift both of his, curving them around the back of her head and drawing her slowly, oh, so slowly, but steadily, towards him. At which point, she stopped arguing.

Nancy closed her eyes, feeling as if some new side of her personality were asserting itself, drowning out the other, louder, argumentative side and telling her to relax and surrender. As Jem's lips touched hers, she yielded, wrapping her arms around his neck and pulling herself closer, moulding her body against his as ripples of excitement coursed through her. This time she had no intention of pulling away. Instead she kissed him thoroughly, meeting every caress with equal enthusiasm, letting herself believe, if only for a few moments, that he'd meant everything he'd just said and he really *did* like her, that he really *did* want to court her, that he'd fallen in love with her at first sight...

She raked her fingers through his hair as his lips moved to her throat, then up her jaw and across her cheek before finding her mouth again. This time he dipped his tongue inside, swirling it around hers, sucking and tasting and sending strange bolts of sensation shooting straight to her stomach. She felt exhilarated, heady, completely unlike herself and yet more like herself than she'd ever been in her life before.

Her entire body felt more sensitive than usual, every inch of her skin tingling as if all of her nerve endings were straining for attention, while her breasts tightened into hard, sensitive peaks. Even her heartbeat no longer felt like her heartbeat, its regular, rhythmic beat replaced by a wild, unpredictable pounding in her ribcage that made it hard to draw breath and impossible to think clearly. Her mind was spinning in the way it once had after she'd drunk too much of her stepfather's ale. She only hoped it wouldn't make her so violently sick afterwards.

Frantically, she slid her fingers across the broad expanse of Jem's shoulders, writhing with delight as he swept his up the sides of her body, skimming her breasts before curving beneath and cupping them gently. And then somehow she was straddling him on the chair, their bodies wrapped tightly together, his hands on her hips, hers on his shoulders, holding each other in place as they started to move. Writhing and swaying and rubbing together in a way that felt so incredibly good and yet not enough.

She could feel the hard length of him through his trousers, but she wanted to be even closer, to feel his skin against hers without the interference of clothing. No, she wanted more than that. She wanted to tug her skirts up around her waist and feel him inside her. She wanted everything right then and there and as quickly and intensely as possible.

'Nancy.' Jem broke their kiss finally, just enough to speak though not enough to separate them completely. 'Is that a yes?'

'A yes to what?' She panted in frustration. She didn't want to talk and, in any case, she had other things to think about, like how to get out of her dress without clambering off him.

'To letting me court you?'

'We can talk about that later.' She wrapped her fingers around his neck, drawing him back towards her.

'No.' He tensed beneath her fingertips, moving his head back so that his lips hovered a tantalising inch away. '*Now.* Is it a yes?'

Nancy held her breath as the room seemed to sway around her. Yes, she wanted to say. Yes, yes and absolutely yes, but how could she? If she agreed, then his family would be horrified and everyone else would think he was mad. *She* was starting to think he was mad. Which meant that she had to be the sane one and stop him from making a terrible mistake. Only maybe not yet…

'Later…' She tried to kiss him again.

'No,' he repeated, more forcefully this time. 'Nancy, I need to know that you're serious. Hell, I need to know whether you even *like* me. Please, just tell me how you feel.'

'I'm not ready to answer that yet.'

'You're not…?' An expression of hurt crossed his face before he lifted her away from him, setting her back on her feet in one fluid motion. 'Then this can't happen.'

'What?' She stared at him for a moment before turning away, mortified, feeling her cheeks flame as she started to rearrange her clothes. 'Fine. If that's what you want.'

'You know it's not.' His voice sounded rough. 'But I can't…*we* can't…if it doesn't mean anything.'

She closed her eyes, her heart clenching. *Of course it means something!* she wanted to scream at him. Did he really think she would have straddled him if it didn't mean something? Did he think she was the kind of woman who straddled men in general? She'd just shocked herself with her own behaviour, but the words froze in her throat. This was the moment of truth. If she was going to save him from himself, then she had to do it now.

'You're absolutely right.' She spun back around, digging her fingernails painfully into her palms so that she couldn't be tempted to change her mind. 'It didn't mean anything. So, no, you can't court me.'

He stood up slowly, his expression sombre. 'So what was that kiss?'

'An apology,' she lied. 'For the way that I've treated you in the past. Now come on, the others are probably wondering where we are.'

'Do you know how many times you've walked away from me?' Jem reached a hand out as she made to walk past him. 'Because I do. One of these days I might do it to you.'

'That's your choice.' She lifted her chin, hardening her voice along with her heart. 'Go right ahead.'

Six weeks later, May

Jem closed up the shop shutters and waved goodnight to the last of his employees with relief. It had been a busy day and he'd been in a strange, disorientated, apprehensive mood ever since he'd woken up that morning. Actually, now that he thought about it, for longer than that, ever since he'd left Bartholomew Square the evening before, full of champagne and good wishes… It wasn't exactly the way he'd expected to feel. Not bad, exactly, but not good either. Just…strange.

He rubbed a hand wearily around the back of his neck as he shut the door of the shop behind him. He felt exhausted enough to go straight to bed, but he still needed to visit Sebastian and Henrietta and tell them his news before they found out by some other means. First, however, he needed to sit down and work out what exactly it was he was going to say. Which really oughtn't to be so hard. They were his friends. They would be pleased for him. Knowing Sebastian, there would be more champagne.

And if they were disappointed that he'd finally given up on Nancy, then…well, surely they would understand that a man couldn't wait for ever? He could only take so many rejections and insults, too. Some feelings were simply destined to remain unrequited and the only thing to do was move on. They would appreciate that and agree with the decision he'd made.

Probably.

The bell above the door jingled just as he stepped into his office. Obviously, he'd forgotten to draw the bolts. Damn it. He groaned inwardly. Another customer was the last thing he needed at that moment. Probably a picky one, too...

'We're closed, I'm afraid.' He retraced his steps and then stopped, his heart slamming to a halt against his chest as he saw who it was. 'Nancy?'

'Jem.' She looked uncharacteristically nervous, pushing a curl out of her eye as she met his gaze.

'Can I fetch you something?'

'No, I didn't come to shop.' She hesitated for a moment before lifting her hands, taking off her bonnet and slowly removing her hairpins. 'I came to see you.'

'Me?' Try as he might, he couldn't resist letting his eyes drop downwards, his blood heating as her red curls, unleashed from their bun, tumbled in a shining heap over her shoulders, all the way down to her breasts.

'Yes. You made me an offer a little while ago.'

'I remember.' He dragged his eyes back to

her face, trying to work out what was happening. He'd scarcely seen her since the night of Sebastian and Henrietta's party. They hadn't exchanged as much as a word since, which made her appearance now, not to mention her behaviour, even more surprising.

For an insane moment, he actually wondered whether she had a long-lost twin because the temptress standing before him *couldn't* be her. Even if she looked and sounded exactly like her—or the Nancy who haunted his dreams anyway... Maybe that explained it, he thought suddenly. He was dreaming. He'd gone into his office and fallen asleep in his chair and this was all his imagination playing tricks on him...

'The thing is,' Dream Nancy went on, 'I've had some time to think and I've decided that, if your offer still stands... I'd like to accept.'

'You would?' The words seemed to scrape the inside of his mouth. Now he *had* to be dreaming. There was only one offer she could be talking about and she'd been adamant about her refusal to that.

'Yes.' She half turned about, drawing the bolts across the front door. 'Shall we go upstairs and discuss it?'

'Upstairs?' Somehow he got the word out although it was indecipherable even to himself.

Honestly, it was becoming painful to speak. He didn't have a huge amount of experience with women, but there was no mistaking her meaning. The sound of the door bolts seemed uncannily real, too, as if he wasn't dreaming at all. But he had to be. Otherwise this was a waking nightmare.

'You have rooms up there, don't you?' She glanced past his shoulder. 'Isn't that where you live?'

'Yes, but...' He dug his feet into the floor, resisting an almost overwhelming urge to move closer. 'Nancy, what's going on?'

'I've realised something.' She took a deep breath as if she were finding it hard to speak, too. 'I shouldn't have said what I said six weeks ago. I shouldn't have walked away from you. I made a mistake.'

'But... I don't understand. You said you didn't want me. You *said* it didn't mean anything.'

'I know, but I lied. I was afraid. That night...' She paused to lick her lips. 'It was all so sudden, I didn't know how to react. At first, I couldn't believe that you really liked me and then I panicked. I wasn't even sure which I was more afraid of, of being dragged down or of doing the dragging. The truth is, I *do* like you and it did mean something, but I thought that sooner or later you'd realise you'd made a mistake and then you'd be stuck with me. I thought that the best thing I could do for you was to walk away. I told myself that you'd thank me for it one day.'

'So why change your mind now? What's changed?'

'A lot of things.' She held on to his gaze, her own clearer and calmer now than he'd ever seen it. 'I've had time to think since Beatrix left and I've come to realise that I've been letting my fears control me. It's so much easier to believe the bad things people say about you than the good, but I don't want to think that way any more.'

She lifted her chin, folding her hands neatly in front of her. 'I've just come from Henrietta. She's had a letter from Beatrix to say that she's staying in Oxfordshire. She's fallen in love with her husband and she's happy. So are Anna and Henrietta with Samuel and Sebastian. It's made me wonder whether I could be happy, too.'

'You mean—?' Jem croaked. He'd listened with a growing sense of horror, every word raising his body temperature by another degree, so that now he felt as if he were standing on hot coals. Surely she couldn't be saying what he thought she was saying? Because if she was, then he had to stop her right now, only he couldn't get the words out…

'I mean that I thought any kind of relationship between us was impossible, but maybe it's not. Maybe we could be happy together.' She moved slowly towards him, stopping an arm's length away. 'So what I'm trying to say is that I'm sorry, *again*, for the way I've treated you and that I'd like to turn the clock back six weeks.' She smiled shyly. 'And if you still want to court me then I'd like to be courted.' She reached for his hands, her own trembling slightly. 'Very much.'

'Nancy.' He curled his fingers around hers, unable to help himself. 'About that offer…'

'Yes?'

'The thing is… It's too late.'

'Oh!' Her eyes widened with a look of mortification. 'Of course. I shouldn't have presumed.'

'It's not that.' He resisted the urge to hold on as she tugged her hands back, practically leaping across the floor away from him. 'There's just something I need to tell you, something that's only happened recently. Yesterday, in fact.'

'It's all right.' She shook her head, already wrestling with the bolts again. 'You don't have to explain anything.'

'Yes, I do.' He went after her, holding one hand against the door so that it wouldn't open. If

he didn't explain now, then he had a strong suspicion that he'd never get another chance. 'You
have to understand, I thought it was hopeless
between us. I thought you'd be glad to be rid of
me finally. Oh, hell!'

'Jem?' She looked up at him, cheeks scarlet,
blue eyes suspiciously bright. 'Whatever it is, it
can't be as bad as all that.'

'Can't it?' He muttered an oath. 'The truth is,
I'm engaged.'

Chapter Seven

Thirty seconds later...

'Engaged?' Nancy repeated the word in a whisper, fervently willing the floorboards beneath her feet to open up and swallow her whole. Or even the ceiling. Honestly, if that could be persuaded to develop a hole and suck her up into the attic, that would work perfectly well, too. All she wanted was to be somewhere else—anywhere else!—at that moment. It was all too horrible. After six weeks of soul-searching, she'd finally come to the life-altering realisation that she'd been pushing away the only man she could ever love out of fear and now he was engaged to somebody else! She had a horrible feeling that every inch of visible skin was the same vibrant shade as her hair. If not actually redder...

'Yes.' To be fair, Jem's cheeks were looking somewhat flushed, too.

'And you're saying that this happened...' she had to take a deep breath just to get the word out '...yesterday?'

'Last night. I haven't even told Sebastian and Henrietta yet.'

'I see.' Her voice sounded different, like that of some high-pitched stranger. Which wasn't really surprising when her mouth felt as dry as a desert and there seemed to be some kind of invisible weight pressing down on her chest, constricting her breathing and making it a wonder that she could speak at all. Which didn't even matter because if Jem was engaged then there was nothing more to say. Nothing except... 'Congratulations.'

'Congratulations?' His brows clamped together as he took a step backwards, moving away as if she'd just insulted him. Apparently she should have stuck with saying nothing.

'Yes.' She wrapped her hands around the door handle, torn between a desire to flee and a desire to save face. 'It's been a big day for news. First Beatrix and now you.'

He cleared his throat heavily, still frowning. 'So Beatrix isn't coming back to Belles?'

'No. She's staying with her Duke. Henrietta

just showed me the letter.' She felt a lump in her throat at the words and scrunched her mouth up, stifling a sudden, powerful urge to cry. No, her best friend wasn't coming back. First Anna, then Henrietta and now Beatrix. One by one, each of them had left Belles, leaving her all alone. The only good thing was that at least it gave her the perfect excuse for her behaviour this evening.

'That's probably the real reason I came to see you.' She swallowed her tears, tossing her hair back over her shoulders instead. 'I mean, Beatrix's letter was a bit of a shock. I was feeling sorry for myself on the way home and before I knew it, I was here. No doubt I would have changed my mind about you tomorrow.'

Jem's brows contracted even further, though he didn't answer. Instead, there was a new intensity about his gaze, one that made the weight on her chest press down even harder, as if he were trying to work out whether or not she was telling the truth.

And the horrible truth was that she was absolutely, definitely, one hundred per cent certain that she *wouldn't* have changed her mind. Not tomorrow or the next day or ever. Beatrix's news might have forced her to admit her feelings, but it wasn't the reason for them. If only the letter had arrived sooner! The day before even! After eight years of arguing and being perfectly horrible to Jem, one single day had made all the difference.

'So, do I know your fiancée?' She tossed her hair again, affecting nonchalance.

'I don't think so.' He took another step away from her. 'Her name's Emily. Miss Emily Robinson. Our mothers are friends.'

'And how long have you known her?' She wasn't sure why she was asking, except that apparently she wanted to torture herself.

'Several years as an acquaintance, but her parents invited me to dinner at their house last month and…'

'One thing led to another? I see. Just last month?'

'Yes.'

'It must have been a whirlwind courtship. How romantic.'

'I suppose so.'

'Well then, like I said, congratulations. I wish you every happiness.' She attempted a smile and failed dismally. 'And I'm sorry. For coming tonight, that is.'

'There's no need to apologise.'

'There is. You're engaged and I suggested—' Her gaze strayed briefly towards the stairs at the back of the shop. 'In any case, I'm sorry, and if you could forget the whole thing I'd be very grateful.'

'Understood.' His expression looked pained. 'I'll do my best.'

'Good.' She twisted the door handle finally. 'In that case, I'll be off.'

'Wait.' A hand closed around her wrist just as her foot touched the pavement.

'What?' She turned back, surprised by the urgent note in his voice.

'Tell me the truth. Did you mean what you just said? That you would probably have changed your mind about me tomorrow?'

Nancy swallowed. Telling the truth at that moment would do absolutely no good in the world, but standing so close to him, staring up into his face, she couldn't bring herself to lie. 'No.' She shook her head quickly. 'I don't think so.'

'If I'd thought...' A muscle leapt in his jaw. 'But you kept telling me to leave you alone.'

'I know.' She tore her wrist away and stepped outside, then decided to really torture herself by looking over her shoulder one last time, fixing the image of him in her mind. 'Goodbye, Jem.'

'Nancy?' Henrietta stopped in the kitchen doorway, her mouth forming a surprised O-shape as she stared at row upon row of Belles biscuits, laid out neatly on trays and in tins. 'What are you doing up so early? I came to help with the baking.'

'Already finished.' Nancy deposited a collection of bowls and spoons into the sink. 'I couldn't sleep so I thought I might as well get on with it.'

'Well, no wonder you look so exhausted. Have you slept at all?'

'I'm not tired. Can I get you something? Tea?'

'No, thank you, I had a quick breakfast with Sebastian.' Henrietta inched towards her slowly. 'Nancy, are you all right?'

'Of course. Why wouldn't I be?'

'You just look a little tense.'

'I'm a tense person. Everybody knows that. Tense, stubborn, bad-tempered…'

'Kind, loyal and honest,' Henrietta spoke over her. 'Now stop criticising yourself and tell me what's the m—'

'Jem Redbourne is engaged!' Nancy wailed, putting down the kettle she'd just picked up from the range. Honestly, she hadn't intended to say it, or to refer to it at all, *ever*, only somehow she hadn't been able to keep the words in.

'What?' Henrietta looked genuinely shocked. 'Since when?'

'That's the worst part. Yesterday! No, the

day before yesterday.' She shook her head confusedly. 'I forgot I haven't slept.'

'But that's impossible! If Jem had been courting someone, then he would have told Sebastian. Who is he supposedly engaged to?'

'Someone called Emily Robinson.'

'Oh...' Henrietta sank down into a chair. 'Oh, no.'

'Why, oh, no? Do you know her?'

'No, but I remember Jem mentioning her name once. I know that his parents wanted the match, but I never thought he'd give in. I thought that he still had feelings for you.' She shrank backwards, as if she were bracing herself. 'Don't be angry with me, but I always thought that one day you'd change your mind about him, too.'

'Me? Ha! After I've done nothing but criticise and argue with him for years! What on earth would put such a foolish notion into your head?' Nancy put her hands on her hips and promptly burst into tears.

'Oh, no...' Henrietta sprang forward to embrace her. 'Oh, Nancy, you *do* like him, don't you?'

'Yes!' she wailed against her shoulder. 'I think I always did, but I was too afraid to admit it until yesterday. Then I went to see him after we read Beatrix's letter and he told me about this Emily

Robinson and I felt so embarrassed and stupid! And it's all my own fault for pushing him away so many times. *Of course* he found someone nicer eventually.'

'How did he seem when you went to see him?'

'I don't know.' She gave a loud sniff. 'Like he always does. Good and kind and honourable. Like he was sorry for me for humiliating myself in front of him!'

'Oh, Nancy, I'm so sorry.'

'I'll be all right.' She pulled away, rubbing the heels of her hands over her eyes. 'I just need some time to get used to the idea. Right now, I feel like I lost him *and* Beatrix in one day.'

'About Beatrix's letter…' Henrietta's voice turned cajoling. 'You know that she invited us to Howden Hall for a visit next month? Well, Sebastian and I have decided to accept, so why don't you come with us? It might be good for you to have a change of scene and routine, especially after what's happened. A fortnight's holiday might be the perfect tonic for a broken heart.'

'I do *not* have a broken heart!'

'A bruised one, then. You and Beatrix are such good friends. I know you're the one she really wants to see.'

'No.' Nancy shook her head emphatically. 'She invited us to celebrate her marriage and I *can't* do that. Remember what her husband was like?'

'He can't be as bad as all that if she wants to stay married to him.'

'He was still proud and haughty and rude.'

'He's a duke! They're probably all proud and haughty. As for rude, it can't have been easy for him with all of us glaring daggers.'

'You didn't glare. You never do.'

'Well, you and Sebastian more than made up for that. Even Jem gave him quite a hard look, as I recall.'

'He did.' Nancy sniffed again. 'I felt quite grateful to him for that.'

'All I'm saying is that it was a difficult situation and none of us behaved very well. Maybe he deserves a second chance.'

Nancy gave one final sniff before shaking her head. 'Maybe he does, but it doesn't matter. If Beatrix says she's happy, then I'll try to be happy for her, too, but I'm not going to stay in some ducal mansion. I don't belong in a place like that.'

'Neither do I or Sebastian.'

'Sebastian's sister is a countess.'

'A countess who once ran a biscuit shop. The same biscuit shop you're managing now, incidentally. And there's no need to worry about not belonging. Beatrix says she's only inviting friends so it'll be just us, Anna and Samuel, and some of the Duke's family.' Henrietta opened her eyes wide with a look of appeal. 'At least say that you'll think about it?'

'I can't. Who'll run Belles if I'm away?'

'No one. Sebastian says you should just close the shop.'

'For two weeks?'

'I know.' Henrietta laughed. 'We'll never make a fortune. Two businesses and both closed, but friendship is more important.'

'Did Beatrix invite Jem, too?'

'Um…possibly. There was a note for him included with the letter.'

'Then there's your answer.'

'I doubt that he'll accept, considering…' Henrietta's voice trailed away awkwardly. 'Anyway, we can talk more about it later. Right now, you should go upstairs and have a lie down. I'll take care of everything here.'

'What about your tea room?'

'Sebastian will manage.'

Nancy opened her lips to refuse and then changed her mind. 'Thank you. Maybe I am a little tired, after all.'

Henrietta squeezed her hand. 'For what it's worth, I really am sorry about Jem.'

'Thank you. So am I.'

'Just *think* about coming to Oxfordshire?'

'All right, I'll think about it,' Nancy lied, trudging up the wooden staircase to her bedroom. She could think about it all day and all night and the answer would still be the same. There was absolutely no way that she was going to Oxfordshire, but at least it gave her something new to think about when every other thought in her head seemed to revolve around Jem Redbourne. She could thank Beatrix and her duke for that.

On an ordinary day, Mr James Redbourne, owner of Redbourne's General Store, was good nature personified. He rarely swore, never shouted and was endlessly patient with both employees and customers alike. He was, in fact, famous throughout the city of Bath for his fair-mindedness and evenness of temper. On the morning of the fifth of May, eighteen hundred and seven, however, he appeared to have turned over a new leaf and not for the better. By noon, he'd snapped at two of his staff, muttered several coarse oaths under his breath and generally behaved like a man who'd just lost the love of his life.

Because the truth was, he had. Ironically, he'd also just become engaged.

If only he hadn't accepted the Robinsons' invitation to dinner the month before! That was the one thought dominating his mind. He'd been fully aware that his mother and Mrs Robinson had been matchmaking, their combined sights set on a union between him and Emily, whom he'd known and vaguely admired for the past five years as a pretty, amiable and intelligent young lady, but whom he'd never thought of as anything more than an acquaintance. On the evening of that fateful dinner, however, only a few days after yet another, this time definitive rejection from Nancy—or so he'd thought—it had soothed his wounded pride to have a woman take an interest in him. An interest that had finally led him to conclude that it was time to give up on the unattainable and move on—the unattainable being Nancy, who had been perfectly clear about her feelings. Crystal clear. Practically transparent. Until yesterday.

He'd decided against visiting Sebastian and Henrietta afterwards, devoting most of the night to sitting in his office and staring at thin air instead. He must have dozed at some point because he'd awoken with a start that morning to find Paul, another of his assistants, standing over him with a panicked expression. As it turned out, he'd forgotten to lock the shop door after

Nancy's departure, though fortunately no thieves had noticed.

In short, it had been a bad day. A *very* bad day for his employees, something he already felt guilty about, but at least now it was over and he could do what he'd intended to do the evening before and follow the sound of enthusiastic singing through Henrietta's Tea Shop to where Sebastian was washing pots in his kitchen. The tune was one of Cimerosa's, if Jem wasn't mistaken, although given his friend's tendency to jump from opera to opera without warning, it could turn into Mozart at any moment.

'Well, look what the cat dragged in.' Sebastian looked up from his task with a grin. 'You look terrible.'

'I feel it.'

'You haven't been out drinking without me, have you? Because if you have, then you deserve everything you get.'

'No, I haven't, although alcohol sounds like a good idea right now.'

'Sounds serious. Sit down and tell me what's happened, although I'll have to keep washing while you talk. Hen's helping out the firebrand today.'

'Is she?' Jem sat down, propping his elbows on the kitchen table and promptly burying his head in his hands. There was no need to ask who 'the firebrand' referred to.

'So?' A cloth waved under his nose. 'What's happened?'

'I've done something.' He pressed his thumbs into the sides of his head, trying to relieve some of the tension there. 'Something that seemed like a good idea at the time. I mean, it *was* a good idea. *Is* a good idea, I should say. It's too late to be anything else now and it's disloyal of me to say otherwise, but—'

'Jem,' Sebastian interrupted, 'what the hell are you talking about?'

'I'm getting married.'

'What? Are you joking?' His friend's jaw dropped. 'You're *not* joking! Well, congratulations! But that's good news, isn't it?'

'It should be. It was. Until last night.'

'So what happened last night? Wait…' Sebastian circled a hand in the air. 'Go back a bit. Who's the lucky woman?'

'Miss Emily Robinson.'

'The lawyer's daughter?' Sebastian made a face and then clicked his fingers. 'Hold on, I've seen her somewhere, I think. At a concert. Hen pointed her out. Blonde hair, tall, willowy figure, but how long have you been courting?'

'About a month. I didn't mention it because I wasn't sure whether it would come to anything.'

'And now you're engaged? That's fast work, my friend. So how did this all start?'

'Well, Emily's mother and mine are friends…'

'Ah.' Sebastian tossed his cloth aside and sat down. 'Your mother. So this was all her idea, then? You know, you take being a good son too far.'

'It's not like that.' Jem stiffened defensively. 'Shouldn't you be washing up?'

'Damn the washing up. This is more important. Now, about your mother?'

'Actually, she hasn't even mentioned marriage for the past couple of months. That's why I've been so worried about her.'

'What do you mean?'

Jem leaned back in his chair with a sigh. 'Remember she took a turn for the worse back in February?'

'Yes.' Sebastian nodded, sombre for once.

'Well, the doctor says she'll recover again as long as she gets plenty of rest, but she's been so quiet recently. It's not like her. She used to pester me incessantly about grandchildren, but there's been nothing like that recently. That's what made me start to think seriously about marriage. I know how happy she'll be when I tell her about Emily.'

'Jem…' Sebastian leaned forward across the table. 'Please don't tell me you proposed just to make your mother happy?'

'No.' He scowled. 'At least, not entirely. Emily's a nice, sweet girl and we've always got along fairly well. I think that we understand each other and, with time, I'm sure we'll come to care for one another, too.'

'So this is some kind of practical arrangement?'

'Yes, with a woman who's actually glad of my company.' He rubbed a hand around the back of his neck, trying to summon an image of Emily into his mind, but it was no use. Her blonde ringlets kept turning into scorching red curls. 'You know, a man can only be rejected so many times. He has to draw a line eventually.'

'Only now you're having second thoughts?' Sebastian nodded sagely. 'Well, that's understandable. You've been pining after Nancy for years.'

'Exactly.' Jem dug his fingernails into his scalp. If he wasn't careful, he was going to tear his hair out from its roots. 'I thought it was time to give up on romance, the way you always told me to.'

'When did I tell you that?' Sebastian sounded aggrieved.

'Lots of times. You always said I was too romantic.'

'I never said any such thing! I love romance!'

'Now you've met Henrietta, you do, but growing up, you said it was all nonsense.'

'Well, why would you listen to me? What did I know?'

'Anyway, I thought that pursuing Nancy was a lost cause. She even told me it was. Then yesterday evening she came to the shop and...well, apparently it's not quite as hopeless as I thought.'

'What? You don't mean...? *Nancy?* And just when you're...' Sebastian tipped his chair on to its back legs and then dropped it forward again with a thud. 'Oh.'

'Oh? That's all you can say?'

'I'm trying not to swear. Henrietta keeps reminding me I'm not at sea any more. So what now?'

'Now I'm engaged and I can't break things off with Emily just because—' He stopped and grimaced.

'Because you want to?'

Jem looked shamefaced. 'I shouldn't even think it. Emily's a nice person. She deserves better from me.'

'She probably deserves someone who isn't in love with another woman either.'

'I'm *not* in love with Nancy. I don't know what I am, but whatever it is, I honestly thought that I was over it.' Jem slammed a hand down hard on the table. 'And Nancy has no right to do this! After all this time, to turn up on my doorstep and just expect me to come running.'

'She's definitely contrary.'

'That's it!' Jem jabbed a finger at his friend. 'Exactly. Contrary and argumentative and fiery! Whereas Emily is calm and mild-mannered. I can't imagine her ever losing her temper. I'm not even sure she has one.'

'Which nobody can say about Nancy.'

'This is so typical of her!' Jem let out a roar of frustration. 'Just when I'm starting to get my life in order, she has to go and confuse everything!'

Sebastian clicked his fingers. 'We should make a list. Advantages and disadvantages of both women.'

'What's the point? I'm engaged to Emily and I can't go back on my word, no matter what any list says. It wouldn't be fair on her.'

'It might help you to feel better about it.'

'That's true. All right, Emily's from a respectable family. We'll have a nice, respectable home and well-behaved children. My parents already like her. They'll be thrilled about the whole thing, my mother in particular. The thought of planning a wedding will probably give her a whole new lease of life. And I like Emily, too, I really do. She's pleasant company. There'll be no arguing, no shouting.'

'No excitement.' Sebastian rolled his eyes. 'Although I have to say, she's very pretty.'

'I suppose so.'

'You *suppose* so?'

'I mean…yes, she is.' Jem made a face. 'It's just that sometimes I wish she wasn't always so neat and tidy-looking. I wish that she'd be messier.'

'And have red hair maybe?'

'Stop it.'

'Have you kissed her?'

'Who?'

'Miss Robinson.'

'We only just got engaged.'

'What does that have to do with it?' Sebastian gave him a pointed look. 'You kissed Nancy when you weren't engaged to her.'

'I'm starting to wish I'd never told you about that.'

'All right, tell me this.' Sebastian leaned forward. 'Does Miss Robinson make you smile?'

'Sometimes.'

'Smile properly, I mean. Does she make your heart sing?'

Jem sucked in a deep breath and then let it out again slowly. 'No. I don't know why not. She ought to be perfect for me.'

'Maybe because she's not Nancy?'

'No.' Jem dropped his forehead on to the table with a thud. 'No, she's not.'

'You, my friend, have a genuine problem.' Sebastian placed a supportive hand on his shoulder. 'I can swear now, if you want?'

'Please.'

Chapter Eight

Three weeks later

Emily was saying something. Jem could tell she was speaking because her lips were moving rhythmically as they walked arm in arm through Sydney Gardens, only he was finding it difficult to focus on what she was saying. Which wasn't her fault necessarily. She just had one of those inflectionless voices. Pleasant enough, but without any hint of emotion. He'd never noticed it before, but now he had the impression that she would have described the sudden appearance of the King with the same flat monotone as she described a cup of tea. Or maybe he *had* noticed before and found it soothing or charming. Either way, something about it today was causing his thoughts to keep wandering off in all sorts of inappropriate directions.

Well, one direction really and it wasn't as much a direction as a person, another woman, one with an *extremely* animated voice. Too animated sometimes, not to mention loud and argumentative... He shook his head, wrenching his thoughts away from the one person he ought not to think about and yet seemed unable not to for more than ten minutes at a time. And it really wasn't fair of him to compare, especially when he ought to be concentrating...

'I know that Mama and Papa would be perfectly thrilled,' Emily was saying. 'Now that the banns are being read, they think it's high time to introduce you to the rest of the family.'

'That sounds like a good idea.' He looked around, surprised to find them halfway along the winding path that led to the faux medieval castle. How had they got there? The last time he'd looked around, they'd been walking alongside the lake.

'Wonderful! So you'll come to Taunton?'

'Taunton?'

'To visit my uncle and aunt.' Emily's emerald-green eyes clouded, though her voice, inevitably, remained completely flat. 'Jem, I don't believe you've listened to a single word I've said since we left the house. Is something the matter? If you didn't want to come for a walk, then you should just have said so.'

'It's not that. Forgive me, I'm just a little pre-occupied today.'

'Is it anything I can help you with?' A gloved hand slid its way up his arm. 'You know you can always talk to me.'

'Thank you.' He smiled, touched by the earnest content of the words, if not their expression. 'But it's nothing of any consequence. One of my suppliers is being difficult, that's all.'

'Oh.' The grip on his arm loosened. 'I see.'

Emily twisted her face away as Jem stifled a pang of guilt. It wasn't a lie, although it wasn't exactly the full truth either. He *had* been thinking about his supplier a few minutes previously, but his thoughts had strayed, as they seemed determined to do, back to a certain redheaded shopgirl he hadn't seen for almost a month, but who'd taken up residence in a corner of his brain and seemed intent on spreading her influence outwards. She'd been doing it gradually for the past eight years, but since her last visit, she'd been expanding her empire faster than ever. If his brain had been a house, she'd be occupying an entire floor by now.

It was distracting. It was maddening. It was completely unfair to Emily. Most of all, it *had* to stop. *She* needed to be evicted. He just needed to work out how to do it.

Silently, he repeated to himself all the rational arguments that were keeping him sane. He was engaged to somebody else. To an intelligent, respectable, gentle-mannered lady who'd never shown the slightest sign of bad temper. He turned his head back towards her, admiring the way the sunlight glinted off her golden hair, making every thread seem to sparkle. She was lovely. Beautiful really. Everything he could ever want in a bride. Everything he *did* want in a bride. His proposal might have seemed like monumentally bad timing three weeks ago, but now he'd come to the conclusion that her acceptance was the best thing that could have happened. Because if he hadn't proposed and she hadn't accepted then he might have taken one more chance on Nancy and ended up being rejected all over again.

So, yes, he assured himself, everything had worked out for the best. His wedding plans were coming along nicely, or so the Robinsons informed him, and he hadn't been glared at or insulted for weeks. He was happy. Happyish anyway. More importantly, his mother was ecstatic. She'd started talking about grandchildren again. And if a small voice at the back of his mind occasionally wondered how long his happiness would last after he said 'I do', then that was surely just premarital nerves talking.

And if a slightly louder voice wondered why he didn't feel any closer to Emily than he had on the night of his proposal, despite all the additional time they were spending together, that was probably only due to his confusion about Nancy. He was absolutely doing the right thing; he just had to keep reminding himself of that fact, especially when Sebastian's question, *Does she make your heart sing?*, kept echoing over and over in his head.

'Mama suggested Thursday.'

He blinked, belatedly realising that Emily was talking again. 'Thursday?'

'For Taunton. Of course, we'll need to leave early to get there and back in one day, but as long as the weather stays nice, I'm sure we'll have a perfectly lovely time.'

'I'm afraid I'm already busy on Thursday.' He shook his head apologetically. 'Sebastian and Henrietta are going away for a couple of weeks and I promised to wave them off.'

'But surely they'll understand if you explain the situation? We have so much to prepare before the wedding! Oh, Jem, please say that you'll come.'

'I wish that I could, but there's also the shop to consider. Paul's wife has been unwell recently so I've given him some time off to look after her. It wouldn't be fair to leave Owen and Agnes to manage alone.'

'It's what you pay them for, isn't it?' Emily's tone sharpened. 'Honestly, James, you really do work too hard. I'm afraid that your employees take advantage.'

'They don't, trust me, and I like working hard. A job's not a job when you enjoy it.'

'*James.*' Emily made a shushing sound as another couple walked past them in the opposite direction, her cheeks reddening slightly. 'I do wish you wouldn't talk about it quite so openly.'

'What? My work?'

'Yes. It's one thing to have your name above the door, quite another to mention *working* in public. You never know who might overhear you.'

'I don't care who overhears me. The shop is a big part of my life. I'm not ashamed of working for a living.'

'And I never said that you should be. You're a successful man and you've every right to be proud of your accomplishments. All I'm suggesting is that perhaps you could be a little more discreet.'

'You've never said so before.' He frowned. Had she? No, she definitely hadn't. 'I've heard your father discuss his work in the street, too.'

'He's a lawyer. There's a difference.'

'How?'

'You know how.'

'Do I?'

'Yes! The law is a gentleman's profession. Now obviously I'm not saying that you're *not* a gentleman, but...'

'You're just hinting at it?' Jem lifted an eyebrow. 'Then I'm sorry I embarrass you.'

'That's not fair.' Emily drew her hand away from his arm, letting it fall to her side as she took a step sideways away from him. 'Now you're putting words in my mouth.'

Jem clenched his jaw. It was true, he *was* being somewhat unfair. Emily had been brought up as a lady. No doubt she'd been taught not to discuss certain subjects in public. It was just one of those adjustments he'd have to make once they were married. Although, as for putting words in her mouth...well, if he *had* then he would have given them slightly more intonation.

'You're right.' He cleared his throat, aware that he was being overly critical again. 'My apologies.'

'Then you're forgiven. I'm sorry to have mentioned it. And if you really feel strongly about saying goodbye to your friends, then of course you must.'

'Thank you. Actually, speaking of the Fortinis, I thought that we might visit their tea shop tomorrow? I'd like for you to get to know them better before the wedding. Sebastian's been my best friend for as long as I can remember.'

'Then I'd be delighted to know them better, but I'm afraid that tomorrow is quite impossible. Mama needs me to accompany her to the dressmaker's. You know, she quite relies on my judgement when it comes to her clothes.'

'Couldn't you postpone?'

'Not easily. I'm afraid she's already made the appointment.'

'I see. Another time, then.'

'Yes. I'm sure we'll have some opportunity after the Fortinis get back from their holiday.' Emily replaced her hand on his arm. 'Do you know, I heard the most outlandish rumour about them the other day. Completely ridiculous since it can't possibly be true, but someone suggested they were going to visit the Duke and Duchess of Howden in Oxfordshire.' She gave a small, tinkling laugh. 'Can you imagine?'

Jem kept his gaze fixed on the horizon. 'Mmm.'

'James?' Emily's head spun round. 'You're not laughing.'

'No.'

'Surely you're not saying it's true?' Her mouth dropped open. 'How on earth would people like *the Fortinis* be acquainted with a duke and duchess?'

Jem gritted his teeth. For the first time in their conversation there was actually a trace of expression in her voice and he didn't like it. He wasn't sure how to respond to the question either. He could hardly tell the truth, that the new Duchess of Howden had once worked as a shopgirl at Belles Biscuit Shop. Only a handful of people knew the former Belinda Carr was now Beatrix Howden and he knew that Beatrix would prefer to keep it that way for her husband's sake.

According to Henrietta, the Roxbury family had been the focus of enough scandal in the past. Besides, it was Beatrix's story to tell, even if it meant keeping secrets from his own future wife. Maybe one day he'd ask permission to tell Emily, but not yet. He'd have to be completely certain that he could trust her first—something which, alarmingly, at that precise moment, he didn't.

'It's complicated.' He took an intense interest in the progress of a beech leaf as it spiralled slowly to the ground in front of them. 'I'm sure you've heard that Sebastian's grandfather was the Duke of Messingham and his sister is the Countess of Staunton.'

'I'd heard those rumours, too, but he was in the navy! And not even as an officer. And now he runs a tea shop!'

'He was always a bit unconventional.' Jem couldn't resist a chuckle. 'Although so was Anna, to be fair.'

'Anna as in the actual Countess of Staunton, *Anna*?' Emily's eyes widened so much he could practically see the cogs of her mind turning. 'So the rumours are true? And you call her Anna?'

'Yes, we grew up together.'

'But I assumed it was all nonsense! Why on earth didn't you tell me this before?'

'It never came up. It probably would have if we'd had tea with Henrietta and Sebastian sooner, but you've been so busy.'

'That's not the point. You ought to have told me.'

'Well, I'm telling you now.'

'But then, if *you* know Mr Fortini and the Countess of Staunton so well, does that mean you're also acquainted with the Duke and Duchess of Howden?'

'A little, although I can't say I know them *very* well. It was kind of them to invite me, too, but—'

'*James!*' Emily's hand clamped firmly around his bicep, bringing them both to a halt. Judging by the sudden ferocious tug on his shoulder she was using her whole weight to do it, too. 'Are you saying that you're invited to Oxfordshire as well?'

'Um…' He grimaced, but there was really no way to avoid answering. 'There was some mention of it.'

'And you *refused*?'

'Yes.'

'But you *have* to go!'

'Why?' Curiously, her voice seemed full of expression now. Or at least she was emphasising certain words in the manner of a military sergeant. 'I thought you said there was still lots to do before the wedding.'

'But they're a duke and duchess! This might be your only opportunity. They might not invite you again.'

'I wouldn't expect them to.' He was starting to wish Emily would go back to speaking in a monotone. 'Anyway, like I said before, it's not easy taking time off from the shop.'

'And like *I* said, that's why you have staff.' She lifted her spare hand to cover the one already digging into his forearm. 'I wonder…'

'What?' he asked doubtfully.

'Well, since the Duke and Duchess have been so generous as to invite you to their home, perhaps we ought to add them to the guest list for our wedding?'

'Mmm. Perhaps.'

'Wonderful, I'll tell Mama. She'll be so excited. And you're quite right about the Fortinis, I really should get to know them better. The dressmaker's will just have to be rescheduled.' She smiled brightly. 'I'd be thrilled to visit their tea shop tomorrow.'

'I'll let them know.' Jem twisted his face away before she could read his expression, which turned out to be a spectacularly bad idea since it meant he saw Nancy directly ahead and felt a wave of jealousy so strong he almost fell over.

Nancy averted her gaze quickly from the sight of Jem's approach, though not before she took in every horrifying detail of his companion. She was a vision of feminine loveliness, a slender, elegant blonde whose perfect deportment and expensive apparel immediately marked her out as a lady. There didn't appear to be a single smudge or wrinkle anywhere on her person. There probably never was. She was probably one of those people who went through life being effortlessly pristine. No doubt she was accomplished, too.

Nancy felt her spirits plummet to rock bottom. As if the evening wasn't proving enough of a trial already! She was starting to wish she'd gone to bed at five o'clock…

She lifted her chin and forced herself to smile at her companion. She could hardly have been any more surprised than when Mr Reginald Palmer, whose pie shop stood three buildings down from Belles on Swainswick Crescent, had asked if she'd like to 'promenade' with him after they closed for the day. As far as she could recall, they'd never exchanged more than polite pleasantries before. To be frank, she'd hardly been aware of his existence, despite his black hair and strong jaw and the fact that he was generally considered an excellent catch, and yet she'd decided to accept his invitation anyway.

It had been an impulsive decision, one based largely upon not wanting to spend another evening at home moping, and the new-found conviction that, after almost a month of sobbing into her pillow, it was time to pull herself together and move on. And so she'd accepted Mr Palmer, who'd seemed pleasant enough, if somewhat overenthusiastic on the subject of pies.

Not that she had anything against pies. On the contrary, she'd been quite pleased with his gift of a large steak and kidney one—she'd insisted on returning the favour with a bag of rose-flavoured Belles—but she would have been happy with a little less detail about pastry. He'd been talking about the exact proportions of water to lard for the past half-hour and she fervently hoped never to hear the word shortcrust again in her life. She'd allowed her mind to start wandering somewhere after Pulteney Bridge and now the sight of Jem and his fiancée walking towards them had just thrown all her thoughts into confusion.

'Miss MacQueen?'

'Hmm?' She was jolted back to the present with a start. 'I'm sorry, what?'

'I just asked what you thought about Kitty?'

'Who? Oh, your sister?' Thankfully, she remembered that detail from somewhere.

'My youngest, yes. I have three, but like I say, there's only room for so many bakers in my shop and you know what they say about too many cooks.' Mr Palmer chuckled at his own joke. 'Anyway, she knows her way around a kitchen and she's a hard worker.'

'I'm sure she is,' Nancy agreed, half of her mind wondering why he was telling her this, the other half calculating the number of footsteps between her and Jem. She didn't dare to look up and meet his gaze, but she could sense his approach. Five footsteps... Four... Three... Two...

'And now that Miss Carr's left...'

'Ha-ha-ha-ha!' She emitted a high-pitched laugh as they came level with Jem and his companion. It was possibly the worst fake laugh in the entire history of fake laughs, but she had to make *some* pretence of enjoying herself.

'Ah-ha-ha-ha,' Mr Palmer echoed nervously, immediately spoiling the effect. 'But still, you must be run off your feet.'

'Not really.' She closed her eyes in mortification as Jem passed by. 'I like to keep busy so— Oh.' Her eyes snapped open again as the words finally made sense. 'You want me to give your sister a job?'

'Um...yes.' Mr Palmer looked both relieved and embarrassed by her sudden comprehension. 'She lives close by, she'll work hard and she doesn't expect much in the way of wages.'

'Is that so?' Nancy arched an eyebrow, beginning to feel sorry for Kitty. 'Well, why didn't you just ask me this morning? You didn't have to invite me out for a walk.'

'It didn't seem polite.' Mr Palmer dropped his gaze to his boots. If she wasn't mistaken, he was veering sideways, too, as if he were trying to put some distance between them.

'Mr Palmer…' Nancy leaned forward and twisted her neck, forcing him to meet her eyes again. 'Are you afraid of me?'

'No!' Mr Palmer's affronted tone was belied by the way he immediately cringed backwards.

'I see.' She sighed and stood upright again. She supposed that she ought to take umbrage at the way he'd deceived her, leading her to believe that he wanted her company when it had only been to ask a favour, but it wasn't as if she'd been enjoying herself either. If anything, she was relieved that he'd just given her an excuse to bring their walk to an end. She had a feeling she was going to be dreaming about pastry as it was.

'So you'll give Kitty a try?' Mr Palmer was a braver man than she'd given him credit for.

'Maybe.' Nancy pursed her lips and then shrugged. 'All right, send her around first thing in the morning and I'll see how good she is at baking. I'm not promising anything, but I suppose I could do with some help.'

'Thank you.' Mr Palmer looked as if he'd just run the gauntlet. 'And I hope you don't think the *only* reason I invited you out was to ask about Kitty, because I can assure you, nothing could be…'

'Further from the truth, naturally, but if I'm not mistaken, *that's* a rain cloud.' Nancy gestured towards an infinitesimal scrap of grey cloud in the distance. 'I think it's time we ought to be getting back, don't you?'

'Oh, yes, definitely.' Mr Palmer nodded eagerly. 'We wouldn't want to get caught in a storm.'

'Quite.' Nancy rolled her eyes as they both pivoted on their heels. Pastry aside, it had been quite pleasant to think, however briefly, that another man had been interested in her, even if she hadn't been particularly interested in him. Unfortunately, the truth was that only one man had ever *really* been interested. In the same way that only one man had ever interested her, too, but all of that was over and, frankly, it was for the best.

Jem was far better off with his vision of loveliness, a real lady, someone who would never embarrass or disappoint him. They looked perfect together—no doubt they were in love, too. Everything that had happened had obviously been for the best.

Despite that, she couldn't quell a pang of regret. She could see Jem ahead of them, albeit in the far distance now, walking away from her in the way he'd once threatened he would. She'd always thought that he could do better and now he had. Unfortunately, his better made her feel a thousand times worse.

Chapter Nine

'So what do you think?' Jem glanced up and down the pavement outside Belles, making sure that he and Sebastian were completely alone before asking the question that had been playing on his mind for the past twelve hours.

'I think that cloud looks like a butterfly.' Sebastian leaned back against the wall, directing his gaze upwards. 'Or maybe an elephant.'

'You know I'm talking about yesterday.'

'Well, in that case, I think the tea was delicious. I made it myself, you know.'

'So you told us. What did you think about Emily?'

'Oh, fine.' Sebastian folded his arms. 'If you can't take a hint then we'll talk about it, but you won't like what I have to say.'

'Because?'

'Because she didn't eat enough for a start. I

put a lot of effort into those sandwiches and she barely touched the cakes.'

'That's not exactly a character flaw.'

'I haven't finished.' Sebastian gave him a look. 'She was also a little too interested in Anna and Beatrix, if you ask me.'

'That's not so surprising.' Jem clenched his brows defensively. 'She only found out I was acquainted with them the day before yesterday. It was natural for her to ask questions.'

'There's interested and then there's *interested*. She hardly talked about anything else.' Sebastian held his hands up. 'And there's no point in looking at me like that. You asked what I thought.'

Jem glanced through the window into Belles. Judging by Henrietta's expansive arm gestures, she was making one last-ditch attempt to convince Nancy to travel with them to Oxfordshire. He didn't rate her chances. 'What does Henrietta think?'

'Oh, you know Hen, not a bad word to say about anyone, even people who look down their noses at her.'

'Emily wasn't—'

'Yes,' Sebastian interrupted shortly. 'She was.'

Jem winced. He couldn't deny that Emily's behaviour the day before had caused him no small degree of embarrassment. She'd acted as if it were the very height of condescension for her to set foot inside a tea shop.

'I'm sorry,' he muttered at last.

'I know. I thought you said she was sweet.'

'She was. *Is*. She's just—'

'A snob?'

He didn't answer, relieved to see the carriage Beatrix had sent to collect Sebastian and Henrietta rolling around the corner of the street towards them. 'It looks like it's time for you to go anyway.'

'Right.' Sebastian put a hand on his arm. 'Look, I'm sorry to be blunt and maybe I shouldn't say this—in fact, I'm pretty sure that I shouldn't— but I'm afraid you got engaged too quickly. You thought that things were hopeless with Nancy and you wanted to make your mother happy so you rushed in.'

'Those weren't the only reasons.'

'But they were the main ones and that woman's all wrong for you.'

Jem took a step backwards, shrugging Sebastian's hand away. 'I'm not saying Emily's perfect. I'll even admit there are certain aspects of her character I wasn't aware of before and don't particularly like, but I'm sure we'll adapt to each other.'

'But—'

'In any case, it would be dishonourable for me to break the engagement off now.' He sighed heavily. 'Look, I'll understand if you can't support me, but I need to know whether you'll still be my best man next month?'

'Next month?' Sebastian's eyes filled with a look of horror.

'Yes. Emily's parents, and mine for that matter, think that a quick wedding would be best.'

'You don't think you ought to take a little more time and get to know each other properly?'

'Says the man who eloped to Gretna Green.'

'That was different. Sometimes you just *know* about a person. Can you honestly say that about Miss Robinson?'

Jem gritted his teeth. No, he couldn't say that, but there was absolutely no way that he was about to admit it. Fortunately, he didn't have to as the front door of Belles opened at that moment and Henrietta stepped out on to the pavement.

'Ready to go?' Sebastian's expression altered immediately, the way it always did when he set eyes on his wife, a warm smile spreading across his face.

'As I'll ever be.' Henrietta took his proffered hand. 'It's going to be just the two of us, after all.'

'So we get to spend three days alone together

in a carriage?' Sebastian lifted her fingers to his lips. 'That doesn't sound too bad to me.'

'See what you've condemned me to?' Henrietta threw one last look of entreaty over her shoulder towards Nancy, standing behind her in the doorway. 'We honestly don't mind waiting if you want to run inside and pack a few things?'

'I think your coachman might have something else to say about that, but I'm completely sure.' Nancy shook her head with a smile. Which meant that she obviously hadn't noticed him yet, Jem thought with a twinge of regret. If she had, she'd be scowling already. 'Now have a good journey, enjoy yourselves and give Beatrix my love.'

'We will, but the invitation will still be open if you change your mind. I'm sure Beatrix would send the carriage back in a moment if you sent word.'

'I won't change my mind.' Nancy lifted her chin. 'Beatrix and I live in different worlds now. It's one thing to go from Avon Street to Belles Biscuit Shop, but a ducal mansion is too much.'

'Speaking of too much…' Sebastian interjected. 'Don't work too hard while we're away.' He winked and then glanced towards Jem before saying the worst thing it was possible to say under the circumstances. 'Keep an eye on her for us, won't you, Jem?'

'I'll do my best.' Jem Redbourne's voice drifted over Nancy's shoulder in a way that made her whole body tense. She hadn't noticed him standing on the other side of the doorway and the sudden awareness of his presence made all the blood in her body rush straight to her cheeks.

'Excellent.' Sebastian's expression had a distinctly devious edge. 'Although you can still change your mind about joining us, too.'

'I know, and it's kind of Beatrix to invite me, but—'

'She *is* kind,' Henrietta interrupted, her voice uncharacteristically angry all of a sudden. 'And all she's asking is for her friends to come and celebrate her wedding like real friends do! Given everything she's been through with her family, I personally don't think that's too much to ask!'

'Well…' Even Sebastian looked taken aback by his wife's vehemence as she stomped up into the carriage. 'On that note, if you *do* change your minds, I'll see you in Oxfordshire. Otherwise, we'll be back in two weeks. Jem, Nancy…'

He tipped his hat and climbed in after Henrietta, closing the door and waving a hand out of the window as the carriage rolled away down the street.

'That was odd,' Jem commented finally.

'I know.' Nancy kept her eyes fixed on the carriage, willing her body to return to a comfortable temperature. Unfortunately, this was the first time she'd been alone with Jem since she'd declared her feelings for him and the memory of that night was doing nothing to cool her down, embarrassment warring with an attraction she no longer wanted to acknowledge. 'I'm not sure I've ever seen Henrietta grumpy before.'

'Maybe she has a point. Maybe it wasn't too much to ask.' Jem took a step forward, moving directly into her eyeline so that she couldn't avoid looking at him. 'I didn't think Beatrix would care too much whether I accepted the invitation or not. To be honest, I assumed she'd only invited me to be polite, but maybe I didn't think about it hard enough.'

'Well, like they said, you could still change your mind.'

'So could you.' He lifted an eyebrow. 'You must want to see Beatrix again.'

She shrugged, fighting the urge to retreat. 'Yes, but things are different now. She's a duchess.'

'She's still your friend.'

'I'm sure they make new ones easily.'

'Real friends are different.'

'Is that so?' She pursed her lips, annoyed as much by his persistence as by the fact that he was right. Only it was a truth she didn't want to accept. 'Speaking of friends, it's one thing for Henrietta to scold me, but you have absolutely no right to do so.'

'Fine.' He shook his head, turning away before changing his mind and swinging around again. 'Do you know what your problem is?'

'I beg your pardon?'

'You're stubborn. You've always been stubborn. Once you get an idea in your head you're like a dog with a bone. And you never consider how those ideas might affect others. Have you ever stopped to think about how other people might feel?'

'Of course I have!'

'Really?' He took two steps back towards her, his dark eyes flashing in a way she'd never seen before—a way that told her he was talking about more than Beatrix, too. 'What about all those times you pushed me away? You admitted you were horrible to me. Did you ever think about my feelings? Do you ever think of them now?'

'I—' Nancy froze, an angry retort petering out on her lips. Because the answer was, no, she hadn't, not really. At first she hadn't believed that a man like him could have feelings for a woman like her and when she'd found out the truth, she'd still focused on her own, rather than his feelings. Even after Henrietta's party, she hadn't really considered how all her rejections over the years might have hurt him. Now, the look in his eyes told her that maybe she'd done more damage than she'd realised. In which case, maybe she deserved the pain she was feeling now.

'I said I was sorry,' she mumbled.

'Then prove it. Think about how Beatrix is going to feel about you refusing her invitation.' He lifted his chin a notch. 'Just because she's a duchess now doesn't mean she hasn't got feelings.'

'All right, I'll think about it!' she burst out, folding her arms indignantly. 'And how was your walk the other evening?'

Jem blinked and swayed backwards slightly, as if he were taken aback by the abrupt change of subject, which was fair enough when she was somewhat startled by it herself. She'd had absolutely no conscious intention of bringing the subject up at all. If it hadn't been her own voice speaking, then she might have thought there was somebody else there.

'Very pleasant, thank you.' He furrowed his brow. 'And yours?'

'Lovely,' she lied. 'I had a perfectly charming evening.'

'I didn't realise that you and Mr Palmer were so well acquainted.'

'Didn't you?' She batted her lashes evasively. Just because she had absolutely no desire to see Mr Palmer again, and vice versa, didn't mean that Jem needed to know that. 'Well then, perhaps you don't know as much about me as you thought?'

He made a small sound like a grunt. It was a very un-Jem-like sound, but at that moment it felt quite rewarding.

'So…?' he spoke again after a few moments.

'So what? I didn't hear you ask me a question.'

'So how do you and Reginald Palmer know each other?'

'That's his shop over there.' She pointed further down the street. 'How do you think we know each other?'

'You know I didn't mean it like that.'

She shrugged. 'He simply asked me to go for a walk one evening and I accepted.'

'Just like that?'

'Is it so surprising?'

'No. I'm just not sure—' He stopped mid-sentence.

'What?'

'I'm just not sure that he's such a good match for you. And, yes...' he hurried on before she could interrupt '... I'm aware it's also none of my business.'

'You're right, it isn't, and I'll have you know that Mr Pa—*Reginald* is a very respectable man and makes excellent pies.' She tossed her hair, unable to think of any more enthusiastic comments at that moment. 'So I'd be obliged if you would keep your opinions to yourself. I don't offer my views on your fiancée.'

'I wasn't aware that you had any.'

'I saw her in Sydney Gardens.'

'And that led to views?'

'Observations. Purely superficial ones, of course.'

'Naturally. And?'

She screwed her mouth up, compelled to admit the truth. 'The pair of you looked very hand-some together.'

His brows contracted. 'Did we?'

'Yes. Like a lady and gentleman.'

'I'm not a gentleman.'

'Yes, you are. In all the ways that count.'

She paused and then added begrudgingly. 'You looked very well suited.'

'Nancy—'

'So everything's worked out for the best, wouldn't you say?' she said hurriedly. 'Now, if you'll excuse me, I have a shop to run and so do you. We should probably both get on with it instead of wasting any more time.'

She whirled about before he could answer, closing the shop door firmly and loudly behind her. Honestly, there wasn't much work to be done. Henrietta had insisted on helping her with the baking and general tidying up before she'd left, which meant that all she had to do now was wait for customers.

Instead, she went through to the kitchen and slumped into the old, tattered armchair by the fireplace, torn between heartache over Jem and guilt over Beatrix. There was nothing to be done about the first, but maybe there was still something she could do about the other... Maybe Henrietta and Jem were right and she *was* being a bad friend by refusing to accept Beatrix's invitation.

Only it would be ridiculous for a person like her to visit a place like Howden Hall! A lady like Miss Robinson might fit in, but she'd be entirely out of place. She'd say all the wrong things and wear all the wrong things and end up making herself look ridiculous. Even among friends, she'd stand out like a sore thumb. She wasn't a lady and she had no desire to pretend to be one. Going to Oxfordshire was a mad idea, insane really, like going to a different planet. Beatrix would understand that.

Hopefully.

Chapter Ten

It was a perfect June day. Nancy tilted her face up to the sun as she strode along Great Pulteney Street, bonnetless, but still wearing her detestable shop dress, letting the rays warm her cheeks. Every time she'd looked out of the shop window that day, it had felt like the world had been calling to her. It had seemed wrong to be shut up indoors, so much that she'd resolved to escape the very moment she closed up. And so here she was finally, enjoying the last of the day's sunshine, under a sky so luminously blue that even Mr Palmer would have had trouble finding a cloud. Not that she would have put it past him.

It had been a difficult week. After the low point of Henrietta and Sebastian's departure, as well as some painful soul-searching over her own past behaviour, she'd descended into a fresh bout of melancholy, where the phrase rock-bottom felt like an understatement. Fortunately, the only way to go from there had been up, with the result that today she was in a much better frame of mind. Not a happy one exactly, but she was working on it. All day she'd kept reminding herself of how lucky she was, of how much she enjoyed her life and work and of how far she'd come from Avon Street.

She was only twenty-two years old and she'd achieved everything she'd ever wanted in life. She was independent and successful and...well, honestly, she was exhausted. So exhausted, in fact, that she was starting to wonder if she ought to go ahead and hire Kitty Palmer, after all. She'd put off the decision in the hope that Beatrix would eventually realise the mistake she'd made in reconciling with her Duke husband and come back to Bath, but since that was looking increasingly unlikely, it was time to find her replacement. And Kitty seemed a pleasant enough girl, as well as reasonably competent in a kitchen. Maybe she would pay a visit to the Palmers' household after her walk...

Yes, she'd been through a difficult patch and come out the other side. As for Jem Redbourne, she was determined to relegate all her feelings for him to the past. He'd been right when he'd accused her of being self-centred. She *had* been.

She'd treated him badly, actually *proving* that she wasn't good enough for him, albeit not in the way that she'd thought. She'd been selfish and rude and downright insulting on occasion. Even when she'd worried about dragging him down, she'd thought of it purely in terms of how *she* would feel.

So it really ought to be no surprise that he'd moved on and fallen in love with somebody else, which meant that the best way she could make amends now was to let him go and do the same thing herself. She'd missed her chance and she had no one to blame but herself. Now he was engaged to somebody infinitely more suitable and soon he'd be married. She was happy for him. As happy as she could be while feeling as though her heart had cracked in half anyway.

And there she was, thinking about Jem again, she realised with a sigh, something she did with infuriating regularity, no matter how hard she tried to forget everything that had happened between them. Of course, she was only a few footsteps from his shop at that moment, which at least explained this particular instance. She only wished she had equally valid excuses for all the other occasions.

Quickly, she crossed to the opposite side of the road, ardently wishing she didn't have to walk past his premises to go into the city, but unless she fancied a long journey round to the next bridge over the river, it was the only way. None the less, she wasn't going to risk meeting him face to face on the same pavement. From now on, they would be nodding acquaintances only. If she ever did happen to find herself in the same room as him, in Henrietta and Sebastian's tea shop for example, a polite 'good morning' or 'good afternoon' would suffice. That would be the extent of their relationship from now on. And if she could just manage that, well, then she'd be back to her old self in no time…

She was just reflecting on how she might actually feel if she ever *did* find herself in the same room as Jem when she spied a group of boys in the middle of the road ahead. They were all familiar, most of them apprentices in the neighbouring businesses. She even knew their names: Philip Cotter, George Wilmer, Noah Heckles and Hugo Dempsey. They were usually good friends, but today something appeared to have gone wrong. Judging by the raised fists and voices, a fight was about to break out. A group of onlookers had started to gather around them expectantly, too, and if she wasn't mistaken, a few bets were already changing hands.

'What's going on here?' She barged straight

into the middle of the argument. 'You four are making quite a display of yourselves.'

'That's what I said.' Noah, the youngest, looked relieved to see her. 'It's all a big fuss about nothing. Tell 'em to stop arguing.'

'It's not nothing!' Philip yelled, squaring up to George. 'I caught him talking to my girl. He wants her for 'imself!'

'Don't be ridiculous.' Nancy rolled her eyes. 'Firstly, whoever she is, she's not *your* girl. She's her own person. Secondly, she can talk to whomever she wants. And thirdly, jealousy is an extremely unattractive quality.'

'Exactly! He's just jealous because I make her laugh!' George jeered.

'She was laughing *at* you, not *with* you!'

'She was not!'

'I'll show you jealous!'

'Oh, for pity's sake!' Nancy stretched her arms out, pushing them away from each other. 'You're acting like a pair of stray dogs…'

'Excuse me, Mr Redbourne?' Agnes's face appeared around the edge of Jem's office door, her forehead creased with concern. 'I think that perhaps you ought to come outside.'

'How many years have we been working together now, Agnes?' Jem put down his pen with a smile. 'And how many times have I asked you to call me Jem? There's no need to be so formal.'

'I know, but I can't.' Agnes shook her grey head with a look of regret. 'I can't help thinking about how your father would react if he heard me.'

'What he doesn't know won't hurt him, but never mind.' Jem pushed his chair back and stood up, conceding defeat. There was no point in arguing. Owen and Agnes would call him Mr Redbourne for ever. 'So what's going on outside?'

'Some kind of disagreement between the apprentices. It's getting louder and louder. I thought I ought to tell you before someone gets hurt.'

'Right.' Jem nodded and strode out of his office, rolling his shirt sleeves up as he went, hearing the racket even before he reached the door. From what he could see, a small crowd had gathered on the pavement outside the store, forming a close circle around a group of four boys, all of whom appeared to be shouting at once. Peering over the top of the crowd, he could see a woman, too, standing in the centre with her arms raised as if she were trying to keep them apart. A woman of average height with bright red hair.

Red hair!

'Stop this!' He flung the door open and surged

forward, practically hurling the onlookers out of the way before grabbing the two ringleaders by the scruffs of their necks and hauling them roughly apart. 'What's going on?'

'*He* started it!'

'No, I didn't. You started it when you—'

'I don't care who started it!' Jem bellowed, tempted to bash both of their heads together. 'It ends now, do you understand? What kind of men do you call yourselves to be fighting in front of a lady?'

'Where?' One of the boys looked around in confusion. 'What? Do you mean Nancy?'

'*Yes, I mean Nancy!*' Jem practically roared. 'Now apologise!'

'Sorry, Nancy.' The two boys looked shame-faced.

'Good.' Jem dropped their collars and glanced towards the woman in question, just in time to catch her staring at him with an expression of wide-eyed admiration, one that dropped completely when she noticed him looking. Still, the fact that it *had* been there made him feel pretty good.

'Get out of here, all of you!' He waved an arm at the disappointed-looking crowd. 'You ought to be ashamed of yourselves. And as for you...' he turned back to the boys '... I suggest that you go home and put this stupidity behind you before I decide to tell your parents.'

'I will if he will,' George muttered.

'I will if he stops looking at my girl.'

'Maybe she likes me looking at her.'

Jem stepped forward, bracing himself as the two boys lunged at each other again, catching one in mid-air and depositing him on the opposite pavement before swinging back for the other. Unfortunately, he wasn't quite fast enough, turning around just in time to see Nancy hurtling through the air as she was knocked to one side.

'Nancy!' He leapt forward, but he could tell it was already too late. She was tumbling in the opposite direction, practically spinning around in mid-air, and there was no one standing behind her, no one to catch her falling body or even break its momentum. All he could do was watch in horror as she hit the ground, her head thwacking hard against the cobbles.

'Nancy?' His pulse slammed to a halt as he dropped down beside her. Her eyes were closed, but she was writhing, twisting her head from side to side and murmuring incomprehensibly.

'I'm sorry.' Philip crouched down on her other side. 'I didn't hit her, I swear. I dropped my fists the moment she stepped in front of me, but I couldn't stop from bumping into her. I didn't mean to knock her down, honest. I would never hit a woman.'

'Nancy?' Jem ignored him, taking her face in his hands to stop her from moving. 'Can you hear me?'

A small furrow appeared between her brows. That was a good sign. Not for him, obviously, but for her.

'Don't move.' He strove to make his tone reassuring. 'I'm sending for a doctor. *You!*' He glared at Philip. 'Go to Forester Road and fetch Dr Thorpe. Run!'

'Yes, sir!'

'And if he's not there, go on to Holburne Park for Dr Harrison.'

'Right.' The boy started away and then stopped. 'What if he's not there either?'

'Then go somewhere else. Just don't come back without a doctor!' He looked around at the other boys. They were all wearing the same stricken expressions. 'The rest of you go, too. Make sure he doesn't take no for an answer.'

'Yes, sir!'

'And no more fighting or you'll have me to answer to!'

'Yes, sir!'

'Jem?' Nancy's voice was so faint he had to bend closer to hear it. 'There's no need to shout.'

'You can talk.' He almost sobbed with relief. 'How do you feel?'

'A bit strange.' Her blue eyes opened, looking up at him with a dazed expression. 'What happened?'

'You got in the middle of a fight.'

'Somebody punched me?'

'I don't think so, not deliberately anyway. From what I can gather, one of the boys knocked you over by accident, but you took a nasty bump on the head.'

'That sounds about right.' She winced. 'Where are the boys now?'

'Gone for a doctor. You can shout at them later.'

'Good. There are a few things I'd like to say.'

'Not if I say them first. Wait.' He put his hands on her shoulders, holding her down as she tried to sit up. 'Don't move. A doctor ought to look at you first.'

'I'm not just going to lie here on cold cobbles.' She made a face. 'Especially with all these people staring at me.'

'What people?' He lifted his head and glared furiously, sending a gaggle of curious onlookers scattering in various directions.

'Problem solved. But you still shouldn't move.'

'I already am.' She twisted her head from left to right to prove it. 'See.'

'Nancy...' He gritted his teeth. 'Is it too much for you to do *one* thing I ask?'

'Yes!'

'Fine. In that case, you're coming with me.' He slid his hands beneath her knees and shoulders, hoisting her up into his arms.

'Jem?' He felt her body stiffen in alarm. 'Wh-what are you doing?'

'Taking you up to my rooms.'

'What? Why? I should go back to Belles.'

'That's too far away.'

'It's just around the corner.'

'That's still too far. You should keep as still as possible.' He tightened his hold, trying to ignore the fact that one of his hands was curled around her upper thigh. There had been times when he'd dreamed of this exact situation, only without the injury part. 'Now stop arguing. I'm not letting you out of my sight until a doctor sees you.'

'Have you always been this bossy?' She sounded genuinely surprised.

'Yes. You just haven't noticed before because you're bossier.'

'Hmm.' There was a disgruntled pause before she laughed. 'That sounds about right, too.'

To his amazement, she actually tipped her

head against his shoulder, her body relaxing as he manoeuvred her carefully through the front door of the shop.

'Nancy?' Pleasant as it was, the gesture alarmed him. It seemed far too acquiescent for her. 'How are you feeling now?'

'A little dizzy. My ears are ringing.'

'How's your vision?'

'All right.' She opened her eyes wide, as if she were testing them.

'Good. Just be sure to tell me if your sight goes blurry or you feel sick. In the meantime, try to stay awake, at least until the doctor arrives.'

'If you say so.'

If you say so? He gave her a worried look before heading up the wooden staircase that led to his living quarters. There was really only one place he could take her, he realised belatedly, since there was only the one bedroom, which wasn't exactly proper, although considering the circumstances, surely no one could accuse him of impropriety? And if they did…well, frankly, at that moment, he didn't give a damn.

'Here we are.' He laid her down on top of his mattress. 'Now don't move.'

'Don't worry.' She gave him a half-smile. 'I'm not going to start dancing.'

'Good. Is the pillow comfortable enough?'

'Yes. Stop fussing.'

He glanced over his shoulder impatiently. Where the hell was the doctor? Maybe he ought to have gone to fetch one himself. Or maybe he should have given the boys some money for bribery. The majority of doctors were responsible, but there were still some who would prioritise a rich widow's nerves over a shopgirl's head injury.

'Ow!'

'What's the matter?' He spun around as Nancy let out a yelp of pain.

'My ankle. I just tried to stretch my legs and now it feels like it's on fire.'

'I told you not to—' He sighed and rolled his eyes. 'You must have twisted it when you fell.'

'Whatever I've done, it hurts.' She tugged the hem of her dress up. Sure enough, one of her ankles was twice the size of the other.

Jem winced in sympathy, resisting the urge to ask permission for a closer look. He'd already carried her to his bed. Touching her ankles was arguably a fantasy too far.

'When I get my hands on those boys…' She narrowed her eyes to slits. 'Do you know, all of that fuss was just over one girl. That's all the fight was about.'

'Some girls are worth fighting for.' He caught

her eye for a second before turning his head sharply back towards the door, heart leaping at the sound of voices below. 'That must be the doctor. *Don't move!*'

Nancy waited until Jem had gone through the door before immediately disobeying his order, heaving herself up to a sitting position and looking around with interest. She was in Redbourne's, she knew that, but she'd never been upstairs or seen this room before. It was bright and airy, with a large casement window, the top half of which was propped open, causing the curtains on either side to waft gently in the light evening breeze, and decorated with only a few items of furniture: a dresser, a chair and the bed where she was lying. There was a jacket draped over the chair and a few personal items on the dresser, which meant that it wasn't a guest room either...

It took her several seconds to fully grasp the implication. As far as she knew, Jem lived alone, which meant that she was lying on *his* bed, on top of *his* sheets and *his* pillow. The realisation caused a flare of guilty excitement in her stomach. Maybe he still cared for her a little, after all...

Truth be told, she still wasn't entirely sure what had just happened. One moment she'd been standing between George and Philip. The next she'd seen Jem lift George into the air and then, out of the corner of her eye, a blur of movement as Philip had barrelled into her with the full force of an aggrieved fifteen-year-old boy, knocking her off her feet.

After that, there had been a succession of disorientating images as the world had seemed to lurch sideways and then spin wildly around her, followed by a painful thud and a high-pitched ringing in her ears that had all contributed to an overwhelming sense of confusion. One moment she'd been looking up at the sky, then at the boys' horrified faces, then at the cobbles on the road, then blackness and then... Jem. And now here she was, in his bedchamber. His surprisingly nice, comfortable, safe-feeling bedchamber. All things considered, it could have been a lot worse.

The sound of footsteps on the stairs alerted her to the imminent arrival of the doctor and she lay down again quickly, putting on an innocent expression as Jem opened the door and practically shoved another man into the room.

'This is Dr Thorpe.' He moved around to the other side of the bed as he spoke. 'I've already told him what happened.'

'Yes, between Mr Redbourne and the boys who came to fetch me, I've heard the story half a dozen times now.' Dr Thorpe smiled, peering at her over the top of a pair of wire-rimmed spectacles, though his view seemed partially obscured by the vastness of his bushy white eyebrows. 'The specifics vary, but the basics are generally the same. You were knocked down and hit your head as you fell, I understand. Possibly twisting your ankle, as well. Are you still in pain now, Mrs Redbourne?'

'Mrs...*who*?' Nancy blinked, suddenly wondering how bad a knock on the head she'd really had.

'It's *Miss* MacQueen,' Jem corrected him. 'Miss Nancy MacQueen. We're not married.'

'Ah, I see. My apologies, Miss MacQueen. In that case, if you could sit up for a moment, I'll take a look at your head first.' He glanced sideways and cleared his throat. 'Forgive me, but if the young lady isn't your wife...'

'What?' It seemed to take Jem a little while to comprehend his meaning. 'Oh. Yes. I'll wait outside the door. Call out if you need anything.'

'I'll stay with Miss MacQueen.' A grey-haired woman with a kindly face passed him in the doorway as if she'd been waiting there for her cue. Her name was Agnes, Nancy recalled, one of Jem's employees. 'If you don't mind, that is, my dear?'

'No.' Nancy shook her head and then winced. 'I don't mind at all.'

'Very well, then.' Doctor Thorpe removed his jacket before taking her face in his hands. 'Let's see what we're dealing with.'

Fortunately, the examination didn't take too long. Dr Thorpe continued to peer over the top of his spectacles as he prodded the back of her skull, murmuring and asking a few searching questions before turning his attention to her ankle, applying some kind of sticky ointment and then wrapping a bandage around it. At last, he nodded with satisfaction and gave Agnes permission to let Jem in again. Judging by the promptness of his reappearance, Nancy guessed that he'd been waiting just outside the door. The idea made her feel inappropriately yet pleasantly warm inside.

'Nothing to worry about.' Doctor Thorpe's tone was positively jovial as he shrugged his coat back over his shoulders. 'You'll be right as rain in a few days, just as long as you keep your feet up and get some rest.'

'A few days?' Nancy pushed herself up on to her elbows in protest, the pleasant warm feeling disappearing abruptly.

'*Complete* rest,' Doctor Thorpe repeated before turning to address Jem. 'Someone ought to keep an eye on her in case of complications.'

'What kind of complications?'

'Unlikely ones, but if she gets a nosebleed or feels sick or has any trouble with her vision, send one of those boys back to fetch me at once. I'm sure it won't be necessary, but head injuries can be unpredictable. Better to be safe than sorry.'

'I'll keep an eye on her myself.' Jem nodded, his face somewhat paler than usual.

'I'll stay, too, as well,' Agnes added.

'There's no need for anyone to watch me. I feel perfectly fine now.' Nancy started to shake her head again and then thought better of it. 'I want to go home.'

'Absolutely not.' Dr Thorpe pushed his glasses up his nose for emphasis. 'I don't want you going anywhere for a few hours at least. I'll come back tomorrow morning and then we'll see.'

'Can she eat anything?' Jem asked.

'Not until the morning, although I'm sure a cup of tea with some sugar wouldn't go amiss.'

'I'll go and make some now.' Agnes hastened down the stairs.

'And make sure she keeps that ankle elevated.'

'Understood.'

'Excellent. Now, try to keep her awake until it gets dark. After that it should be safe to sleep.'

'Ahem!' Nancy cleared her throat loudly, infuriated by the way *her* doctor was addressing all of his comments to Jem. 'So sorry to interrupt, but you can't honestly expect me to just lie here for the next twenty-four hours, drinking tea and staring at the ceiling?'

'Yes, I do.' Dr Thorpe didn't move his eyes away from Jem. 'As for breakfast, a little broth would probably be best.'

'I have a business to run!'

'Oh, no, you don't.' Jem gave her a stern look. 'As from this moment, Belles is closed until further notice. Give me the key and I'll put up a sign and make sure all the shutters are down.'

'You will not.' She thrust her chin out at his authoritative tone. 'I'll make my own arrangements, thank you very much.'

'Not from that bed, you won't, and you're not going anywhere.'

'*I'm* in charge of the shop!'

'Yes, but it belongs to Sebastian and Henrietta and they asked me to keep an eye on things.'

'Sebastian only said that to annoy me.'

'I know, but he still said it.'

'If somebody could just show me out?' Doctor Thorpe sounded very much as though he wanted to escape. 'My dinner ought to be ready about now.'

'Of course, Doctor. My apologies.' Jem gestured towards the door with one hand while holding the other out towards Nancy. 'Key.'

'Fine.' For once, she realised the futility of arguing, reaching into the pocket of her pelisse. 'Here.'

'Thank you. I'll go and see to it right now.' He inclined his head. 'This way, Dr Thorpe, and thank you for coming so promptly.'

'Yes, thank you, Doctor,' Nancy mumbled.

'No need for that, my dear. Just follow my instructions and you'll feel like yourself again in no time.'

'I'll make sure of it.' Jem fixed her with a gimlet stare. 'Agnes will be back with that cup of tea in a couple of minutes. In the meantime, don't even think about getting out of that bed or I'll tie you to it.'

'How dare you!' Nancy spluttered, trying to hide the blush that immediately sprang to her cheeks at the idea. 'I'll do what I want!'

'Of course you will, but only when it's safe for you to do so.' Jem narrowed his eyes mercilessly. 'Until then, you're going to lie there and let Agnes tell you about each of her grandchildren. She has eight altogether and I'm sure she'll be thrilled to tell you about every single one in great detail. Then I'll be back to read you the newspaper.'

'Oh, joy.'

'Quite. Now settle down and I'll be back before you know it.'

Chapter Eleven

"'The trial was heard at assizes at twelve o'clock, where the defendant pleaded guilty to all charges.'" Jem sat back in his chair and folded the paper with a flourish. 'And that concludes the news for today.'

'Fiiinally!' Nancy rolled her eyes. 'I thought you were trying to keep me awake, not send me into a stupor.'

'I thought it was quite an interesting trial personally, but if you'd rather I got Agnes back in here…?'

'Don't you dare!' She swatted at his arm as he made to get up. 'And she doesn't have eight grandchildren. She has *nine*. Her eldest daughter had another son three weeks ago.'

'Ah, so she did.' Jem clicked his fingers. 'Simon, wasn't it?'

'Simon Andrew Owen Carruthers, yes, and

he's going to be tall just like his father. She can tell because he was a long baby, just like her other sons Alan and—'

'Stop!' Jem put his hands over his ears with a laugh. 'I know all about how long Simon is. She's extremely proud of her family.'

'And they sound very nice, but I could have done with a little less detail.'

'It makes her happy to talk about them, but I'm sorry for doing that to you. In my defence, it was for your own good.'

'Why is it always men who say things like that?' She lifted her eyebrows pointedly. 'I've lost count of the times I've been told that things were for my own good or that I shouldn't worry my head about them. Every time by a man.'

'We get lessons. When we're ten years old, we get taken aside in school and taught how to be patronising. Of course, I probably shouldn't tell you. It's all top secret.'

Nancy gave a surprised laugh. 'Well, that explains a lot.'

'In this case, however, it really was for your own good. You look better already.'

'How bad did I look?'

'Not bad, just not quite yourself.' He gave her a sidelong look, his eyes glinting in the candlelight. 'You were behaving oddly, too. You even put your head on my shoulder at one point.'

'I remember.' She dropped her gaze quickly, suddenly very aware of the fact that she was sitting on his bed.

'You gave us all quite a scare.' His voice sounded husky. 'Anyway, I'm just glad you're all right.'

'So am I. Thank you for fetching a doctor. And for insisting I stay, too. I know that I said otherwise, but I wouldn't have wanted to be on my own.'

'You're welcome.' He gave an abashed-looking smile and then sobered. 'Would you like me to fetch anyone? Mr Palmer, perhaps?'

'Why? Oh…no.' She shook her head quickly. 'I wouldn't want to worry anyone.'

'He might want to know.'

'Honestly, there's no need.'

'What about your mother? Should I send a message to her?'

This time, she laughed. 'What on earth for?'

'Because she might have heard about what happened. She might be worried about you.'

'She won't be. I haven't even seen her for the past month.'

'So the two of you—?'

'Are still arguing most of the time? Yes.' She

made a face. 'And no. Actually, things aren't so bad. After I told you to confront your father that time I decided I ought to do the same with my mother. So I told her how much money I could give her each month and in return she stopped my stepfather from asking me for more. We still argue, but things have been much better ever since.'

'I see.' Jem dropped the newspaper on to the floor and leaned forward. 'But don't you think she ought to at least know where you are?'

'Look…' Nancy folded her arms. 'I know you mean well, but where my mother's concerned, it's best to leave well enough alone. If people saw me get knocked down then they'll also have seen you carrying me in here. She can find me if she wants to. Which she won't. Trust me.'

'All right.' He sat back again. 'If that's what you want.'

'It is.'

'What does your mother look like anyway?'

'Why?' She tilted her head suspiciously.

'In case she comes asking questions?'

'Dark hair, green eyes.' She shrugged. 'A permanently disappointed expression.'

'You get your hair from your father then?'

'Hmm.' She grimaced. 'That and freckles.'

'I like freckles.'

Nancy pressed her lips together, trying not to smile at the compliment. 'Just don't trust my stepfather if he shows up, asking questions. No matter what he says about being worried about me, if he comes round here, it'll only be to steal something.'

'Is he really that bad?'

'Worse. You know, I don't remember much about my real father, but everyone says he was a good man. They always said he would do anything for anyone. I'll never understand how my mother could have gone from one extreme to the other.' She ground her teeth for a moment, letting the old bitterness wash over her. 'You know, I've always thought that when a person loves someone, *really* loves someone, then it ought to be just that one person for ever. Because there could never be anyone else.'

'I used to think that, too.' A shadow crossed his face before he looked away, fixing his gaze on the window. 'But there are different types of love. Some are instinctive and passionate, others are…quieter. And sometimes people move on, not because they necessarily want to, but because it seems like the best thing to do.'

She bit her lip, following his gaze to the window. It was completely dark outside now. It made the room feel enclosed and intimate, like they were cocooned away from the rest of the world. She wondered, too, if they were still talking about her mother. She didn't think so. It felt instead like he was saying goodbye, although being Jem, he was doing it in the nicest way possible, trying to protect her feelings even as he told her that he was in love with another woman.

'But I also think that when a person has cared for someone, truly cared—' He stopped suddenly. 'Then some of it always remains. You never stop, no matter what. Even if, sometimes, you can't be together.'

'If it's too late, you mean?'

He didn't answer at first and when he looked back, his eyes were hooded. 'Yes.'

She swallowed, feeling her pulse thump heavily in her neck. 'You know, I've been thinking about what you said, about me never considering other people's feelings, and you were right, I haven't always, especially yours.'

'I shouldn't have said that. It was too harsh.'

'No, it wasn't. I needed to hear it.' She sighed. 'Recently it feels like all I do is apologise to you.'

'Then you should stop, especially since, right now, I should be the one apologising to you.'

'Why?'

'For not waiting longer.'

'You don't need to apologise for that. Eight years is a long time.'

'Still…' He lifted a shoulder and then cleared his throat. 'Does this mean we can finally be friends?'

'I suppose so.' She gave a half-hearted smile. She had a feeling that being friends with him would be even more painful than being enemies, but it was the right thing to do. Besides, at that moment, he really did feel like a friend. 'And in the spirit of friendship, I really do wish you and Miss Robinson every happiness.'

'Thank you.' His gaze locked on to hers before he put his hands on his knees, bracing himself to get up. 'Well, I think I've kept you awake for long enough. It's time you got some rest.'

'I do feel tired.' She stretched her arms above her head for emphasis. 'You know, you really don't have to watch me all night.'

'Yes, I do. Agnes and I are going to take turns. She's taking a nap in the parlour right now.'

'You have a parlour up here?'

'Yes, and another two rooms. Unfortunately, I use them as storerooms and they're full at the moment.'

'It reminds me of Belles. Warm and cosy.'

'I can't think of a greater compliment.'

'But I'll never get any sleep if you're sitting there staring at me.'

'Don't worry. I have some accounts that need doing and Agnes has some knitting. We won't be watching you all the time. We'll just be here if you need us.'

'That's a waste of candles.'

'If you say so. Now, that's enough arguing. Go to sleep.' He leaned forward and reached a hand out, smoothing his fingers over her cheek briefly before standing up. 'Goodnight, Nancy.'

'Goodnight, Jem.'

Nancy arched her back and rolled her neck from side to side, unable to remember the last time she'd slept so well. She'd fallen asleep before Jem had even opened his book of accounts, as soon as her head had touched the pillow in fact, a pillow infused with the scent of him, she'd realised as she'd rubbed her cheek against it. As she opened her eyes now, however, there was no sign of him in the room, nor any trace that he'd been there except for a folded blanket on the chair by the bed. She was aware of a stab of disappointment. Typical that she'd finally spent the night with him and missed it.

On a more positive note, she felt almost back to normal again. Optimistically, she lifted her ankle in the air and moved it in a slow, painful circle. All right, maybe not completely back to normal, but definitely better.

'Time for breakfast.' Agnes bustled into the room just as she lowered her leg back down to the bed. 'You're not exerting yourself, I hope?'

'Just testing my ankle. And I don't see what harm a little exertion will do anyway.'

'Doctor's orders, my dear.' Agnes placed a tray across her lap and went to open the curtains. 'It's a beautiful morning.'

'What time is it?' Nancy blinked in surprise as sunlight streamed into the room. Normally she was up and baking in the dark.

'Eight o'clock.'

'Eight?' She sat bolt upright.

'You obviously needed some sleep.' Agnes gestured at her tray. 'Now here's some broth like the doctor suggested, but I thought that a little hot toast wouldn't go amiss either.' She raised a finger to her lips and winked. 'Don't tell Mr Redbourne.'

'I won't.' Nancy smiled conspiratorially. 'Speaking of Mr Redbourne, where is he?'

'Preparing to open the shop, but he'll be up to see you soon, I expect. Although...' Agnes's expression wavered.

'Although what?' Nancy paused in the act of

blowing steam away from her spoonful of broth as Agnes threw a surreptitious look towards the door. She had the expression of a woman who had something important to say, but didn't know the right words. 'Is something wrong?'

'Not exactly, but…well, yes.' The older woman sat down on the edge of the bed. 'It might not be my place to say so…'

'But?'

'But I'm afraid that you being here, which isn't your fault, of course, might lead to talk.'

'Talk?'

'I mean, *we* know there's nothing untoward going on, but some people have wicked minds.'

'Oh.' Nancy put her spoon down, abruptly losing her appetite. 'I see.'

'And with Mr Redbourne being engaged…'

'Yes, of course.'

'His fiancée might not approve.'

Nancy closed her eyes, mortified that she hadn't thought of that herself. Maybe because she hadn't wanted to. Which meant that she'd been thinking of herself and not Jem's feelings again. *Of course* his fiancée wouldn't approve of her staying in his bedchamber. What kind of fiancée would?

'I'll go home right away.' She started to put the tray aside.

'There's no need for that. You need to see the doctor again first.' Agnes pushed the tray back, lowering her voice to a discreet whisper. 'Only it would probably be best to leave before tonight.'

'I understand.' Nancy nodded. 'And about last night, thank you for keeping an eye on me.'

'I wish I could say that I did, my dear, but I had a perfectly good night's sleep of my own.'

'But I thought—'

'Mr Redbourne insisted he wasn't tired.'

'You mean, he sat up with me all night?'

'Yes, my dear.' Agnes seemed to be avoiding her eyes suddenly. 'All night.'

'Oh.' She stared down at her tray, not knowing what to think about that.

'Ah, there you are.' Nancy swallowed the last of her illicit toast a few seconds before Jem entered the bedchamber a few minutes later. 'We need to talk.'

'Soon.' He looked sterner than usual. 'I have some visitors for you first.'

'For me?' She brushed a few tell-tale crumbs away from the blanket. 'Who?'

'You'll see. Just don't make this easy on them.' He planted his feet apart, looking altogether quite masterful, before twisting his head over his shoulder and calling, 'You can come in now!'

Nancy lifted her eyebrows in surprise as the four apprentices from the day before came trudging into the room, heads and eyes lowered.

'Well?' Jem folded his arms. 'What do you all have to say for yourselves?'

'We're sorry,' all four mumbled at once.

'And?'

'And we shouldn't have been arguing in the street in the first place.' George shuffled his feet.

'I never meant to knock you over,' Philip added. 'It was an accident. But it was all our fault,' he added quickly as Jem shifted position.

'And we've learned our lesson.' George took over again. 'There won't be any more fighting.'

'I should hope not.' Nancy lifted her chin, giving them all a superior look. 'And what have you learned about that girl you were fighting over?'

'What do you mean, miss?' The youths exchanged a look of confusion.

'Who is she *allowed* to talk to?'

'Whoever she likes,' they intoned in unison.

'Good. As long as that's understood, you can go.'

'Not yet,' Jem contradicted her. 'There's one more thing they want to say.'

'We want to make it up to you,' George mumbled, though he could hardly have sounded any less enthusiastic. 'When you're better, we'll do any jobs you need doing around Belles. We'll work in the evenings. For a whole month. *Each.* Any time you think of something, we'll come straight away, no matter what.' He scuffed his foot along the edge of a patchwork rug. 'I'll go first.'

'Well…' Nancy struggled to keep a straight face at the boy's miserable expression. 'That's good to know. I'm sure I'll think of a few tasks for you.'

'*Now* you can go.' Jem jerked his head towards the door. 'Remember, I'll be checking up on you.'

'Yes, sir.'

'Free work for a month each?' Nancy queried after they'd all trailed out in a sheepish line.

'It's the least they can do.' Jem's expression was implacable. 'Personally, I think they're getting off too lightly.'

'It should really only be the two who were fighting. The other two were trying to stop them.'

'Not hard enough.'

'It was still an accident.'

'One that shouldn't have happened.'

'That's the definition of an accident.'

'It'll still be a good lesson for them.' He unfolded his arms finally and sat down on the edge of the bed. 'So what was it you wanted to talk about?'

'Mmm? Oh, that.' With him sitting so close, she was having a hard time remembering. 'I think that it's time for me to go home.'

'Absolutely not.' He shook his head adamantly. 'You shouldn't be alone for a few days.'

'I know. Which is why I've decided to go to my mother's house.'

'Oh.' His expression wavered. 'I thought you said that things were still bad between you.'

'I know, but she's still my mother. She won't turn me away. Probably.'

'You don't have to go.'

'Yes, I do.'

'Ah.' He glanced meaningfully towards the door. 'Has Agnes said something?'

'Only the truth. It would be indiscreet of me to stay here.' She paused and then went on. 'It wouldn't be fair to Miss Robinson either.'

Jem stood up abruptly, going to stand by the window as if there were something he desperately wanted to look at outside. 'No, I suppose not. However, we'll wait for Dr Thorpe before making any decision.'

'All right. But after that—'

'After that, if he says it's safe, I'll arrange some transport.'

'I can—'

'You *cannot* walk.' He swung around, looking imperious again. 'I won't let you.'

'Let me?' She lifted her chin. 'You know, if I didn't know better, I'd think you enjoy telling me what to do.'

'Maybe I do.' His lips twitched, though there was a flicker of something else, something like regret, in his eyes. 'It must be the novelty.'

Jem drove the cart himself. It was one he used for deliveries around the city and was sturdily built, albeit not very elegant.

'Are you sure you're comfortable?' he asked, climbing on to the bench beside Nancy.

'Yes, thank you, and warm enough, too, before you ask again.' She smiled. 'Honestly, I'm feeling much better. There was no need to carry me downstairs.'

'Except for a sprained ankle.'

'Only a light sprain, the doctor said.'

'I'm still not taking any chances.'

'Stop worrying!' Nancy rolled her eyes. 'You're making me feel like one of those delicate women who come to Bath to take the waters for their nerves.'

'Somehow I can't imagine that.' He laughed as he flicked on the reins. 'I've never thought of you as delicate.'

'Is that a compliment or not?'

'It definitely is. You're one of the most capable women I've ever met.'

'Thank you.'

'Which isn't to say that you can't accept help once in a while. Now remember, when you get to your mother's, if you start to feel dizzy or sick or have any pain at all…'

'Then I should send you a message at once.' She jabbed an elbow into his ribs. 'Yes, I know, you've told me at least a dozen times.'

'I'm still not convinced you're listening. I need you to promise.'

'Jem…' She heaved a sigh. 'I don't mean to sound ungrateful, but you've done enough already. I'm quite capable of sending a message to the doctor myself— the doctor *I'm* going to pay for incidentally.'

'You will not. I sent for him. That means I get to pay.'

'*I* was the one he treated!'

'That's not the point.'

'It's very much the point.' She thrust her chin into the air. 'I can take care of myself.'

'Then you're welcome to do so from now on, but as for Dr Thorpe, it's too late.'

'What?'

'I paid him this morning.' He lifted a shoulder, hearing her sharp intake of breath.

'Then I demand that you let me pay you back.'

'You can demand all you like.'

'*Mr* Redbourne—'

'*Miss* MacQueen.' He turned his head just in time to catch the expression of furious indignation on hers before she whipped her face away again. 'I didn't mean to offend you.' He spoke more quietly. 'I just felt responsible for what happened.'

'How could you possibly be responsible?'

'Because I ought to have protected you. I shouldn't have turned my back on those boys.'

She looked round at him then, her eyes wide with surprise. 'That's one of the most ridiculous things I've ever heard.'

'Maybe so, but it's how I feel.'

'Fine.' She sighed again. 'I won't pay you back.'

'Thank you, and if things don't work out at your mother's… Well, you know I'm here for you.'

They carried on through the city in silence, though he found himself sneaking occasional sideways glances and not just to make sure she was all right. All his emotions were in turmoil. He felt as though he was being torn in two directions at once and no matter what his head told him, his heart refused to listen. Somehow just sitting beside her, with their legs only inches apart, gave him a sense of rightness. A completely false one since feeling that way was completely inappropriate and wrong, but maybe just for one hour, for one journey, he could stifle his guilt about Emily and enjoy it. Surely that wouldn't be so bad…would it?

'Turn this way.' Nancy pointed across him, gesturing to the left as they entered the Avon Street district. 'And when we get to the house, it would be best if you don't come in.'

'Any particular reason?'

'Yes. I'd like for you to still have a cart when you come out again. You don't leave things on the street around here.'

'I see.'

'It's that one.' She pointed to a narrow wooden building squeezed between two others. It had obviously seen better days—quite a long time ago, too. The paint was peeling and the top half was leaning sideways, resting against the gable of its neighbour, as if the house itself were dozing.

'Here we are, then.' He drew on the reins and

jumped down, going to knock on the door. Based on what Nancy had told him, he wasn't entirely sure what kind of reception they were going to get.

'What is it?' A small woman with dark hair opened the door.

'Mrs MacQueen?' he queried, although there was really no need when the face in front of him was so familiar. She might have inherited her hair from her father, but Nancy's features were the mirror image of her mother's.

'No. Mrs Naylor.'

'But Nancy MacQueen's mother?'

'Yes.' A flicker of panic crossed the woman's face. 'What's wrong? What's happened to her?'

'Nothing that won't mend,' Nancy called from the cart behind him. 'Hello, Mother. I've come home for a visit.'

Chapter Twelve

'What a shame that you couldn't join us for dinner last night,' Mrs Robinson commented, holding out a plate of biscuits towards Jem. They looked like pale imitations of Belles, he thought, lifting his palm to decline—too small, too thin and frankly unappetising by comparison.

'It was…' he smiled politely '…but I'm afraid it couldn't be helped. A friend of mine was injured and I had to make sure they were all right.'

'Very laudable. It wasn't anything too serious, I hope?'

'No, thankfully. She took a nasty bump on the head and twisted her ankle, but the doctor believes she'll make a full recovery.' He lifted his teacup to his lips, trying to swallow the memory. It was still hard to talk about. Every time he thought of it, he was aware of the same rush of sheer, unadulterated panic that had flooded his system when he'd seen Nancy falling.

'*She?*' his future mother-in-law repeated sharply.

'Yes.' He took another mouthful of tea, aware that both she and Emily were now watching him very intently, their twin gazes as piercing as arrows. 'Miss Nancy MacQueen. She works in one of the shops on Swainswick Crescent. Some apprentices were arguing and she got knocked over by accident.'

'Poor woman, but I don't understand...' Mrs Robinson made a strange high-pitched sound, somewhere between a gurgle and a squeak. 'I mean, without wishing to sound uncharitable, surely there were others who might have helped her? Why would some shopgirl's injury cause you to miss dinner?'

'Actually, most of her friends are away at present.' He felt a stab of irritation at the words. *Some shopgirl?* Even if they hadn't referred to Nancy, the comment would still have offended him. 'Whereas I was there and saw what happened first-hand. Consequently, I thought it best to take Miss MacQueen upstairs to my own rooms and call for a doctor.'

'*Your* own rooms? You mean you didn't return her to her own residence?'

'No. She's living alone at present and considering that it was a head injury—'

'For pity's sake, Mama,' Emily interjected. 'James was helping the poor girl. What does it matter where he took her? I'm sure that she's back to wherever she belongs now.'

'She is.' He inclined his head. 'I escorted her back to her mother's house before I came here.'

'You're so good and thoughtful.' Emily placed a supportive hand on his arm, albeit a little more tightly than was necessary. If he wasn't mistaken, he could actually feel her nails digging into his skin. 'Which is why I know you never meant to cause us any inconvenience. Our dinner party was to tell you some good news, but we can just as easily share it now.'

'Oh?'

'Well…' She let go of his arm to clasp her hands together. 'It's about Oxfordshire. Mama and I have been talking and we've thought of a way to persuade you.'

'Persuade me?' He lifted an eyebrow, struck with the horrible feeling that he already knew what was coming. 'To do what exactly?'

'To go there, silly! I've felt so guilty about you not being able to visit your friends just because of our wedding arrangements. So…' She turned and gestured to her mother. Almost as if they'd rehearsed, Jem thought sourly.

'It's such a coincidence!' Mrs Robinson took over enthusiastically. 'A relative of mine, a second cousin, wrote to me just yesterday, inviting Emily and me to stay. Naturally I wouldn't have dreamed of accepting normally, not with so much wedding planning to do, but considering your own situation, it seemed too good an opportunity to miss. Dear Lucinda lives just outside Oxford and since we wouldn't want to travel alone and you know my husband is suffering so dreadfully with gout at the moment, you'd be doing us the greatest of services if you would escort us.' She paused, briefly, for breath. 'And then, of course, you could go on to Howden Hall yourself.'

'I see. That really is a coincidence.'

'Isn't it?' Mrs Robinson's smile was a little too bright to be convincing.

'You seem to have thought it all through.'

'Jem.' Emily's eyes widened with a look of apparent hurt. 'You don't seem pleased at all.'

'It's not that.' Jem decided to put his teacup down before he snapped the handle off. 'However, I have a shop to manage. I don't have time to go to Oxfordshire.'

'But surely you wouldn't deny Emily the

chance to meet a duchess?' Mrs Robinson stood up for the sole purpose of taking a seat closer to him.

'I thought that you wanted me to escort you to your second cousin's house?'

'Yes, but perhaps we might pay a visit one day and be introduced? Surely the Duchess would be delighted to meet your fiancée? You must be good friends since she saw fit to invite you to visit.' Mrs Robinson sidled closer. 'Although I don't think you've ever mentioned how you happen to be acquainted with so important a personage?'

'No, I don't think I ever did.' Jem drank up the last of his tea. The room was starting to feel a little claustrophobic for his liking. He could almost have sworn the walls had just moved in a little. 'Now I must be going.'

'You're leaving already?' Mrs Robinson threw a panicked look at her daughter as he stood up. 'I'm sure that I didn't mean to offend.'

'You haven't.' He made a polite bow. 'I just have some work to catch up on after all the excitement yesterday.'

'So you'll think about Oxford?'

He clenched his jaw. 'If it means so much to you, yes.'

'And do come for dinner another evening this week. Tonight, perhaps?'

He hesitated. The last thing he wanted to do was subject himself to another visit like this, but perhaps he owed it to Emily. It was bad enough that he'd barely thought about her for the past twenty-four hours—worse still that, even now, half of his mind was on Nancy. Maybe he owed it to Emily to take her to Oxfordshire, too. It was what any decent fiancé would do.

'That would be very pleasant.' He reached for Emily's hand and pressed a kiss to her knuckles. 'Until tonight, then.'

Nancy was dreaming. She was lying on the surface of a lake, arms spread wide as waves lapped gently around her. She didn't usually nap, but today she felt completely relaxed, more than she had in a long time, longer than she could remember, and yet, even as she thought it, the water started to recede, lowering her gently down to the pebbles on the lake bed until...

'Mama?' She opened her eyes and stared in disbelief. Her mother was crouched on the floor next to the improvised pallet bed by the fire, smoothing a hand over her hair. 'What are you doing?'

'What I used to do when you were a little girl.'

Her mother's eyes looked suspiciously moist. 'You used to say you couldn't get to sleep without it.'

'I remember.' Long-forgotten memories stirred at the back of Nancy's mind. 'Sometimes Father would tell a story at the same time.'

'So he did. He always slowed his voice towards the end, trying to lull you off to sleep, but you'd never drop off until he was finished.'

'He told the best stories.'

'He did.' Her mother's tone was bittersweet. 'I used to enjoy them, too. You were such a lovely little girl.'

'Unlike now, you mean?'

Her mother's hand stilled. 'That wasn't what I meant.'

'Wasn't it?'

'No.' Her mother turned away and went to sit on a chair on the opposite side of the fireplace. 'You talk as if all I do now is criticise you.'

Nancy pushed herself up to a sitting position, looking around her childhood home and vaguely wondering if she was still asleep and dreaming. Floating in a lake struck her as several times more believable than her mother's current behaviour. She seemed different. Softer. As if for once, she wasn't about to start listing her faults.

'I haven't been the best mother to you, I

know.' Her next words were even more surprising. 'I wouldn't blame you for despising me. I've said some cruel things over the years, but you always wanted so much more from life than I could give. I thought you needed bringing back down to earth for your own good. I wanted you to understand that fairy tales aren't for the likes of women like us. It's not fair, but it's the way things are. I didn't want you to be disappointed in life.'

'So all those insults were to *help* me?'

'I suppose I told myself that.' Her mother looked shamefaced.

'You never used to say such things. Not before…' Nancy screwed her mouth up, letting the unspoken implication sink in.

'I know.' Her mother stared into the fire for a few seconds. 'I suppose that was part of it, too. I knew you resented me for taking up with your stepfather. You thought I was a fool.'

'I never thought—'

'Yes, you did.' Her mother smiled sadly, drawing the sting from the words. 'You've never been any good at hiding what was going through your mind.'

'But I never despised you,' Nancy protested. 'I just thought that you deserved better, especially after Father.'

'Maybe I did, but it's not easy raising a child on your own. It's hard work and it's lonely. It didn't feel safe either.'

'And you thought my stepfather was *safe*?'

'He wasn't always so bad. He might have been lazy, but he wasn't such a drinker when I met him. Even now...he drinks and gambles too much, but he's never hit me. Or you either.'

'That doesn't make him a good husband.'

'No...' Her mother's face twisted. 'No, it doesn't. I know the difference because your father *was* a good husband. I loved him very much, but I'm not strong like you. I didn't want to be on my own.' Her expression turned pleading, as if she were begging her to understand. 'I know I've defended your stepfather too much over the years, but it's not easy, admitting when you've made a mistake, especially when you've a temper like us.' She sniffed again. 'And as for all those things I said, I didn't mean half of them.'

'Really?'

'Yes. You're very pretty.'

'No, I'm not.'

'Yes, you are. Not like your friend Henrietta, maybe, but you're one of a kind, Nan. You're more vibrant than anyone else I've ever met. It was wrong of me to criticise you, especially when you've proven me wrong so many times.

You wanted more from life and you got it despite me.'

Nancy swung her legs over the side of the pallet bed. 'Why are you telling me all this now?'

'Because I was scared. Yesterday, when that man, that Mr Redbourne, came to the door, I thought that something terrible had happened. It made me realise how much I love you. How much I've missed you, too. It's good to have you back, even if it's just for a while. Sometimes you don't appreciate a person properly until she storms out in a temper.'

'Well, that's something I'm *very* good at.' She went to crouch down by her mother's chair, touched by the words. 'I'm sorry for all the times I've lost my temper, too. And if it helps, I don't think you're a fool any more.'

'Well, that's a relief.' Her mother's lips curved. 'In that case, you might be pleased to know that I took your advice and hid some of that money you gave me away. I have a reasonable amount saved now.'

'You have?' Nancy grinned. 'I'm impressed.'

'Aye, well, you've been better to me than I've deserved. Anyway, I'm truly sorry for the past. I just never thought that anything I said would ever hurt you, not really. You've always been so independent.'

Nancy dropped her eyes to the floor, hiding their expression. Her mother's words *had* hurt, and deeply, but she didn't want to talk about that, not now. She was tired of feeling angry and bitter. She didn't want to spoil the moment. More than anything else, what she wanted was a fresh start.

'In that case…' she peered up again hopefully '…maybe we should both make a promise never to criticise each other ever again?'

'I'd like that.' The deep creases in her mother's brow softened. 'It's good to have you back, Nan.'

'It's good to be back.' Surprisingly, she actually meant it. 'Where is you-know-who anyway?'

'Upstairs.' Her mother jerked her head to the ceiling. 'I'm surprised we can't hear his snoring from here.'

'Would you like me to pour a bucket of water over him?'

'Let's give it an hour.'

Nancy grinned and wrapped her arms around her mother's neck, only to drop them quickly again at the sound of a knock on the door.

'Who's that now?' Her mother brushed a hand over her eyes before getting up to answer it. 'Oh, Mr Redbourne.' She threw a flustered look over her shoulder as she took a step backwards. 'This is a surprise.'

'Jem?' Nancy leapt to her feet.

'My apologies for disturbing you again so soon.' Jem removed his hat and handed her mother a box. 'I hope this will compensate for the trouble.'

'A whole leg of beef?' Her mother's mouth dropped open as she peered inside. 'I don't know what to say.'

'Then please don't say anything. I just came to see how the patient was doing.'

Nancy stiffened, part touched by his concern, part horrified by the fact that she was still in her nightdress with her hair practically standing on end. Quickly, she threw a shawl around her shoulders and dragged a hand over the unbrushed curls, her pulse kicking a frantic, and frankly painful, tattoo against her chest at the sight of him. She wished that it wouldn't. She wished that her body wouldn't respond at all. It wasn't right to feel this way about an engaged man! Unfortunately, the knock on her head seemed to have made him more attractive than ever.

'I'm feeling much better, thank you.' She thrust her chin upwards, doing her best to look composed. 'Ready to get back to work.'

'So soon? What about your ankle?' His gaze dipped, though if she wasn't mistaken, it lingered on her hips before it reached her legs. For once, she couldn't quite bring herself to feel offended.

'As good as new.'

'It is not,' her mother interjected. 'I saw you limping just now.'

'*Almost* as good as new then, but I don't want Belles to be closed for any longer than necessary.'

'Don't be silly. Your health is a lot more important than biscuits.'

'I don't know.' She made a sceptical face. 'Some of our customers would say there's *nothing* more important than biscuits.'

'I'm sure they'll survive for a few days.'

'I agree with your mother.' Jem sounded serious.

'Of course you do.' Nancy put her hands to her hips, glad of the opportunity to argue. 'What a surprise.'

'*And* I have the key to Belles,' he added pointedly. 'So you can't go back until I say so.'

'Mmm.'

'Good. Then it's settled.' Her mother gestured towards an empty chair. 'Won't you take a seat, Mr Redbourne?'

'Thank you.' Jem inclined his head as if he were addressing a lady. 'I won't take up much of your time, but there was a matter I wished to discuss with your daughter, if neither of you has any objections, that is?'

'None at all.' Nancy plonked herself back down on her pallet bed.

'It's about the Duchess.'

'What?' She sat up straighter. 'Is Beatrix all right?'

'Perfectly, as far as I know. However, there's a chance I might be travelling into Oxfordshire this week, after all.' He shifted position, toying awkwardly with the hat in his hands. 'Miss Robinson and her mother have decided to visit a relative near Oxford and they've asked me to escort them.' He cleared his throat. 'It struck me that it would be rude to travel so close to Howden Hall and *not* to accept the Duchess's invitation so I'll be going on there afterwards. Just for a brief visit. A few days at most.'

'I see. Yes, that sounds like an excellent idea.'

'In short, there's still a chance for you to come, too, if you were tempted to change your mind?'

'You mean…' Nancy stared at him disbelievingly for a few seconds. 'You're suggesting that I travel with you and your fiancée and her mother?'

'Yes.' If she wasn't mistaken, he was trying extremely hard not to wince. 'I appreciate that it's not exactly an ideal situation, but I couldn't go without asking you to join us and I'm sure… since we're all mature adults, we could all get along…and it would really be for the Duchess.'

'She'll go,' her mother answered from across the room.

'What?' Nancy jerked her head around.

'It sounds perfect to me. You need to rest and if you stay here, you'll only be back in that shop tomorrow and don't pretend that you won't.' An eyebrow lifted towards Jem. 'I wouldn't put it past her to break a window to get in.'

'That doesn't mean I should travel to Oxfordshire instead!'

'Why not? You'll enjoy yourself. You always said Beatrix was one of your dearest friends.'

'She is, but she's a duchess now!'

'But still the same person underneath.'

'*You're* telling me to go to the home of a duke and duchess? *You* are?' Nancy gaped in bewilderment.

'Yes, *I* am. So it's decided, then.'

'No, it's not. I haven't agreed to—'

'In fact, you'll go if I have to drag you there

myself.' Her mother rubbed her thumb and fore-finger across her chin. 'That's not such a bad idea actually. I could do with a little holiday. I could find myself a nice little corner in the stables while you're out wining and dining with the aristocracy.'

'You'll do no such thing.'

'Then you'd better say thank you and that you'd be delighted to accept Mr Redbourne's kind offer, hadn't you?'

'Fine.' Nancy folded her arms. 'I'll come. *Apparently.*'

'I'm glad to hear it.' Jem looked from her to her mother in bemusement. 'In that case, I'd like to wait a few more days to make sure you're well enough to travel, but how does Wednesday sound?'

'Is that when your fiancée and her mother want to travel?'

'It'll have to be.' He got back to his feet, his tone leaden. 'In the meantime, I'll write to the Duchess and let her know that we're coming.'

'You know, you can still call her Beatrix.' Nancy rolled her eyes. 'We won't have to use all that "Your Grace" nonsense until we get there.'

'You'll do things properly,' her mother interrupted again. 'I didn't raise my daughter to be ill-mannered.'

'Who *are* you today?'

'A mother making up for the past. I'll bring her to your shop first thing on Wednesday morning, Mr Redbourne.'

'I'd be more than happy to collect her.'

'Absolutely not.' Her mother shook her head emphatically. 'You can't bring a carriage down 'ere, especially not one with two ladies inside. No, I'll bring her to you and that's an end to it.'

'As you wish. Until Wednesday morning, then.' Jem bowed. 'No breaking any windows in the meantime.'

Nancy gave a pained smile as he went out, waiting until the door was firmly closed behind him before rounding on her mother. 'What was that? You just condemned me to three days in a carriage with him and his fiancée!'

'So?'

'So I'm sure it wasn't what he wanted!'

'He offered.'

'He was being polite!'

'And why would he do that?'

'Because he's nice!'

'Nice?' Her mother's expression turned sly. 'How come you know him so well anyway?'

'I don't. He's simply an acquaintance who happened to be there when I hit my head.'

'An acquaintance who couldn't keep his eyes off you.'

'Probably because I look such a mess.'

'Your cheeks are looking a little flushed as well.'

'Because I'm standing next to the fire.'

'He still needn't have come here to check on you. Most people avoid places like this, although, given the size of him, he can probably take care of himself.'

'Mmm.' Nancy pursed her lips, refusing to dwell on that particular comment. She thought about Jem's shoulders far too often as it was.

'All I'm saying is that it seemed to me like he wanted to see you again.'

'He's engaged! To a lady, as well.'

'But not married yet.'

'Mother!' she gasped in shock. 'There's no difference. And what happened to fairy tales not being for women like us?'

'Says the girl who's spent her life proving me wrong.' Her mother came to sit on the pallet bed beside her. 'Anyway, I've changed my mind. Why shouldn't fairy tales be for women like us, too?'

'Because…because—' Nancy opened her mouth and then closed it again.

'Listen to me.' A prematurely wizened hand

folded itself around one of hers. 'There are good men and bad men out there. I ought to know since I've been married to both, but mark my words, *that* was one of the good ones.'

'I know that.'

'And I think he really likes you.'

'Not any more!' Nancy practically wailed. 'He used to, but now he's engaged to somebody else and if you're suggesting what I think you're suggesting then forget it. I would never try to break up an engagement.'

'Maybe you don't have to. Maybe you should just be yourself and see what happens.' Her mother's shoulder nudged against hers. 'At the very least, you can have a nice holiday. What's the worst that can happen?'

'*Nothing* is going to happen.' Nancy stuck her nose in the air resolutely. She'd never had a very high opinion of men, but women were a different matter. If there was one thing she'd learned at Belles, it was the importance of female friendships—of women standing up for each other—and she wasn't about to stab one of the sisterhood in the back. And even if she had been entertaining treacherous thoughts, albeit briefly…well, she was thinking about Jem's feelings from now on and that meant respecting his choice.

He'd chosen Emily, which presumably meant

that he loved Emily, and even if he had some residual feelings for *her* then it would do no good to confuse matters. If she went to Howden Hall, then she would be calm and contained. She would act like a lady, as much as she could anyway. She was even prepared to like Miss Robinson. No, more than that, she was *determined* to like her.

She would go to Howden Hall and absolutely *nothing* would happen.

Chapter Thirteen

He'd had bad days in his life before, Jem reflected, sitting in a hired carriage beside his future mother-in-law and facing his fiancée and the woman he'd pined over for years, but this was, without the tiniest sliver of a doubt, the absolute worst of his life so far. To be fair, he'd thought the same thing on the first day of the journey, then again on the second, but this time he *really* meant it. If he'd been trying to torture himself, he could hardly have come up with a better scenario than trapping himself in a tight space with two of the most significant women in his life. Women he'd hoped would never meet, let alone spend time together.

And it had been all his own doing. *He* was the one who'd invited Nancy to travel with them, but only because he hadn't in all conscience *not* been able to invite her. He certainly hadn't expected her to accept and, judging by the look on her face when he'd made the offer, she hadn't intended to either. It had all been down to her mother! Just like Emily's sudden, spontaneous trip into Oxfordshire was due to *her* mother! Or so he chose to believe because he wasn't entirely convinced that his fiancée wasn't complicit in that one… In any case, what did it matter? He was here, they were here and he was slowly but surely going mad.

He tipped his head back and groaned inwardly. Facing backwards was disorientating enough, but Nancy's injured ankle on the seat beside him was having an equally discomposing effect. He'd insisted that she keep it elevated despite her protests and now his eyes seemed determined to wander in that direction every few minutes. Every so often the lurch of the carriage would cause her leg to bump against his, too, sending tiny but searing pulses of awareness shooting through his body and making it impossible for him to do anything as simple as nap the time away. His nerves were exhausted.

He clenched his jaw with frustration, wondering if Nancy was finding the situation as unbearable as he was. If so, then she was showing no sign of it. Instead she looked remarkably, uncharacteristically calm. Tranquil even. Completely *un*like herself. Maybe she'd changed her mind about him again and didn't mind the situation at all. Which was both good in principle and mortifying in practice. Emily was the one who was constantly fidgeting and sighing and asking when their next stop would be, although he noticed she was also casting occasional sharp glances at Nancy when she thought nobody else was watching. The exact cause of these stares he was unsure of, although he supposed that his recent behaviour might have struck his fiancée as somewhat strange.

In his defence, and as he'd already asserted several times, he would have acted the same way towards anyone who'd been knocked down on the street outside his shop, although perhaps— and this part he admitted only to himself—not quite so assiduously. Perhaps he wouldn't have given them his own bed and then slept on a chair beside them for the entire night either.

'How much further can it possibly be?' As if on cue, his fiancée started moaning again, looking and sounding more petulant than ever.

'Hush, dearest.' Mrs Robinson smiled at her daughter and then at Jem apologetically. 'We're going as fast as we can.'

'The roads have been rougher than antici-pated, but we ought to reach your cousin's house by mid-afternoon.' Jem forced a smile, tempted to add that their description of *dear Lucinda's* house being 'close' to Oxford had been somewhat exaggerated. It wasn't even in the same county. Now their circuitous route was going to take them almost ten miles north-west of Oxford, thereby adding another few hours to the journey, after which he and Nancy would travel on together to Howden Hall. Alone. In a closed space. As if his nerves weren't frayed enough…

'Actually, Mama and I have been talking and it occurred to us—perhaps we ought to go to Howden Hall first?' His fiancée exchanged a surreptitious look with her mother. 'We discussed it at the last stop and we're afraid it might look rude if we don't stop to pay our respects to the Duke and Duchess.'

'I'm certain they won't think so. Besides, we won't reach Howden until this evening. Then it would be too late for you to turn round and go back to your cousin's.'

'But *I'd* feel that I was being rude.' Emily batted her lashes. 'All things considered, I think it would be far better if we all went there first. Besides, there's poor Miss MacQueen's condition to consider.'

'Are you feeling unwell?' He turned his head sharply towards Nancy.

'Never better.'

'You're just being polite, I'm sure.' Emily sighed condescendingly. 'But we don't want you to suffer a relapse.'

'And there's the matter of a chaperon,' her mother interjected, notching the condescension up yet another level. 'Not that we don't trust Mr Redbourne, of course, but travelling in a closed carriage together could be misinterpreted by some people. There's your reputation to consider.'

'My what?' Nancy's expression suggested she'd just grown two heads. 'I'm not a lady.'

'No, but still—'

'Only *ladies* have chaperons. What do I care what people say about me?'

'None the less, I think it would be far better for us all to go to Howden Hall first.' Emily's tone brooked no argument. 'Then Mama and I will go on to dear Lucinda's. I'm sure that we won't mind the additional travel,' she added, contradicting her behaviour for the past two days. 'And you'd still come with us, wouldn't you, James?'

'Of course.' Jem inclined his head reluctantly. At that moment, a pit filled with rabid dogs sounded infinitely preferable to getting back into a carriage with her and her mother, but he could hardly send them on alone. 'However, I really think—'

'Then it's settled.' Emily clasped her hands in her lap. 'And perhaps the Duke and Duchess might be so good as to offer us some refreshment before we continue our journey? You can never be sure of the quality of food in these coaching inns.'

Coaching inns that *he* was paying for, Jem thought silently, catching Nancy's eye before they both turned to stare out of the window. If he wasn't mistaken, at that precise moment, their thoughts were in perfect accord.

It was no use. After almost three days in the company of Miss Emily Robinson, Nancy was forced to concede defeat. Supporting other women was all very well, but liking her rival had proved substantially harder than she'd anticipated. Emily Robinson was a prize pain in the posterior and, frankly, that description was too generous. She was a pain in other areas, too. After one day in the same carriage Nancy's head had been throbbing with the effort of *not* thinking critical thoughts. Three days and it felt close to exploding. Listening to Jem's fiancée moan about the distance and discomforts was like being in the company of a spoilt and excessively vocal four-year-old. Which, judging by the way that Mrs Robinson pandered to and cajoled her, was exactly what she was. Not to mention a liar. The pair of them certainly hadn't discussed any change to their itinerary at the last stop—she'd been with one or the other of them the whole time—and as for any concern about *her* health... Well, if Jem believed *that* then he wasn't as intelligent as she'd always given him credit for.

She'd spent most of the journey so far staring out of the carriage window, keeping her face averted in case her mother was right and her opinions really were too obvious on her face, trying to ignore the atmosphere. Most of all, she'd avoided looking at Jem. There had been only a few occasions when she hadn't been able to resist, usually after Miss Robinson had asked, yet again, how long it would be until they arrived, and she'd had the distinct impression that he'd been as irritated as she was. They'd both looked away quickly, but the thought had been there, fleeting but unspoken, between them.

On the whole, it had been a strange journey. After running a whole gamut of emotions over the past month from humiliation to jealousy to eventual acceptance, she'd settled on feeling strangely calm. Calm enough to be actually looking forward to seeing Beatrix again and not terrified by the prospect of staying in a ducal mansion. She was even quite proud of her behaviour so far. She was being tranquillity and dignity personified, without as much as a hint of temper. And if she couldn't actually like Miss Robinson, then she was at least learning to tolerate her. That, as she kept telling herself, was what a calm person would do.

Still, at this point they couldn't reach Howden Hall soon enough and she'd never thought she'd say that...

It was late afternoon when the carriage finally rolled beneath the great gatehouse of Howden Hall—a structure so massive it looked like a castle itself. Nancy peered out of the window with trepidation. Now that they were almost there, she felt more of an impostor than ever, though it was some consolation to know she at least had more right to be there than the Robinsons.

She'd barely stepped down from the carriage, however, before Beatrix came flying out of the massive front door and down a flight of equally massive steps, themselves flanked by a pair of massive stone lions, to embrace her, almost knocking her off her feet with enthusiasm.

'You came! I don't believe it! We didn't know

when you'd be arriving exactly so I've been watching all day and...well...' Beatrix caught her breath and beamed. 'I'm just so pleased to see you!'

'It's wonderful to see you, too.' Nancy hugged her back, craning her neck to stare up at the house in amazement. There were entire streets in Bath that took up less space. *Hall* didn't seem quite a big enough word for a building so immense, though thankfully it didn't seem to have had any detrimental effect on her friend. Beatrix looked just the same as ever, albeit a little neater, in a blue chemise gown with her chestnut waves swept back into a neat, understated bun. 'So this is the place you gave Belles up for?' She pulled away finally, holding Beatrix at arm's length with a teasing smile. 'Honestly, I expected something a little grander. Are you sure we'll all squeeze in?'

'We'll manage somehow.' Beatrix glanced over her shoulder, her expression turning faintly anxious. 'You remember Quin?'

'I do.' Nancy tried not to tense. She'd noticed the Duke advancing down the steps towards them, looking just as arrogant and haughty as she remembered. Well, all right, not *quite* as arrogant. Not particularly arrogant at all, in fact, considering the fact that he was actually smiling, only she'd never seen his face do that before and her brain was taking a few moments to catch up.

'Miss MacQueen.' He bowed in front of her. 'I believe we got off on the wrong foot the first time we met. Perhaps we might start again? I'm delighted that you changed your mind and came to join us.'

'So am I and a new start sounds like an excellent idea.' Nancy bent her knees slightly, making a token attempt at a curtsy. 'I appreciate the invitation.'

'Thank you,' Beatrix whispered, linking arms before turning to greet the other new arrivals. 'Jem! Thank you for bringing her and for coming, too. It feels just like old times.'

'Your Grace, I'm honoured to be here.' Jem made his own bow.

'And that's quite enough of that. My name's Beatrix and this is Quin. There'll be no "your gracing" anyone, thank you very much.'

'As you wish.' Jem's lips quirked. 'In that case, *Beatrix*, might I present my fiancée, Miss Emily Robinson, and her mother, Mrs Robinson? They're on their way to visit some relatives near Oxford and wanted to pay their respects.'

'Mrs Robinson, Miss Robinson.' Beatrix's smile didn't waver. Which obviously meant, Nancy reflected, that Henrietta had prepared her. 'I'm pleased to make your acquaintance. Welcome to Howden Hall.'

'Your Grace.' Both the Robinsons dropped into floor-skimming curtsies, though for once Mrs Robinson seemed at a loss for words, her lips opening and closing soundlessly.

'Perhaps you'd care to join us for a cup of tea before you carry on with your journey?' Beatrix went on.

'Oh, we would be honoured.' Miss Robinson appeared to have no trouble answering.

'Not at all. Mr Redbourne is *such* a good friend. It's the least we can do.' Beatrix threw a warm smile in Jem's direction. 'Of course, you would have been more than welcome to stay here, if you hadn't already made plans.'

Nancy twitched, struck with the sudden urge to clamp a hand over her best friend's mouth… Unfortunately, a single glance at Miss Robinson showed that the damage had already been done.

'But we could easily change those!' Miss Robinson's eyes flared with excitement. 'If you really mean it, then we'd be thrilled to stay.'

'What about your cousin?' Jem sounded shocked. 'She'll be expecting you.'

'Oh, I'm sure she'll understand if I send a message to explain why we're not coming, won't she, Mama?'

'I…' Mrs Robinson found her voice at last. 'Why, yes, I'm sure.'

'Perfect!' Miss Robinson actually clapped her hands together with glee. 'It was going to be such a trial to leave dear James, even for a few days, but this way we can all stay together.'

'Um, yes…' Beatrix, by contrast, now appeared to be having some trouble maintaining a welcoming expression. 'In that case, I'll ask my housekeeper to prepare some more rooms. If you're certain, that is?'

'Perfectly.' Miss Robinson simpered. 'The truth is, I've been simply longing to meet you, Your Grace. Jem has told me *so* much.'

'Has he?' Beatrix's eyes flickered with a look of alarm. 'Well then, do come in. Most of my husband's family are away in Scotland at the moment, making a tour of the Highlands, but these are our friends, the Earl and Countess of Staunton.' She gestured to Samuel and Anna waiting at the top of the steps beside Sebastian and Henrietta. 'And Mr and Mrs Fortini you know.'

'Of course.' Miss Robinson smiled in a way that set Nancy's teeth on edge. 'How charming to see you again.'

'Isn't it?' Sebastian sounded as if his teeth

were gritted, too, though his gaze was focused on Jem, Nancy noticed.

'This way.' Beatrix gestured for everyone else to precede them before tipping her head sideways and lowering her voice. 'We need to talk.'

'Get the man some brandy. Quickly.' Sebastian gestured to one of the red leather sofas beside the fireplace in Quin's private office, waiting for Jem to fling himself down in one before putting a hand on his shoulder. 'You're a braver man than I am, my friend.'

Jem rubbed his hands over his face, still feeling somewhat dazed. Tea had been a strained, though mercifully brief, affair, after which Emily and her mother had been shown upstairs and the men and women, by tacit agreement, had separated into different rooms.

'Is he?' The formidable Duke of Howden reached for a decanter. 'Surely the journey can't have been that bad?'

'Three days in a carriage with the woman he's engaged to *as well* as the woman he loves? Not to mention a possible future mother-in-law? I'd say that's pretty damn brave.'

'I second that.' Samuel, Earl of Staunton, gave a naval salute before propping an arm against the mantelpiece.

'And I third it.' Quin's younger brother Corin sprawled in one of the armchairs opposite. 'Either that or completely insane.'

'I appreciate the summary.' Jem shot a dark look towards Sebastian, although he had to admit that brandy sounded like an excellent idea. He wasn't quite sure how it had happened, but somehow the torture of having Nancy and Emily together in the same place was being extended by another week. If he'd thought that he could have got away with it, he would have climbed straight back into the carriage and returned to Bath. 'And don't call her that.'

'Call who what?'

'Don't call Nancy the woman I love. I admit I used to have feelings for her, but I never claimed it was love. And in case you hadn't noticed, I'm engaged to Emily now.'

'So you're saying that you absolutely don't have *any* feelings for Nancy any more?' Sebastian lifted an eyebrow.

'Maybe we should give the man a chance to recover before he answers any questions.' Quin handed over a glass.

'All right.' Sebastian held a hand up. 'But don't think I won't ask again.'

'Don't.' For the first time in his life, Jem found himself wanting to punch his best friend.

'I'm only trying to stop you from making a terrible mistake.'

'No, you're interfering.'

'Interfering, helping… So how did you convince Nancy to come, just out of interest? I would have bet everything I own against it.'

'I didn't. Her mother did.'

'Her mother? But I thought—'

'I know. A lot's happened since you left.'

'Evidently.'

'You know, I've heard a great deal about Miss MacQueen over the past few months,' Quin interceded, gesturing at the already empty glass. 'Another?'

'Please.'

'Beatrix is very fond of her. I confess that, at one point, I was afraid she was going to choose her and that biscuit shop over me. Thankfully it didn't happen, but I'm hopeful that Miss MacQueen and I might still become friends.'

'Good luck.' Sebastian snorted. 'She has a low opinion of the opposite sex and once she's formed an opinion about someone, she doesn't change it easily. Remember the twelve tasks of Hercules? Expect something like that. Times ten. The first time I met her, she dropped a pile of books on my head. I shudder to think what might have happened if Henrietta hadn't rescued me.'

'You seem to be friends now.'

'Yes, but I'm charming.' Sebastian grinned. 'And I'm not a duke. In this particular case, that's a definite advantage. She's not keen on the aristocracy either.'

'You know, I used to think Anna was abrasive, but I'm starting to see I had an easy time of it.' Samuel rubbed his chin thoughtfully.

'It's not that I don't *want* Emily to stay here,' Jem interrupted, trying to drag the conversation away from Nancy. 'It's just...' He pushed his hands through his hair. 'It's all so damned confusing.'

'Well, this ought to make for a very entertaining week, I must say. I'm already looking forward to it.' Corin chuckled, earning himself a remonstrative glare from his brother. 'What?'

'What on earth are you all doing?' Nancy watched in bemusement as Beatrix made her way methodically around her private sitting room, peering beneath every piece of furniture. Which would have been strange enough behaviour on its own, but to make matters worse, Henrietta and Anna were also doing it, wrenching back curtains and peering behind doors as if they were afraid of mice. 'Is this some kind of bizarre Oxfordshire custom I ought to know about? Or is it just what the aristocracy do? Because if it is, you all have far too much time on your hands.'

'It's nothing like that. We're checking for someone, but she's not here.' Beatrix gave a satisfied nod before spreading her hands out apologetically. 'I'm *so* sorry for inviting Miss Robinson and her mother to stay. I only said it to be polite!'

'I know and you're forgiven.' Nancy perched on the edge of a chair. 'Miss Robinson is Jem's fiancée, after all.'

'Ye-es…' Beatrix exchanged a look with Anna and Henrietta before all three sat down in a row on the sofa. 'But what's going on with the two of you? I couldn't believe it when I got his message saying you were travelling here with him.'

'No, I couldn't quite believe it myself. It's a long story.'

'We have time.'

'Well…' Nancy drew in a deep breath and then sighed it out again, making her voice as matter of fact as possible. 'The long and short of it is that I had a bit of an accident a few days ago and Jem took care of me. So we're friends now. Sort of. Then I went to convalesce at my mother's and he came to visit and said that he was escorting the Robinsons to stay with some relatives near Oxford and asked if I wanted to travel with them, too. So I said no, but my mother said that I ought to because you're a friend and I eventually decided she was right and coming with Jem was the only way.'

'I see.' Beatrix blinked a few times. 'What kind of an accident?'

'I hit my head on a pavement and, yes, before you ask, I saw a doctor.'

'So you and Jem are really friends now?'

'We are.' She lifted an eyebrow towards Henrietta. 'I suppose you told the rest?'

'I *might* have mentioned something about you changing your mind about Jem and it being too late because he was already engaged.' Henrietta looked embarrassed.

'It's not her fault,' Beatrix interceded. 'I practically dragged it out of her. But I would happily have sent a carriage if it would have made things easier for you.'

'I know, but then it would have looked like I had a problem travelling with them, which I didn't.'

'Really?'

'No, but I coped with it. Anyway, I'm happy for Jem and I'm sure that he and Miss Robinson are going to be very happy.' She paused. 'Just as long as they don't travel together very often. She's not very patient.'

'She's completely wrong for him.' Henrietta shook her head sorrowfully. 'Did you see how she just *forgot* about visiting her family? Jem looked horrified. He would never do something like that.'

'No-o, but—'

'Jem is so very genuine and down to earth,' Anna commented, 'whereas Miss Robinson appears rather—'

'Insincere and ingratiating?' Beatrix suggested.

'Yes, and no matter what she said, she was *not* delighted to see me and Sebastian again.' Henrietta folded her arms. 'The last time we met, all she wanted to do was talk about the two of you and your husbands. I'm surprised she even remembers who we are.'

'Stop it!' Nancy moved her head from left to right along the sofa, wondering what had happened to her usually kind-hearted and generous friends. 'What's going on? You're supposed to be the nice ones.'

'You're right.' Beatrix hung her head. 'It's wrong of us to judge anyone so quickly. I suppose nobody's at their best after three days in a carriage.'

'It's just that you and Jem are so perfect for each other!' Henrietta burst out. 'You're obviously meant to be together. Beatrix, Sebastian and I have always thought so.'

'Have you?' Nancy swallowed the lump in her throat. 'Well, you might have said something sooner.'

'How could we when you used to bite our heads off for even mentioning his name?'

Nancy opened her mouth to deny it and then sighed heavily. 'I know. I've brought all of this on myself. Only what was obvious to you wasn't obvious to me. And by the time I came to my senses and decided to take a chance…' She heard her voice crack and cleared her throat. 'Well, he's engaged to someone else now and that's that.'

'But what if—?'

'There *are* no what ifs. Anything there might once have been between me and Jem is over.'

'What we need to do,' Henrietta went on as if she hadn't spoken, 'is find Miss Robinson someone else.'

'Someone richer. With a title.' Anna nodded enthusiastically. 'I bet she'd throw Jem over in a second.'

'What? No! Think how Jem would feel!' Nancy protested. 'I've rejected him enough times. He'd be devastated if his fiancée did it, too.'

'Or he might be relieved.' Beatrix tapped a finger against her chin. 'I mean, what if the engagement was a mistake? What if he rushed into it too quickly when he thought you didn't care for him? What if, given the choice, he'd choose you?'

'It still wouldn't matter. I've no idea what he feels for me now, if anything, but I know that he proposed to her. That means he must care for her and I won't put him in the position of choosing.' Nancy clamped her brows together. 'I want him to be happy and if Miss Robinson makes him that then…well, it's all for the best.'

'Oh, Nancy.' Beatrix reached for her hand and squeezed it. 'I'm so sorry.'

'I wonder if Corin might like her?' Henrietta murmured thoughtfully.

Chapter Fourteen

Jem descended the great staircase with a heavy heart. One that seemed to get heavier with every downward step. It had been a long day and it was about to get even longer. Ungrateful as it sounded, given the grandeur of his surroundings, what he really wanted was to go to bed, preferably with Quin's bottle of brandy, and sleep the next week away. He was dreading dinner. And breakfast. And every meal afterwards until he could go back to Bath and make some attempt to restore his sanity. The thought of listening to his future wife fawning over everyone with a title was enough to turn his stomach. He was having a hard time recognising the softly spoken lady he'd proposed to. A few more days and he might not know her at all.

He reached the bottom of the staircase and turned in the direction of the drawing room where they'd all gathered for tea earlier. The door was slightly ajar, but there was nobody else around, which gave him the perfect opportunity to pause, tug on the hem of his waistcoat and brace himself to get the evening over with. Because frankly, the sooner he put this day out of its misery, the better…

'*Jem?*'

He swung around at the sound of his name, uttered in a loud whisper from the direction of the shadows beneath the staircase.

'Nancy?' He peered closer, catching a tell-tale glimpse of red hair. 'Is that you?'

'*Yes!*' A hand stretched out of the shadows, beckoning him closer.

'What's the matter?' He closed the distance between them in two strides and then stopped short, alarmed by her appearance. Her skin looked pasty, her breathing sounded laboured and she was chewing her lip so frantically she seemed in danger of drawing blood.

'I don't know.' She gave an embarrassed-sounding laugh. 'Beatrix said she'd come to fetch me when it was time for dinner, but I said not to be so silly and that I was perfectly capable of coming downstairs by myself. Only, as it turns out, I'm not. Or I *was*. Until I wasn't. I don't know what happened.' She jerked her head towards the drawing room door, her voice wavering. 'I just know that I can't go in there.'

'It's all right.' He put his hands on her shoulders, lowering his voice to match hers. 'They're all friends.'

'I know, but…' She stopped and put a hand to her chest as if she were trying to calm herself. 'Just look at this place! When I was little, there were days when we didn't have enough bread to eat and now look where I am! I even have my own maid!'

'It's how they do things here.'

'Beatrix offered to lend me a dress, but I thought this would suffice.' She plucked at the waist of her gown. It was cornflower blue and had obviously seen better days, although the colour perfectly matched her eyes. 'Now I just feel ridiculous.'

'Well, you don't look it.'

'Maybe I ought to have accepted her offer, but I was afraid that I'd feel like a fraud in silks and satins. Like I was betraying where I come from.'

'You wouldn't be.'

'But I'd *feel* like I was.' She looked up at him, eyes bright. 'Just being here feels hypocritical. I've always thought it was wrong for some people to have so much when others are starving on the streets.'

'I agree.'

'You do?'

'Absolutely. What's more, I'm sure that Beatrix does, too.'

'I know.' A guilty expression passed over her face. 'I wasn't criticising her. I know she's not the sort of person who would forget about those less fortunate and I'm sure that she does a lot of good with all this. It's just so overwhelming.'

'I understand.' He squeezed her shoulders again. 'I've never personally been starving, but this isn't exactly the sort of place I ever expected to find myself either. Honestly, I'd be a lot more comfortable if we were staying in the local hostelry. I wouldn't have to wear this ridiculous cravat for a start.'

A nervous laugh escaped her lips. 'It's strange to see you dressed up.'

'Strange good or strange bad?' he couldn't resist asking.

'Good! You look very handsome.' Her lashes dipped. 'Only, on balance, I think I prefer you in shirt sleeves.'

'Then we're in agreement about that, too.'

'So we're both revolutionaries?'

'In spirit.' He smiled conspiratorially. 'Only we should probably keep that to ourselves for the next week.'

'You might be right.' Her lips curved. 'Thank you. I feel better already.'

'You're welcome. I'm glad that I could help.'

He tipped his head and ordered himself to let go of her shoulders. Standing so close in the darkness reminded him too strongly of an alleyway and a kiss and the way it had felt to hold her in his arms, to feel the warmth of her body and the strength of her heartbeat through their clothes. Despite the years between, his pulse still accelerated at the memory, tempting him to pull her against him again. Not necessarily to kiss her, but just to hold her and comfort her and... damn it, he was deluding himself if he honestly thought that he could stop there. And in case he'd forgotten, a voice in his head shouted, he was *an engaged man*!

'Well, if you're feeling better...' He took a step backwards, crooking an arm and offering it to her. 'We'll go in together.'

She started to lift a hand and then froze, a hesitant expression crossing her face before she lowered it again. 'Thank you, but you go ahead.'

'I'd rather not leave you out here on your own.'

'I'll follow in a few moments, I promise.'

'Still...'

'Please.' She darted a look around, as if she

were afraid of anyone else seeing or overhearing them.

'All right.' He drew his brows together, moving away from her reluctantly. 'If you're certain, but don't be too long or I'll send Beatrix out to get you.'

Emily was already in the drawing room, dressed in an elegant white satin gown, talking with Anna and Samuel while her mother stood to one side, listening placidly. Henrietta and Sebastian were standing close by, too, Jem noticed, certainly close enough to be included in the conversation, but Emily's attention seemed focused exclusively on the Earl and Countess. He wished that he could feel surprised.

'James.' Emily gave a little wave when she saw him. 'We were just talking about you.'

'That sounds worrying.' He put on a smile, nodding a greeting to the others. 'Good evening.'

'Well, it was really more about *us*,' Emily went on, 'and where we're going to live once we're married. We really ought to hurry and find somewhere. There's only a month until the wedding.'

'You know, as luck would have it, there's a house available on our street.' Mrs Robinson perked up abruptly. 'Wouldn't that be convenient?'

'Indeed.' Jem felt his smile stiffen. Honestly, at that moment he couldn't think of anything more terrifying. 'Fortunately, we can always live above the shop until we find somewhere we like.'

'The shop?' Emily burst out laughing. 'Oh, James, you're so droll sometimes.'

'Am I?'

'Of course! You can't possibly mean that.'

'I admit that it wouldn't be suitable in the long term, but it's warm and dry.' He paused and then couldn't resist adding, 'Some people think it's cosy.'

'Cosy?' Emily's expression turned to one of horror. 'It's tiny!'

'It only seems that way because I use a couple of the rooms for merchandise, but I can clear them out easily enough. I'm sure we could manage for a few weeks.'

'Weeks? How could I possibly entertain my friends there? I'd be humiliated!'

'Humiliated?' Temper flared in his chest. 'My parents always lived above their shop. *I* grew up above a shop. I didn't realise it was something to be ashamed of.'

'You know, it looks like the weather's going to

be fine tomorrow,' Anna announced suddenly. 'I noticed a pink glow in the sky earlier.'

'I noticed that, too.' Henrietta took a step closer. 'Hopefully, it'll be a nice day for a walk. The park here is so beautiful. Oh, Nancy!' She turned in the direction of the doorway. 'There you are.'

Jem stiffened, resisting the urge to look over his shoulder, conscious of Emily's still-enraged eyes on his face. She'd made several references to finding a house since he'd proposed, but he'd thought there was plenty of time. Apparently not. Apparently she wasn't averse to insulting him and making a scene about the matter either. No, he had absolutely no idea who she was any more. And at that moment, he didn't want to spend another minute, let alone the rest of his life, with her.

The dining room was huge. No, Nancy corrected herself, it was enormous. Colossal. *Gargantuan.* Whichever duke had built this hall had either expected a lot of guests or simply liked entertaining. Even the dining table was huge, although thankfully she was seated at the opposite end to Miss Robinson.

'I remember the first time I ate in here,' Beatrix murmured as she took a seat beside her. 'We were all so far away from each other, I thought we were going to have to shout to have any conversation.'

'It's very impressive.'

'It's ridiculous, but on the other hand, there are twelve of us tonight.'

'Twelve?' Nancy looked around, counting. She'd been introduced to the Duke's brother Corin at tea, but she had no idea who the little girl with curly black hair sitting a few places down could be.

'That's Helen, Quin's little sister,' Beatrix explained. 'We thought the journey to Scotland might be a little exhausting for her. She's only ten and somewhat shy.'

'I'm surprised you let her eat in the dining room.' Nancy shook her head quickly. 'Not that I mind, obviously. I just thought the upper classes liked to keep their children in the nursery.'

'I believe that's the way usually, but I think it's good for her to sit with us.' Beatrix smiled. 'And I put her between Sebastian and Henrietta for a reason. They're both so good with children.'

'True.' Nancy muttered an awkward thank you as a footman placed a dish of soup in front of her. 'So the rest of the Duke's family live here most of the time, too?'

'Yes. His mother, his sister Antigone and his brother Justin.'

'And how is that?' Nancy reached for her glass of wine. It was red and fruity and tasted expensive. 'Living with your in-laws, I mean?'

'We had a rocky start, but it's actually going quite well. His mother offered to move to the dower house, but it's not like we don't have enough space.'

'I really must compliment you on your decor,' Mrs Robinson interjected from the other side of the table at that moment. 'I'm quite speechless with admiration.'

Nancy took another sip of wine, sincerely wishing that were the case.

'Thank you.' Beatrix inclined her head politely. 'Although, I confess, it's mostly due to my mother-in-law. I haven't done much redecorating myself.'

'Well, it's perfect as it is.' Mrs Robinson tittered and then blinked, tilting her head to one side abruptly.

'Is something the matter?' Beatrix queried.

'Oh, no, it's just…forgive me, but for a moment there, you looked so familiar.'

Nancy stiffened, aware of a lull in all of the conversations around them. Only Beatrix looked completely calm.

'Do I?'

'Yes. I know it's impossible, but I could almost swear that we've met somewhere before.'

'I probably have one of those faces.'

'Oh, no!' Mrs Robinson sounded horrified. 'No, indeed, you're a duchess.'

'Our faces are nothing out of the ordinary, I assure you.'

'Well…' Mrs Robinson seemed torn between her desire to agree with everything Beatrix said and her instinctive horror to such a radical idea. 'Well…'

'Let's begin our soup, shall we?' Beatrix reached for her spoon. 'I don't know about anyone else, but I'm famished.'

'May I join you?' The Duke of Howden walked up beside Nancy as she stood admiring a painting of a lady on horseback in the drawing room after dinner. The gentlemen had decided not to linger over their port, joining them for coffee only a quarter of an hour later.

'Of course, Your Grace.' She inclined her head, resisting the urge to point out that since it was his house, he could stand wherever and with whomever he pleased.

'Call me Quin.'

She hoisted her eyebrows upwards. 'I really don't think I—'

'*Please.* It would make Beatrix happy.'

She glanced towards her friend, sitting beside the fireplace with Anna and pretending not to watch them. 'In that case, you might as well call me Nancy.'

'I'm honoured.'

'Mmm.' She caught her bottom lip between her teeth, repressing a smile. Obviously the Duke was making an effort on Beatrix's behalf, enough to almost make her like him, although 'honoured' was taking it a bit far.

'Do you ride?' Quin went on.

'I'm sorry?'

'Do you ride? I noticed you were admiring the painting.'

'Actually, it was the lady I was looking at.'

'Ah. That's my mother.'

'Really?'

'Yes.' He looked quizzical. 'Is it so surprising?'

'No, it's just…' She stopped, suddenly regretting the conversation.

'What?'

'Nothing.'

'Except?'

'Her expression.' She waved a hand towards it. 'She looks so sad.'

'She probably was. My parents' marriage wasn't very happy.'

'I'm sorry.' She gave him a sidelong look, but he was staring at the painting now, too, his gaze distant.

'In her defence, it was entirely my father's fault. He was a vindictive man as well as a gambler. My childhood left me with a profound antipathy towards marriage, I'm afraid.' He turned to face her again. 'Perhaps that's why I was such a terrible fiancé to Beatrix, not that I'm trying to excuse my behaviour. In retrospect, I can't blame her for running away from me.'

'At least she gave you another chance.'

'And I know how lucky I am, believe me.'

'Just be sure not to forget it.' Nancy narrowed her eyes and then relented. 'But I suppose I can understand how you felt. I've never had a very high opinion of marriage either.'

'Have you never been tempted to change your mind?'

She gave him a sharp look, wondering how much Beatrix had told him about Jem. 'Once, but sometimes people run out of chances.'

'I'm sorry to hear that.'

'The past is the past.' She tossed her head. 'As

for riding, however, I've never sat on a horse in my life.'

'Are there any other pastimes you enjoy?'

'Pastimes?'

'Things you particularly like to do in your spare time. My whole estate is at your disposal. Anything you wish to do, you've only to ask.'

'Um… I don't know. I've never really thought about pastimes.'

'I think that what Miss MacQueen is trying *not* to say is that there isn't much free time when you're running a business.' Jem came over to join them at that moment. Which would have been quite pleasant, Nancy thought, if Miss Robinson hadn't been hanging on to his arm like a sullen-looking limpet. Judging by the atmosphere in the drawing room when she'd finally summoned the courage to enter earlier, there appeared to have been some kind of disagreement between them and the effects were still evident. 'She's the hardest-working person I know.'

'Second only to one other.' She gave him an arch look in reply.

'Not for much longer,' Miss Robinson interjected. 'It's high time for James to stop working so hard and start enjoying the finer things of life.'

'I told you, I enjoy what I do.'

'But I worry about you.' Miss Robinson batted her eyelashes at the Duke. 'He's going to employ a manager once we're married.'

'What?' Sebastian whirled around from where he was standing a few feet away. 'That doesn't sound like you, Jem.'

'It's not.' Jem cleared his throat. 'It's something we've discussed, but nothing's been decided.'

'Why would you even consider it? You love your shop. You always have,' Sebastian persisted. 'And what would I do without you as a neighbour? Who would I chat to on the doorstep every morning?'

'I would have thought a *real* friend wouldn't hold Jem back from moving up in the world.' Miss Robinson's eyes flashed tiny green lightning bolts.

'Meaning?'

'Seb.' Henrietta put a hand on her husband's arm. 'Perhaps it's none of our business?'

'You're absolutely right, he can make his own decisions.' Sebastian lifted a cup of coffee to his lips. 'Best of luck, old friend, you're going to need it.'

'That's enough,' Jem replied sharply. 'I haven't made any decisions about the shop yet and I've no intention of doing so tonight.'

'But—' Miss Robinson clearly didn't know when to stop arguing.

'*Not* tonight!'

'Do you know what I'd really like to do?' Nancy announced, breaking the awkward silence that followed. 'I'd like a sleep-in. Remember how we used to fantasise about those, Henrietta? We used to say that one day we'd sleep until noon, even though we knew we'd never be able to.'

'Then you must. Tomorrow.' Quin inclined his head. 'Sleep for as long as you like.'

'That sounds like bliss.'

'And after that, I propose a stroll around the park, followed by a picnic luncheon by the lake, if you're awake by then, that is.'

'Perfect.' She gave a genuine smile. 'I think that picnicking could make for a very enjoyable *pastime*. Now I can hardly wait to get to bed.'

Chapter Fifteen

Nancy stood in the doorway to the breakfast room, wondering what to do. The mahogany sideboard that stretched the entire length of one wall was covered with a variety of covered dishes, all of them smelling mouth-wateringly delicious. Unfortunately, she appeared to be the only person there. As it turned out, sleeping in wasn't so easy when you were accustomed to getting up in the dark and she'd already spent too long sitting around recently, recuperating and travelling, to enjoy the novelty. Besides, she'd woken up feeling ravenous. Given the fact that she was *still* sharing a roof with Jem and his fiancée, she hadn't expected to have much of an appetite, but apparently she'd underestimated herself. Her mouth was already salivating. So what was she supposed to do now?

No sooner had the thought entered her head

than a footman appeared at her side. 'Can I help you, miss?'

'What?' She almost jumped out of her skin in surprise. 'No. I mean, yes. That is...' She lifted her arms out to the sides and then dropped them again, deciding to just tell the truth. 'Look, I don't know anything about etiquette. Am I supposed to wait for everyone else or can I start eating? I suppose I could go back to my room for an hour.' She glanced towards the sideboard mournfully. Leaving all that food to just sit there would be a wrench, but it might be the ladylike thing to do...

'That won't be necessary.' The footman threw a quick glance over his shoulder before giving her a conspiratorial grin. 'The family dine whenever they're ready. You're welcome to start eating.'

'Well, thank goodness.' She smiled a thank you and strode into the room, piling a plate high with toast and eggs before selecting a chair opposite one of the windows. The parkland outside was covered with a thin layer of low-hanging mist, a grey gauze broken only by a few tree skeletons, though the sky was lightening fast. Yellow streaks were already beginning to pierce through the gloom. It wouldn't be long before they burnt it away completely.

'May I prepare you a drink, miss?' The footman made her jump again. 'Tea, coffee, chocolate perhaps?'

'Chocolate?' Her stomach grumbled at the word. 'Oh, yes, definitely that.'

'Excellent choice.'

'Have you worked here long?' She watched as he picked up a silver pot and poured her a steaming cupful.

'Almost ten years. Since I was fourteen, miss.'

'Is it a nice place to work?' She tipped her head towards the door. 'It's all right, you can be honest. I'm not a spy, I'm just curious.'

'Yes, it's a nice place.' The footman placed the cup in front of her. 'Much better since the Duchess arrived.'

'Beatrix has that effect. I'm Nancy, by the way.'

'I'm Luke, but we're not supposed to call guests by their first names.'

'You can if I say you can.' She thrust her hand out. 'Pleased to meet you, Luke.'

'Likewise, Nancy.' He shook her hand and then sprang back suddenly, turning into a living statue as Jem appeared in the doorway.

'Good morning.' Jem's gaze darted curiously between them, his eyes narrowing slightly at the other man. 'I thought that you were planning to stay in bed until luncheon?'

'It's not as easy as it sounds.' Nancy took a mouthful of toast. 'Besides, I'm still later than usual. Most days, I'd have almost finished baking by now.'

'True. I expect Sebastian and Henrietta will be next. We're all early risers.'

'You mean the ones who actually work for a living?' She winced. 'Sorry. That sounded mean-spirited. I'm sure that dukes and earls work sometimes, too.'

'Just later in the day perhaps?'

'Tea, coffee or chocolate, sir?' The footman approached the table again, staring at a point in mid-air.

'Tea, thank you. So…' Jem waited for the tea to be poured before continuing. 'How are you feeling this morning? About being here, I mean. Any better?'

'Yes.' She nodded, surprised by her own admission. 'It's still strange, but I don't feel quite so ridiculous any more, thanks to you. And Beatrix seems very happy. Marriage obviously agrees with her. Even the Duke seems less…' She scrunched her mouth up. 'You know.'

'Autocratic and dictatorial?'

'I was trying to think of a polite way to put

it, but, yes. Maybe he's not so bad after all.' She grinned at the footman. 'You can tell him I said so.'

'I wouldn't dream of it, miss.'

'Spoilsport.' She looked back at Jem, surprised to find him frowning. 'So are you coming for a walk this morning?'

'No. Quin, Samuel, Seb and I are going for a ride and then meeting you for the picnic, I believe. There was some talk of cricket afterwards.' His frown deepened. 'Are you sure you're up to a walk with your ankle?'

'Absolutely. I told Beatrix about the bump on my head, but she doesn't know anything about my ankle and I've no intention of telling her.' She fixed him with a stern look. 'And I don't want you to either. In fact, I insist that you don't.'

'Insist?'

'All right, I want you to promise.'

'As long as you say something if it hurts.'

'Agreed. You worry too much.'

'I worry about *you*.' He murmured the words into his teacup, though so quietly she wondered if she'd misheard them. 'Anyway…' He pushed his chair back abruptly and made his way to the sideboard. 'Breakfast.'

As expected, the mist had cleared completely by mid-morning, leaving a turquoise-blue sky in its wake. Perfect for something called a wilderness walk, Nancy thought, as she and Beatrix strolled arm in arm through some woodland, Anna, Henrietta, Miss Robinson and her mother just ahead of them.

'This really is a beautiful place.' Nancy caught a glimpse of the hall through the trees. She'd thought she might have got used to its size by now, but, no, it looked just as immense as ever.

'Yes…' Beatrix sighed wistfully '…but there are still times when I miss my attic room in Bath. It was the first place that felt like a home in a long time. I'll always love it for that.'

'It's that kind of place, but I'm glad things have worked out for you here, too.'

'Honestly?'

'Well, I wasn't at first, but now…' She chuckled. 'Your husband's not *so* bad. For a duke.'

'Thank you. That means a lot.' Beatrix squeezed her arm so that they were walking shoulder to shoulder. 'We did have some fun at Belles, didn't we?'

'We really did.'

'Do you remember the time you taught me how to defend myself? First we went to the park, but people kept staring at us so we went back to Belles and moved all the furniture aside in the parlour and you taught me how to break someone's nose with my elbow. Then we ate too much bread and cheese and ended up rolling around the rug clutching our stomachs.'

'I remember I couldn't look at a piece of cheese for months afterwards.'

'I still remember everything you taught me.' Beatrix's voice quavered. 'I haven't had occasion to use most of it, thank goodness, but I remember how you took care of me. I never thanked you properly for that.'

'It was Henrietta who took you in and gave you a job.'

'But you let me stay when she went north with Sebastian. You put up with all my mistakes in the kitchen and never shouted at me or got angry.'

'*Me?*' Nancy made an incredulous face. '*I* never shouted?'

'Not at me anyway.' Beatrix laughed. 'So thank you. For being a good friend, my *best* friend, when I needed one.'

'You're welcome, but that compliment works both ways. I'm lucky to have a friend like you, too. I should have come when you first invited me.'

'You're here now. That's all that matters.' Beatrix dashed a hand across one of her cheeks. 'Anyway, how are things at Belles?'

'Busy. I'm thinking of taking on a new assistant.'

'You don't have one already?'

'No, I've been putting it off. It just feels like such a final thing to do. You know, the end of an era.'

'At least the end of an era means the start of a new one.'

'I know. It's just hard to feel enthusiastic about that at the moment.' She took a deep breath and then blew it out again. 'But I will be, and as much as I miss you, I'm happy for you, Beatrix. Truly.' She gave a loud sniff, horribly afraid that she might start crying. 'Now, where's that picnic? It's been an age since breakfast.'

'What is it about the countryside?' Sebastian queried as Quin, Corin and Samuel thundered ahead on their mounts. 'It seems like everyone wants to either shoot it or trample it underfoot. I've always preferred a more leisurely pace myself.'

'Is that your version of an apology?' Jem wasn't prepared to laugh at his friend's humour just yet.

'I suppose so.' Sebastian turned his head, meeting his gaze squarely. 'But I'll say it out loud, too. I'm sorry for stirring things up after dinner last night. Henrietta says it was wrong and unfair of me.'

'She's right.'

'It's just that I don't want you to end up—'

'Don't.' Jem lifted a hand. 'If you're about to criticise Emily again, then just don't. I told you, I'm not breaking off our engagement. It would be dishonourable.'

'So make her break it off instead. Tell her she can't make you leave the shop.'

'She's not *making* me do anything, but she's consented to be my wife and I need to try to make her happy.' He rubbed a hand across his forehead, trying to soothe the ache that had taken up permanent residence behind his eyes. 'And if that means me spending a little less time at work then so be it.'

'So you're going to change who you are for her?'

'No, I'm compromising in order to give our marriage a chance. I'm trying to make the best of things.'

'What about giving up the woman you love?'

'For the last time, I've *never* said I loved Nancy.'

'No, but it was written all over your face. You know, it's odd, but she seems different now. Calmer.'

Jem clenched his jaw. That much *was* true, Nancy was being oddly calm. It seemed that both she and Emily had turned into different women since leaving Bath. As if he hadn't been confused enough...

'You know, I'm not altogether sure I like it,' Sebastian went on. 'It seems unnatural somehow.'

'All the pair of you ever did was squabble. Don't tell me you miss that?'

'But I do.' Sebastian shrugged. 'Anna was always far too sensible to argue with me. Nancy is like the little sister I never had. It would have been nice to have her officially join the family.'

'You know *we're* not actually related.'

'Not by blood, but you might as well be my brother. That's why I can say all of this without fear of you thumping me.'

'Brothers still hit their brothers sometimes.'

'But you won't. Speaking of families, how's your mother?'

'Much better.' Jem nodded his head, glad of the change of subject. 'I had a letter from her just before we left actually, full of ideas for the wedding.' Not that Emily had seemed to appreciate any of them when he'd told her.

'So maybe you don't need to worry about giving her another shock?'

'I *can't* break off my engagement.' Jem drew on his reins in frustration. 'Look, I'm not entirely happy with the situation either. I'm making more compromises than I wanted to for Emily, but, Sebastian, I need you to make them, too. I don't want my best friend and my wife to be enemies. I've got enough to worry about.'

'You're right.' Sebastian looked genuinely shamefaced. 'To be fair, Henrietta said all of this, too.'

'So?'

'So I'll make more of an effort with Miss Robinson from now on.' Sebastian managed to look almost virtuous for two whole seconds before a cynical gleam lit his eyes again. 'Although she might not want me to, not if there's somebody more important with a title around.'

Despite the lakeside picnic, Jem's grumpy mood had increased tenfold by the early afternoon, which made the thought of hitting a ball with a bat sound extremely appealing. Unfortunately, he hadn't anticipated everyone else wanting to join in with the game of cricket, too. Even Emily had declared that she was 'simply longing' to play, although not until Beatrix and Anna had said something similar, he noticed.

'Right. Teams.' Quin strode authoritatively

into the centre of the front lawn, cricket bat tucked under his arm. 'I suggest we draw lots.'

'That might not be such a good idea.' Corin hammered the wickets into the ground. 'What if one team gets all the best players?'

'Do we even *know* who the best players are?' Sebastian looked around speculatively.

'Not me,' Henrietta chirped up. 'I've never played cricket before in my life.'

'Me neither,' Beatrix agreed. 'Although I've been forced to watch it more times than I care to remember.'

'So have I,' Emily interjected. 'But I've always thought it looked rather fun.'

'And I played a little with Sebastian and Jem when we were children, but not for at least ten years,' Anna added. 'I'm sure it'll come back to me though.'

'I see.' Quin rubbed a knuckle between his brows. 'Perhaps we ought to have discussed this during the picnic. Do any of you know the actual rules?'

'Oh, I wouldn't worry too much about those.' Sebastian tossed the ball high into the air and then caught it again. 'Far more fun if we make them up as we go along.'

'No *rules*?' Quin looked aghast.

'How about married couples together?' Samuel curved an arm around Anna's waist. 'That sounds like fun to me.'

'What about those of us who aren't married?' Corin objected.

'You can team up with Nancy.'

Jem picked the second bat up off the ground and made a few practice swings, keeping his gaze firmly away from Corin as he did so. The thought of Nancy being paired with another man made him feel unreasonably, unfairly and nerve-twitchingly jealous.

'Hang on…' Sebastian held a hand up. 'There are ten of us and we need an equal number in each team. That means we can't all stay in pairs.'

'All right, how about this?' Quin snapped his fingers. 'Anna, Samuel, Sebastian and Henrietta play against Beatrix, Jem, Miss Robinson and me. Then one team can have Corin and the other, Nancy.'

'All right, let's toss a coin for them.' Samuel drew a shilling out of his pocket. 'Heads we get Nancy, tails Corin.' He flipped the coin and then bowed gallantly. 'You're with us, Miss Mac-Queen.'

Jem watched, wrestling a profound sense of disappointment as Nancy made her way to join the other team. It seemed fitting somehow, as if they were destined to always remain apart. He only hoped her ankle was recovered enough and she wasn't just feeling obliged to play because everyone else was. He'd have to keep an eye on her for any sign of pain. Purely for medical reasons, of course…

Another coin toss and his team was up to bat first, Quin leading the way with Corin as second batsman, which meant that he, Beatrix and Emily didn't have a great deal to do for some time. If he hadn't known better, Jem would have thought the brothers were playing for money. Each seemed determined to outdo the other in competitiveness, which would have made sense if they hadn't been on the same team.

Samuel and Sebastian, meanwhile, were taking a more relaxed approach, laughing and joking with their wives as they bowled and fielded respectively, though, thanks to an improbably accurate throw from Henrietta, Corin was run out after half an hour. Fortunately, their team had already scored enough fours and sixes to make Emily and Beatrix's subsequent combined total of nine runs seem of little consequence, while his own tally of thirty-two took their final result to one hundred and five runs before he was finally caught out by Anna, whose surprised expression was accompanied by a distinctly unladylike whoop of triumph.

Samuel and Sebastian were the first to bat on the opposing team, scoring fifty-seven runs between them before Quin took over from Corin as bowler and knocked them both out in minutes, swinging his arm as if his life depended on it. Following that, Anna and Henrietta made a respectable showing of twenty-eight runs, assisted by some decidedly more generous bowling from Quin, before Anna was caught out by an apologetic-looking Beatrix. Which left only one batsman. Or, more precisely, batswoman.

Having opted for the position of wicketkeeper, Jem was perfectly placed to watch as Nancy accepted the bat and made her way to the stumps. She hadn't had a great deal to do during the first half of the game, occupying a space in left field, although she'd laughed heartily at everyone else's jokes. As far as he could tell, she wasn't limping either.

'How are you enjoying the game?' he asked as she approached.

'I'd like it better if we were winning.' She flashed a quick smile before taking up a position in front of the wickets, planting her feet firmly apart and wiggling her hips in a way that made him glad he was crouched down. 'By my count, we need twenty runs to draw even.'

'There's only you and Henrietta left.'

She threw a swift glance over her shoulder, eyebrows raised. 'Are you saying you don't think we can do it?'

'Not to sound ungallant, but I've been watching Henrietta.'

'I see.' The eyebrow arched higher. 'In that case, maybe you'd care for a small wager?'

'A wager?' He chewed the inside of his cheek, considering. 'You know, now that I think about it, I don't recall you mentioning whether or not you've played before.'

'Didn't I?'

'No. So have you?'

'Played before?' She turned away, though not before he saw her lips curve. 'A little. The games weren't quite as civilised as this, but I know how a bat works.'

'Should I stand a little further back?' He found himself smiling, too.

'That's up to you.' She adjusted her stance one last time. 'The trick is to keep Henrietta where she is.'

'You mean, not to let her bat again? You'd need to hit all fours or sixes to make sure.'

'Yes, I would.' Her tone was a tiny bit wicked. 'But then you *did* tell me not to use my ankle.'

Jem braced himself, preparing to catch, as Quin ran towards them, though if his hunch was correct, there wasn't much point. None the less, he waited, poised, as the Duke of Howden swung his arm in a leisurely circle, obviously still in a generous mood. It was a slow ball, so slow that for a moment, Jem thought that Nancy wasn't actually going to move at all. Then she lunged suddenly, sweeping the bat forward in a fluid, powerful arc and sending the ball hurtling towards some distant trees.

'I'd call that a six, wouldn't you?' She placed the tip of the bat on the ground, crossing one leg over the other and leaning casually against it.

'I would.' Jem lifted a hand to his forehead, shielding his eyes from the sun as he watched the ball disappear into the foliage. None of the fielders were anywhere near close enough to catch it, though Corin was optimistically sprinting in that direction.

'Some women can do embroidery.' Nancy examined her nails casually. 'Some of us can swing a bat.'

'Remind me never to play poker with you.'

'Pity. I'm quite good at that, too.'

'This may prove to be a more exciting game than I'd anticipated.' Quin put his hands on his hips as he walked towards them. 'Well played.'

'Thank you.' Nancy dipped into a full curtsy. 'But I'm just warming up.'

* * *

'Why don't we have some dancing?' Anna announced as the men entered the drawing room after dinner. 'I'd like to waltz.'

'Feeling energetic, my love?' Samuel smiled affectionately.

'Very.' She held her hands out. 'So come here and perform your husbandly duty.'

'Always.'

'What about you, Wife?' Sebastian made an elaborate bow in front of Henrietta, flourishing his arms above his head before dropping them almost to the floor. 'Would you care to waltz?'

'I don't know. I ate a lot of dessert at dinner.' Henrietta tapped a finger against her chin. 'But since it's you...'

'Emily?' After a momentary hesitation, Jem bowed over Miss Robinson's hand. 'Would you care to?'

'I'd be delighted.'

'And I'll play the piano.' Mrs Robinson leapt to her feet. 'How delightful.'

'Which just leaves Beatrix, Quin and... Oh.' Anna flushed.

Which just left *her*, Nancy thought, since Corin had gone to visit some neighbours for dinner. Sometimes friends could be just as unintentionally cruel as enemies.

'Don't mind me.' She feigned a yawn. 'I'm worn out from this afternoon anyway. It's not easy getting fifty runs on your own.'

'You made it look that way.' Henrietta laughed. 'I might as well have taken a nap on the pitch for all the use I was. Not that I'm complaining since we won.'

'It was a well-deserved victory,' Quin agreed magnanimously. 'However, you're not getting out of the evening's entertainment that easily.' He extended a hand towards Nancy. 'I'd be honoured if you'd dance with me.'

'You should dance with Beatrix.'

'And I will, but first I'd like to dance with one of the finest cricketers I've ever played against. Next time, you're on my team.'

'We'll see about that.' Nancy looked past his shoulder to where Beatrix was smiling encouragingly. And maybe Quin wasn't just asking her to dance out of pity. Maybe he really wanted to dance with her. And why shouldn't she dance with a duke?

'All right, then.' She put her cup of coffee aside and stood up. 'But you'll have to show me the steps. We didn't do much waltzing in Avon Street.'

'I'd be delighted.'

They made their way to join the others and

then Mrs Robinson started playing and they all began dancing and she thought that maybe the waltz was quite fun, after all. It felt positively liberating, in fact, twirling and spinning and whirling around the room. And then the music finished and they all changed partners and she was with Sebastian, who swung her around with just a little too much enthusiasm, and then Samuel, who proved to be lighter on his feet than anyone, and then…then there was only one partner left. She looked towards Jem, just finishing his dance with Beatrix, glad that her cheeks were already flushed from all the exertion, to find his eyes already fixed upon her. At which point, the lid over the piano keys snapped shut abruptly.

'Well, you must all be exhausted. I certainly am from playing.' Mrs Robinson got up from the piano stool and moved back to her seat by the fireplace. 'That's quite enough of that.'

Chapter Sixteen

Ten o'clock. How could it *only* be ten o'clock? Jem glared at the clock in the hallway on his way to bed. He wasn't really tired, but he couldn't stand the atmosphere in the drawing room a single second longer. Quin and Beatrix were excellent hosts, but it was no use. The whole situation was torture and it had to stop. *He* had to make it stop. His nerves were shattered and his emotions raw from being constantly torn in two directions at once. Tomorrow, he'd find a reason to leave Howden, to either take Emily and her mother on to *dear cousin Lucinda's* house or to return to Bath. It was the only way that he was going to hang on to even the tiniest sliver of sanity. If it wasn't already too late for that.

He was just mounting the staircase when he spotted a door leading to the back of the house and slipped through it instead, emerging into the cool night air with a groan of relief. Slowly, he walked to the waist-height stone wall that ran along the edge of the terrace and curled his fingers around it, letting the tension ease from his body as he gazed at the moonlit park. No doubt it was a beautiful scene, but he was too bone-weary to appreciate it tonight. At that moment, all he wanted was to stop thinking and feeling and simply stare into the darkness.

It was only a few seconds, however, before the tension returned, brought back by the sound of footsteps coming from the left side of the terrace towards him. He didn't need to turn to know whose footsteps they were. He knew the brisk way that she walked, the very rhythm of her tread... Meanwhile, his own feet seemed frozen to the spot, unable to carry him away.

'Jem? What are you doing here?' Nancy's own surprise at seeing him was evident in her voice. 'I thought you were retiring?'

'I intended to.' He shrugged without turning, afraid of what his face might reveal, even in moonlight. 'Then this seemed like a better idea.'

'It's getting cold.' She came and put her hands on the wall beside his. True enough, there were goosebumps on her arms. He wondered if she had a shawl for the evening or whether she felt 'ridiculous' wearing that, too. He wished that she wouldn't. No matter what she wore, she was always the most beautiful woman in the room to him. And if that wasn't another reason why he should hurry up and leave then he didn't know what was.

'I could say the same thing to you,' he commented, resisting the urge to remove his jacket and wrap it around her shoulders. Touching any part of her would be a supremely bad idea. 'What are you doing out here?'

'It was getting stuffy in the drawing room so I thought I'd come outside and take a walk before bed. I just wanted some air.' She sounded defensive suddenly. 'I didn't follow you.'

'I never thought you did. I suppose we both had the same idea.'

'Yes.' She paused. 'But I can go if you want to be alone?'

Jem opened his mouth to agree and found the words frozen on his tongue. He *ought* to agree. Telling her to leave; or leaving himself, would undoubtedly be the wisest thing to do, only he couldn't bring himself to say it. He didn't want to say it. He'd done everything he could to avoid this exact situation, but now that it was here, he wanted to stay like this, with *her*, for as long as he could. 'No, I don't want you to go.'

'Jem...' She sounded concerned. 'Are you all

right? You haven't been yourself since we left Bath. You don't seem happy.'

'Happy?' He gave a hollow laugh and tipped his head back, looking up at the night sky. There must be clouds, he thought, since most of the stars were veiled. 'I don't know what I am.'

'You're starting to worry me.'

'Am I? You know, you're acting oddly, too.'

'I am not!' He heard the indignation in her voice.

'You're not being yourself.'

'I'm behaving properly. I'm being calm and reasonable.'

'That's what I meant.' He drew in a deep breath and then let it out again slowly. 'You know, when I went to your mother's house and asked if you wanted to come with us, I never thought that you'd accept.'

'Then why did you ask?'

'Honestly? Because I couldn't not. It would have felt wrong.'

'Sometimes you're too nice for your own good.'

'Don't do that.' He clenched his jaw. 'Don't call me nice.'

She moved closer, touching her fingertips to his shoulder. 'I'm sorry. I meant it as a compliment. It's one of the things I—' She stopped mid-sentence and dropped her hand again. 'Anyway, I'm glad that you asked me *and* that I came, although I'm sorry if it's caused you difficulties. It's been good to see Beatrix again. It's made me realise that she's done the right thing. So thank you.'

'You're welcome. I'm glad that some good has come out of this mess.'

'*Mess?* Jem, what do you mean?'

'You. Me. Emily.'

There was a heavy silence, so heavy he actually heard her swallow. 'Why is that a mess? The two of you are engaged. You're in love.'

'Who told you that?' He whipped his head around, looking at her finally.

'Well...no one. I just presumed. I mean, you proposed to her.'

'Not because we were in love.' His voice was harder than he'd intended. 'It's not that I didn't care for her. I did. When I asked her to marry me, I truly thought we could make a life together, only she's not the person I thought she was. She's definitely not the woman I proposed to.'

'Oh.' Nancy's chest seemed to be rising and falling very quickly. 'Maybe you shouldn't judge her on the past few days. Some people get overwhelmed by places like this. By titles and money, too. I'm sure she'll get back to normal soon.'

'What if this *is* her normal?' He felt something inside him snap, all the emotions of the past week catching up with him in a sudden torrent. 'What if I only asked her to marry me because it seemed like a sensible arrangement that would make my parents happy and now it turns out that I didn't know her at all?'

'I shouldn't be listening to this.' There was a faint look of panic on Nancy's face. Panic mixed with shock and something that looked like excitement. Something that gave him the confidence to go on.

'Yes, you should.' He reached for her hands, lifting them to his chest. 'Nancy, I've made a terrible mistake. It turns out there was only one woman in the world for me and I gave up on her a day too soon.'

'Jem…'

'I *don't* love Emily.'

'Hush!' She threw a swift look towards the house.

'I know I shouldn't say so, but she knows it already. Love was never part of our arrangement. I thought that we'd grow closer and learn to care for each other, but if anything, we're further apart than we were. I don't even *like* that woman in there. What's more, I don't think she likes me either. I can't understand why she accepted my proposal when all she wants is to turn me into someone I'm not.'

Nancy stared at him, opening and closing her mouth wordlessly a few times before finding her voice again. 'I don't know what to say.'

'Then don't say anything, just listen.' He looked down at their hands for a moment, gathering the words he wanted to say. 'Nancy, I've done what was expected of me my whole life. I've done everything I could to make the people I love happy and yet somehow I've made myself miserable in return. That can't be right, can it?' An image of his mother's face flashed into his mind. His engagement *had* brought her a great deal of joy, but surely if he explained the situation openly and honestly then she'd understand? Like Sebastian said, it wouldn't necessarily make her ill again…

'Maybe we should talk about this in the morning?'

'No.' He tightened his grip on her fingers as Nancy started to pull away. 'I can't wait any longer. These past few days, I've felt like I've been going mad, wanting you and being honour-bound to Emily. I need you to be honest with me now before it's too late. That evening when you came to my store, when you told me that you'd changed your mind about us and wanted to accept my offer, do you still feel the same way? Or are you and Mr Palmer—?'

'There is no me and Mr Palmer,' she interrupted before he could finish the question. 'There never was.'

'But I thought the two of you…?'

'We only went walking together that once and, as it turned out, he had ulterior motives.'

'What kind of ulterior motives?'

'Oh, not *that* kind.' She obviously noticed the furious look on his face. 'He just wanted me to give his sister a job.'

'Damned fool.' Jem shook his head, relieved and indignant on her behalf at the same time. 'I mean I'm glad, but the stupid, damned fool.'

'I thought so, too.' Her lips quirked. 'But it's nice to hear somebody else say it.'

'So you're free?'

'Ye-es.'

'Then what about us? What about my offer? Because if you still want me, I'll ask Emily to end our engagement.'

'Jem! You can't ask me questions like that!' She tore one of her hands away, lifting her fingers to cover his lips. 'It's impossible.'

'No, it's not. There's still time.'

'No, there isn't. I know you. I know how honourable you are. If you go back on your word, you'll be miserable.'

'I'll feel guilty, yes, but miserable?' He peeled her fingers away and pressed his lips to the centre of her palm. 'With you? Never. I'm tired of being honourable, Nancy. I want you. I always have. If I'd thought there had been even the slightest chance of you changing your mind about me, I would never have proposed to Emily. I would have waited until you agreed to let me court you and then I would have proposed every single day until you said yes.'

'Proposed?'

'Yes! I love you. I've fought and denied it for years, but it's the truth. I've been head over heels from almost the first day we met. I'm not asking for a promise, I just need to know if there's any hope for us? Tell me that and I'll do whatever it takes for us to be together.'

'I do…' Nancy started to speak and then stopped, her voice trailing away until all he could hear was their breathing. They both sounded ragged. Slowly, he drew her closer, lifting her knuckles to his lips and kissing each one in turn, staring deep into her eyes all the while.

'Jem…' She whispered his name and he let go of her hands, slipping his arms around her waist instead. It was wrong, he knew. He was supposed to marry someone else in less than a month. And yet everything about holding Nancy felt right. Her body moulded to his as if they were two parts of one whole, as if they were meant to be together and for ever, too.

He lowered his head, touching her lips with his own. Softly, gently, asking a question, sliding his hands lower when she didn't push him away. And then all the questions and guilt faded away and there was only him and her and the most perfect, intoxicating kiss in the world—so perfect, he wished it could go on for ever. If he could just hold on to this moment...

'No!' She lifted her hands to his chest, pushing him away abruptly. 'Your honour is one of the things I've always admired most about you. It's a big part of who you are. I'd never want you to lose it, not even for me.' She shook her head frantically. 'Who's to say we'd be any good together anyway?'

'We would be. I've never been so certain of anything in my entire life.'

'Really?' Her expression wavered and then hardened again. 'Maybe you're right, but it's no use. You might think you can ask Miss Robinson to end your engagement and live with yourself, but I know you better and I won't let you do it.' She took a few steps backwards. 'You told me once that I never considered your feelings. Well, I'm doing it now and I'm saving you from yourself. I *know* that you'll never forgive yourself if you do something dishonourable and you'll never look at me in the same way again either.' She lifted her shoulders, her expression hopeless. 'Because I'd be the woman who'd made you do it.'

'You wouldn't be making me do anything. It would be my decision.' He advanced towards her as she retreated. 'This is our last chance, Nancy.'

'I know.' She jerked her chin up, her expression almost desperate. 'Which is why I'm telling you that there's no hope for us. You have to do the right thing. You have to marry Emily and be happy.' She held her hands out, effectively ordering him from coming any closer. 'You deserve to be happy, Jem.'

'I won't be. Not without you.'

'*Try.*'

He stood, rooted to the spot as she walked, then ran, back in the direction she'd come, fleeing from him as if he'd just suggested something indecent, not told her he loved her. After a few moments, he turned around and slammed his hands down hard on the wall. It was a good thing that Howden Hall was well built because at that moment he felt like he could have knocked down a hundred stone walls with his bare fists and not felt a thing. Nothing compared to the pain of feeling as if his heart were being pulled apart by wild horses.

'Well, well, well…' A new voice spoke from the darkness suddenly. 'That was all very interesting, I must say. I think it's about time that you and I had a little talk, James. Only let's find somewhere more private, shall we? You never know who's listening in a place like this.'

Chapter Seventeen

Nancy stumbled headlong into the empty library, flinging the door shut behind her and throwing herself back against it. She didn't know how she'd found the strength to run away from Jem, but somehow she had. Her ladylike veneer had stood her in good stead. She'd stayed calm and composed and hadn't cracked even when he'd said that he loved her, though the pained look in his eyes had cut her to the quick. It had taken all of her willpower not to fling her arms around him and proclaim that she loved him, too, but instead, she'd done the right thing.

Hopefully at some point in the future she'd feel good about that, but at the moment, she felt utterly wretched. Heartbroken times a million. She'd destroyed her own future chance of happiness and told the man she loved to marry someone else—a woman he didn't love and who didn't love him in return! All because she knew him better than he knew himself and she loved him enough to let him go.

She pressed her palms to her face, trying to force back the tears already pooling in her eyes and seeping down her cheeks. She didn't want to cry, or at least not yet, where somebody else might come in and find her, sobbing by candlelight like a heroine in some Gothic novel—and now that she thought of it, there really were a surprising number of lit candles in an empty room. No, she'd cry later in the safety of her own bedchamber, but right now she needed to compose herself to go back into the drawing room and bid everyone goodnight as if nothing had happened. She needed to—

Her nerves prickled at the sound of footsteps approaching the door. No! If it was Beatrix or Anna or Henrietta then there would be questions and consoling hugs and she couldn't bear the thought of either just yet. And if it was anyone else then it would just be *too* awkward. What if it was the Duke? She'd die of mortification. Quickly, desperately, she ran around the edge of the room, looking for another way out, but there were no other doors and only one window and she didn't have enough time to open that and jump out. Given her recent luck, she'd probably land in a patch of nettles anyway.

At last her gaze fell on an oval-shaped table set in front of one of the bookcases, conveniently covered with a floor-length, lace-trimmed table-cloth. Frankly, it looked somewhat out of place and unnecessary in a library, not that that mattered given the circumstances, she reminded herself, throwing the edge of the cloth aside and diving beneath, only to find herself face to face with a small girl with black curls and blue eyes. *Helen.*

'Oh!' She gave a startled yelp and then clapped a hand to her mouth as the door creaked open and two sets of footsteps entered the room.

'Yes, this is much better.'

Nancy dropped her hand again, recognising Miss Robinson's voice instantly, though it sounded less sweet and simpering than usual. In fact, it had a sharp, angry edge that was completely new. None the less, she wished both it and its owner a thousand miles away. The last person she wanted to find her was Jem's fiancée!

Nervously, she glanced towards Helen, wondering if the little girl was about to leap out and yell surprise, but her companion only shrugged and smiled as if she were happy to have her there beneath the table with her. Looking around, she noticed an assortment of velvet cushions, as well as a pile of books set next to a plate of biscuits and glass of milk. It was a den, she realised, with an overwhelming sense of relief, and an extremely cosy one, too. If it hadn't been for the scene taking place beyond the tablecloth, she might have felt quite comfortable. It was definitely a place she wanted to visit again tomorrow.

'So?' Miss Robinson demanded, her voice even louder and sharper than before. 'What do you have to say for yourself?'

'I agree that we need to talk.'

Nancy gave a jolt, almost bumping her head on the underside of the table. Whoever Miss Robinson was talking to sounded a lot like Jem, but it couldn't be. She'd left him on the terrace barely a couple of minutes ago. How could he have got here so soon with Miss Robinson and why would she be speaking to him in such an accusatory manner unless—her stomach lurched—unless his fiancée had just seen them together! Kissing! And now she had a terrible feeling she knew what Jem was about to do next...

'Yes, we need to talk!' Miss Robinson snapped, sounding as if she were actually spitting. 'How could you? With *her* of all people?'

'What's that supposed to mean?'

'She's a shopgirl! I mean, I knew you were

interested. I'm not a fool. I've seen the way you look at her, the way your friends look at the two of you, too, but I never imagined you'd lower yourself so badly!'

'Now, wait a minute—'

'As if all the freckles weren't bad enough!' Miss Robinson was clearly on a roll. 'But her hair is the most vulgar colour imaginable and as for her accent... She sounds like a milkmaid!'

'Enough!' Jem sounded angry now, too. 'I won't let you insult her. And, in case you haven't noticed, I have an accent, as well.'

'Yours isn't quite as strong.' Miss Robinson sniffed. 'Besides, it's something we can work on.'

'*Work on?* Emily, I don't want to "work on" my accent. I'm perfectly happy with my voice as it is. As for Nancy—'

'*Don't* say her name!'

'All right, as for Miss MacQueen, I'm sorry that you saw what you did just now. It's not the way I would have wanted you to find out, but I'm not sorry that it's happened either.'

'What?'

'Emily...' Jem sounded as if he were struggling to retain his temper '...how much did you hear?'

'Not much. A lot about honour, but your voices were muffled. Why? What does it matter?'

'It matters. The truth is, Nan—Miss Mac-Queen and I have known each other for a long time. Years. I've had feelings for her for a long time, too, although when I proposed I honestly thought that was all in the past. I never imagined anything like this could possibly happen, but now that it has…' There was a heavy silence, so long and filled with meaning that Nancy actually started to wonder whether either of them was ever going to speak again. She only realised that she was holding her breath when a small, warm hand covered hers.

'Now that it has, *what*?' Miss Robinson's voice sounded uncertain all of a sudden.

'You know what. I'm sorry, Emily. Truly. I never meant to hurt you, but even if I didn't have feelings for Miss MacQueen, it's time for us to face the truth. We're not suited. If our mothers hadn't wanted the match, then we would probably never have got engaged. Maybe we saw what we wanted to see in each other, but if these past few weeks have shown me anything, it's that we want different things in life. You must have realised that, too.'

'I've realised no such thing.'

'I'm never going to be a gentleman. I don't even want to be.'

'How can you say that? Look at where we are! Look at this house! We could be a part of this world. A part of society!'

'It's a nice house, yes, but this kind of lifestyle isn't for me. I'm a businessman. I *like* being a businessman. The last thing I want is to stop working.'

'But…'

'But nothing. You can give whatever reason you want for ending our engagement. I'll take all the blame.'

'I see.' Footsteps approached the table, the heels clicking sharply on the wooden floor. 'Well, you seem to have thought of everything.'

'I haven't. I'm just trying to do what's best for everyone.'

'For you and Miss MacQueen, you mean?' A pair of boots peeked beneath the bottom of the tablecloth, their pointed, dagger-like tips stopping only a few inches away from Nancy.

'And you, too. I know this must be as hard for you as it is for me.'

'How generous, but what if I don't *want* to end our engagement?' There was a sound like rain, as if fingernails were drumming on the tabletop.

'I don't understand.'

'What if I decide to ignore your little indiscretion?'

'Why would you do that?'

The boots pulled away again, making a scraping sound as they swivelled about. 'Because you're right about this all being our mothers' idea. I never deluded myself into thinking you loved me. You were always honest with me about how you felt. And I certainly never loved you.'

'So?'

'So why should you kissing *that* woman make any difference?'

'Because I love her! I've loved her from almost the first moment I saw her, only I didn't realise it until now. She's the *only* woman I could ever marry.'

'Well, that's a problem because you're going to marry me.'

'Emily...'

'You know, I witnessed the whole thing out there. I saw her go outside after you went to bed so I followed her just in case. I kept to the shadows and waited. As it was, I believe that your meeting was an accident, but it made for quite a touching scene. You both looked *so* overcome with passion and guilt-ridden at the same time.' There was a hint of mockery in her voice. 'You know, in her own way, she seems to be just as stupidly honourable as you are.'

'Emily, this is madness. You can't want to marry me now!'

'Why not? I was prepared to tolerate all your faults before. You're not exactly the kind of man I would have chosen. Personally I would have preferred someone a little more...what's the word? Oh, yes, *civilised*. But we can't always have what we want, James. I had to lower my standards, thanks to my parents.'

'What do you mean?'

'The truth is, *I* wanted to marry someone else, too, only as it turned out, he didn't want me either. Not enough anyway.' She sniffed. 'We met two years ago in the Assembly Rooms. His name was Captain Matthew Skelton. He asked my father's permission for my hand and, for one whole evening, I thought that I might die from perfect happiness. Then the next day they sat down to discuss practicalities and, as it turned out, he was expecting a bigger dowry. A much bigger one. Only my parents...well, you know what terrible spendthrifts they are. I half thought you might break things off when you found out what a pitiful state their finances are in, but money doesn't seem to matter to you.'

·

'It matters.' Jem's voice was like granite. 'Only there are things that matter more.'

'True, but having one fiancé leave me is bad enough. Two would be *too* much to bear. I'd be a laughing stock. So you see, I simply can't release you from our engagement.'

'So you'll marry me just to save face?'

'Not just for that, no. There's your money, too, and money means security. Believe me, if it wasn't for that, I would never have said yes in the first place.' She sighed. 'Look, it's not that I don't like you. In fact, if you were just a little bit more of a gentleman, I think I could like you very much, but as it is…' She clucked her tongue. 'Pity.'

'I'm happy with who I am, Emily.'

'Oh, don't look so angry about it. You'll thank me for this one day. You can't honestly think that Miss MacQueen feels the same way about you that you do about her? At least *I'm* open about wanting your money.'

'She's not like that.'

'Are you really so naive? Oh, dear, apparently you are.'

'She just told me *not* to break our engagement!'

'And what?' There was a sound like a hiss.

'Do you want me to thank her? I wouldn't thank that brazen, little h—'

'That's enough!'

Nancy reached an arm around Helen's shoulders, seeing the girl jump at Jem's roar.

'Quite right.' Miss Robinson cleared her throat. 'It *is* enough. Now I'm tired, I want to go to bed and I think we've both said all that needs to be said. You'll marry me and do as you're told.'

'I'm not a dog, Emily.'

'Oh, but I think you'll do what I say anyway. Furthermore, I think that you'll give up your work and Miss MacQueen, too. I heard her say one thing I agreed with, that you'd be miserable if you did anything dishonourable. Personally I don't believe you're capable of breaking our engagement yourself, but just in case…'

'Just in case, what?'

'Just in case…' Miss Robinson sounded like a cat toying with a mouse. 'You should know that if you do, I'll tell the whole of Bath just who your friend, the so-called Duchess of Howden, really is.' There was a meaningful pause. 'Or *was*.'

'I've no idea what you mean.'

'Oh, don't play coy, James. I *never* forget a face. It just takes me a while to place them sometimes. I should have realised sooner, given the connection with the Countess of Staunton and the fact that she invited a person like Miss Mac-Queen to a place like this, but it was just so hard to believe—impossible, really—and yet it's the truth, isn't it? Your precious Duchess was a shopgirl at Belles herself. She might have used a different name, but it's definitely her. *That's* why you're all friends. You got your hands dirty together.'

'No one will ever believe you.'

'Why would I make it up? In any case, I wouldn't be so crass as to accuse her directly. There are plenty of ways to make things known without actually saying them. Oh, no, my own hands will be completely clean, I assure you, but as for your Duchess, just imagine the damage to her reputation. A duchess who reeks of the shop.' She gave a sharp trill of laughter. 'I can hardly wait for the rumours. Gossip takes on a life of its own, I always find. Give it a year and who knows what else she might have done for a living.'

'Don't you dare.' Jem's voice held a warning note.

'Or what? What will you do to me?' She laughed again before her voice sharpened. 'Let me tell you what you'll do. You'll marry me, pay off my parents' debts, give up your little shop and buy us a respectable house in the city. And *this* conversation will remain entirely between the two of us.'

'And what's to stop me from going through to the drawing room and telling Beatrix all of this right now?'

'Nothing, except that you're not the kind of man who tells tales, James. Besides which, you know that if you do then the Duke will throw me out. I've seen enough of him to know that he won't respond to blackmail and yet, even if I *were* thrown out, you'd probably still feel hon-our-bound to escort me back to Bath, because that's just the kind of person you are, and then I'd simply spread rumours in retaliation. I won't be silenced. And it would be all your fault. You were the one who brought me here and intro-duced me to your friends, after all.'

'Believe me, I've regretted it ever since.' Jem sounded appalled. 'Emily, how can you want to marry a person you're blackmailing?'

'I told you. Money. Security. And I rather like the idea of my husband being friends with a duke and duchess.'

'You're mad.'

'Why? Because I won't allow a *greengrocer* to leave me for a shopgirl?'

'She's a better person than you are.'

'None the less, you can let me know your decision in the morning. I trust that you'll make the right one.'

Footsteps preceded the click of a door opening and closing and then…nothing. Nancy pressed a finger to her lips, exchanging a quick look with Helen, before bending down and tentatively lifting one corner of the tablecloth. As she'd suspected, Jem was still there, standing with his back towards her, his hands wrapped around the back of a chair on the other side of the room. Her heart clenched at the sight. Half of her wanted to go and comfort him. The other half didn't want to admit that she'd been eavesdropping, which she *had* been, albeit unwillingly.

She really *ought* to have come out and announced herself as soon as she'd known who they were, but under the circumstances it had seemed a lot easier to hide. And once they'd started arguing, well, her mind had been whirling with so many emotions, she would have found it hard to articulate just one. Shame, pity, guilt, blinding rage… She felt exhausted by the maelstrom.

There was a loud splintering sound as the chair came apart in Jem's hands, followed by a crash as he flung the remnants across the room and let loose a series of virulent oaths.

Quickly, Nancy dropped the tablecloth, placing her hands over Helen's ears until the swearing finally stopped and the door opened and closed a second time.

'Phew.' She lay down on the cushions once she was certain they were alone. Cramped as it was, she didn't want to get out from under the table just yet.

'I don't like her,' Helen announced, her small fists clenched. 'She's a horrible woman!'

'Yes, I think she is, too.'

'Is she really going to spread rumours about Beatrix?'

'Not if I have anything to do about it.'

'Should we go and warn her?' The little girl's face took on a guilty expression. 'I'm not supposed to come down here again after my bedtime. I'll have to tell my brother.'

'Oh, don't you worry about that.' Nancy put a hand on her shoulder and squeezed. '*I'll* deal with this.'

Half an hour later, after escorting Helen to the nursery and then returning to say goodnight to the others in the drawing room, Nancy laid her head on her pillow with a smile. For the first time in a long time, her mind was clear. It was one thing to come between a man and a woman in love—or if not in love then in a respectable relationship—but it was another thing entirely to come between a man and a woman who was blackmailing him. *She* might have acted badly by kissing Jem, but at least it had forced Miss Robinson to reveal her true nature. And her true nature was nowhere good enough for him.

You're not exactly the kind of man I would have chosen.

Those had been the most infuriating words of all. How dare the woman insult him and then still demand that he marry her? The nerve! Frankly, Nancy was amazed she hadn't shot out from beneath the tablecloth and attempted to strangle her at that moment. Fortunately, the words also meant that she no longer had to feel guilty. Jem didn't need to be honourable any more and neither did she. She didn't have to play the calm, polite lady either. She could be herself.

In the morning, she would talk to Beatrix and together they would come up with a plan, one that would free Jem from his engagement and convince Miss Robinson to keep her mouth shut and then... *Then* she could tell him that they finally felt the same way at the same time. She could answer yes to all of his questions. She could tell him with complete honesty and with a clear conscience that she was in love with him, too.

* * *

It was the best night's sleep she'd had in three months, so deep and refreshing that she actually stayed in bed until nine o'clock, arriving in the breakfast room the next morning with a spring in her step and a sparkle in her eye, ready to do battle.

Unfortunately, as she discovered almost immediately, Jem, Miss Robinson and her mother had already left. They'd come downstairs several hours earlier with their cases packed, intent upon leaving as soon as possible. At that precise moment, they were already on their way back to Bath, their engagement still very much on.

Chapter Eighteen

'What a shame we couldn't stay any longer.' Mrs Robinson looked nervously across the carriage at Jem. It was the fifth time she'd said the same sentence, apparently in the hope that someone would tell her what had precipitated their sudden flight from Howden, but he had no intention of explaining anything. It was surely obvious that he and Emily had argued. The atmosphere between them was practically vibrating with anger—anger that hadn't abated one single iota from the night before.

That was why he'd sent a message to her room just after dawn, instructing her and her mother to be packed and ready before breakfast. The longer they stayed at Howden, the more ammunition she could gather against Beatrix, which had meant that the best thing he could do was get her away from his friends as quickly as possible. He should never have brought her in the first place and there had been no way in hell that he was going to sit down for another meal and pretend that everything was perfectly all right.

'I told you, Mama, James has remembered some urgent business he needs to attend to.' Emily's voice was perfectly even. She probably *would* have dissembled at breakfast, given the chance, he thought bitterly. No doubt she would have sat next to Beatrix and smiled and laughed and not given the faintest hint of the malicious, mean-spirited intentions beneath. He was coming to heartily dislike his fiancée.

'Well, it's been a most enjoyable stay, I must say.' Either Mrs Robinson was trying to make the most of a bad situation or she really had no tact at all. 'I'll have so much to tell people about.'

'I said the very same thing to James last night.' Emily's gloating tone actually made him shudder. 'I've made so many interesting observations.' She turned her head, smiling sweetly. 'But I think we've made the right decision overall, don't you, dearest?'

'I think there was no choice.'

'How true. By the way, I've been thinking that we ought to bring forward the wedding. I know we were planning a big event, but we don't need so much fuss, do we? The banns have already been read and I'm sure the rest could be arranged quickly enough. Honestly, I see no reason why we shouldn't just get on with it as soon as we get home.'

'But what about all our plans?' Her mother looked stricken. 'What about the dress? The flowers? The food?'

'What about my parents?' Jem glowered.

'I know, it would be a terrible shame for them to miss it, but I wonder if the journey would be too much for your mother anyway. Their village is a couple of hours away.'

'I'm sure they'd still like to be there.'

'They'll be the first people we visit after we're married.' Emily continued as if she hadn't heard him. 'Just think how surprised they'll be!'

'If that's really what you want, dearest?' Her mother sounded nervous again.

'Oh, it is.' Emily looked Jem straight in the eye, her smile not wavering for as much as a second. 'It definitely is.'

Jem gritted his teeth to stop himself from saying anything improper. And maybe she was right and it *would* be better to get it over with. At least he knew where he stood with Emily, which was more than he could say about Nancy. Surely— *surely*—if she'd cared for him the way he cared for her then she would have said so the night before? Even if she'd been saving him from himself, as she'd called it, wouldn't she have fought harder for them to be together? Wouldn't Nancy of all people have fought? Wouldn't she have said if there was any hope at all? It had been their last chance and she'd rejected him yet again. At this point, he didn't know why he was even surprised.

'What do you mean, *gone*?' Nancy dropped her plate in shock, sending scrambled eggs and bacon tumbling all down the front of her dress and over the breakfast room carpet. 'Where?'

'Back to Bath.' Beatrix leapt up from her seat. 'Oh, dear, your gown.'

'Bother my gown!' Nancy grabbed hold of her friend's upper arms, trying not to panic. '*Why* have they gone? And why so early?'

'Honestly, I don't know. Jem left a note, but it didn't make a great deal of sense.'

'What did it say? Can I read it?'

'Of course.' Beatrix reached into her pocket and pulled out a folded piece of paper.

'Dear blah blah…' Nancy read the contents aloud, aware of Quin, Anna and Samuel all exchanging glances in the background. 'Thank you for your hospitality… A situation I'd forgotten about…urgent reason to return to Bath… Apologies for not saying goodbye in person… Oh, hell!'

'And good morning to you, too!' Sebastian chuckled as he and Henrietta entered the room at that moment. 'Not the usual greeting, but we're on holiday, I suppose.'

'Jem's gone!' Nancy thrust the note at him.

'What?' He sobered at once. 'When?'

'Early this morning. That bi—' She bit her tongue. 'That woman made him leave!'

'I don't think so.' Quin spoke up from the end of the table. 'I saw them all leave and Miss Robinson didn't appear to be exerting any pressure.'

'So you didn't notice anything odd?'

'Well, I admit Jem seemed a little subdued and there was some strange apology about a broken chair, but Miss Robinson and her mother were their usual exuberant selves.' He winced. 'Frankly, it was a bit much to take before breakfast.'

'Urgh! Right, sit down, everyone.' Nancy hurried to close the breakfast room door. 'Now listen. She's *blackmailing* him. I overheard them in the library last night. She said that if he didn't marry her then she'd spread rumours about Beatrix working at Belles.'

'What?' Beatrix leapt straight back out of her seat again.

'She recognised you. I'm not sure when exactly, but she said that she never forgot a face. She must have shopped at Belles.'

'But why would she need to blackmail Jem? They're already engaged.'

'Because she thought that he wanted to call things off.'

'Jem would never do that.' Sebastian snorted. 'He's far too honourable.'

'None the less…' She cleared her throat, aware of a swathe of heat spreading up her neck and across her cheeks. 'She might have seen something earlier that made her think otherwise.'

'She *might* have?' Sebastian leaned forward, brown eyes twinkling.

'Fine.' Nancy tossed her head. 'She *did*.'

'No! So she's guessed that he's in love with you?'

'Something like that.'

'Well, it took her long enough! Then what happened?'

'Then he asked *her* to end their engagement.'

'He did? Bravo!' Sebastian punched the air. 'Well done, Jem!'

'Well done, nothing. It only caused her to threaten him.'

'And she said all of this in front of you?'

'Not exactly.' She twisted her hands together

and shuffled her feet. 'I was already in the library, but when I heard them coming, I…well, I hid. Under a table. They had no idea I was there.'

'A table?' Quin lifted an eyebrow. 'I don't suppose you met anyone else under there, by any chance, did you?'

'That would depend.' She pursed her lips. 'Not if it gets the other person in trouble.'

'I see.' He rubbed a knuckle between his brows. 'We have far too many tables in this house.'

'Helen likes them…' Beatrix placed a hand over his reassuringly '…and if they're what she needs to feel comfortable then I don't mind. She's far better than she was and lots of children like cosy spaces.'

'Um…' Nancy looked between them, perplexed by the tangent the conversation was taking. Little girls hiding under tables wasn't exactly their biggest concern at that moment. 'I agree, but the point is, Miss Robinson *knows* that Beatrix used to be a shopgirl.'

'Yes and that's unfortunate, but we've already discussed it, haven't we?' Beatrix glanced back at her husband, who nodded. 'I mean, given the fact that we're all friends, it seemed likely that somebody would recognise me or guess the connection eventually, and we're not going to stop being friends just to evade suspicion. So we've already decided what to do.'

'Which is?'

'I'll call for the carriage.' Quin pushed his chair back.

'Which is?' Nancy repeated.

'We'll go to Bath, too.' Beatrix picked up her cup of tea and smiled serenely over the rim. 'Back to Belles. And if anyone recognises me, let them say so to my face.' She shrugged. 'Or behind my back. It doesn't matter. People can say what they like. The point is, Miss Robinson won't be able to blackmail Jem any longer.'

'Hold on.' Nancy held her hands up. 'Are you sure about this?'

'Yes. My father was in trade and I see no reason to be ashamed of having once worked for a living. I'm *not* ashamed of it.'

'And I don't give a damn about anyone else's opinion. Not any more.' Quin paused with his hand on the door handle, his expression softening. 'In fact, I'm starting to quite enjoy our eccentric reputation.'

'What about the rest of your family?'

'They all love Beatrix far too much to object. They'll understand. When is Jem's wedding date, incidentally?'

'Not for another few weeks.'

'Good. In that case, we have plenty of time, but I presume you'd like to follow him as soon as possible?'

'Yes... Thank you.' Nancy subsided into a chair, her knees giving way beneath her.

'Are you all right?' Henrietta put an arm around her shoulders.

'Yes. It's just... That was a lot easier than I expected.'

'*That* was the easy part.' Sebastian leaned across the table. 'You might be able to break Miss Robinson's hold over Jem, but you know how honourable he is. He might *still* feel unable to break the engagement himself and if Miss Robinson won't release him...'

'Seb, that's really not helpful right now.' Henrietta gave him a chiding look.

'It's the truth. There's only one thing that might overcome that honourable streak.'

'What?' Nancy clenched her brows suspiciously.

'You! This *something* that happened between you and Jem last night. I don't suppose it involved you finally admitting you love him, did it?'

'That's none of your business.'

'You're right, it's not, but I'm willing to bet that he still isn't sure how you feel. So maybe it's about time you told him that you're just as head over heels about him as he is with you. It's been perfectly obvious to everyone else for years.'

'It has *not* been perfectly obvious!'

'It's been blinding! I'm blinded right now.'

'I was going to tell him this morning *actually*!'

'So you *do* love him?'

'Of course I love him!' she burst out. 'I'd be mad not to. He's the best, most lovable person in the whole world. I love him more than I ever thought I could love anybody and if that woman gets her talons into him then I think my heart might actually shatter into a hundred million pieces!'

'Then what are we waiting for?' Sebastian leapt to his feet. 'Let's get after him!'

'*We?*'

'You don't think I'd miss this, do you?'

'Oh, Nancy.' Beatrix dabbed a handkerchief to her eyes.

'Samuel and I are coming, too.' Anna sniffed. 'We'll all confront Miss Robinson together, if necessary. There are a few things I'd like to say to her.'

'Two carriages, then,' Quin commented from the doorway, though his voice had a faint huskiness about it, too. 'I suggest that we be ready to leave in an hour. They've had a reasonable head start, but you never know, we might be able to catch up with them on the road.'

Chapter Nineteen

'Here we are.' Beatrix craned her neck as the Roxbury family carriage finally rolled to a halt in front of Redbourne's General Store in Bath. As it turned out, they hadn't been able to catch up with Jem and the Robinsons on the road, after all, and their progress had been slowed by near incessant rain ever since they'd left Howden Hall. 'Oh… That's odd.'

'What's odd?' Nancy lunged across her, noticing a large notice in the shop window. 'It looks like some kind of announcement. *Agnes!*' She opened the door and leapt out as Jem's assistant emerged from the shop at that moment.

'Why, Miss MacQueen.' Agnes beamed at the sight of her. 'You're back, too? And looking very well, I might add. How was your trip?'

'Never mind that. I need to find Jem.'

'Oh.' Agnes's smile faded, her expression

turning sympathetic. 'Oh, dear. I'm afraid he left a little while ago.'

'Is he coming back soon?'

'Well, no-o. Not until after the wedding anyway.'

'Wedding?' Nancy lifted a hand to her chest, afraid that her heart was about to burst through her ribcage.

'Yes, he's getting married this morning.' Agnes shook her head. 'Although it's all very strange, if you ask me. I know I shouldn't say so, but he doesn't seem particularly happy about it. He only arrived back late last night and he hasn't even had time to send for his parents.'

'But…this morning?' Nancy felt winded, her whole ribcage trembling with aftershocks. 'At what time?'

'Half past eleven, which means I only have an hour to freshen up and get myself to the church, if you'll excuse me? Lovely to see you again, Miss MacQueen.'

'Wait!' Nancy put a hand out. 'Do you happen to know where Miss Robinson lives?'

'I'm afraid not.'

'I do!' Anna called, her head sticking out of the second carriage. 'Mrs Robinson mentioned it the other day. Number Four, Bartholomew Square.'

'Then that's where we're going!' Beatrix, whose head was also sticking out of a carriage, gave an authoritative nod to her coachman. 'There's still time. Anna and Henrietta, come and get into our carriage. Quin, you go and join Samuel and Sebastian.' She winked at her husband as he passed her. 'You know what to do.'

'What's he going to do?' Nancy looked around, confused, as Anna and Henrietta swapped places with Quin.

'The men are going to open up Belles for us. I know it's a little late in the day for baking, but they can still sell a few biscuits.'

'They're doing *what*?' Nancy gaped in astonishment as she climbed back into her seat. 'A duke and an earl are going to work in a biscuit shop?'

'Don't forget Sebastian.' Henrietta clucked as the carriage started to roll away. 'Actually, he's in charge since he's the only one who knows how to bake. They don't teach it at Eton, apparently.'

'It's a good thing that Samuel and Quin were both officers.' Anna laughed. 'At least they know how to take orders.'

'Yes, but they both outranked Sebastian.'

'Well, today he outranks them.' Henrietta smiled placidly. 'I think he's going to enjoy himself immensely.'

'But I don't understand.' Nancy turned back to Beatrix. '*Why* are they opening Belles?'

'Because if anyone's going to reveal my secret then it ought to be us.' Her friend folded her hands neatly in her lap. 'We're making a point and this is the strongest way we can make it.'

'Oh…' Nancy sank back against the carriage cushions. 'Are you absolutely sure about this?'

'Positive.' Beatrix peered out of the window and sighed wistfully. 'It's good to be back. I've missed Bath—Belles especially. To be honest, I'm a little jealous of the men getting all the fun.'

'We have more important matters to attend to. We're not letting Jem be blackmailed into anything.' Henrietta sounded uncharacteristically fierce.

'So what's the plan?' Anna clenched her fists. 'I say we just burst into her house and accuse her!'

'Considering that Jem will be married in less than an hour otherwise, I don't think we have any other choice.' Beatrix looked directly at Nancy. 'As for Jem, he's all up to you.'

'There's a carriage outside the house!' Anna was practically bouncing in her seat with excitement by the time they arrived. 'That means they haven't left early!'

'Thank goodness, but we still need to hurry!' Beatrix banged on the roof, barely waiting for the carriage to roll to a halt before grabbing Nancy's hand and dragging her out, along the pavement and up the front steps of the Robinsons' house.

'Wait!' Nancy stopped and dug her heels in, pulling Beatrix back before she could knock. 'I need a moment.'

'You don't have a moment. They could come out at any second.'

'I know, I just…' She closed her eyes, took a deep breath and then wrenched her shoulders back. 'All right, I can do this. I just need to do it alone.'

'Are you certain?' Henrietta asked as she and Anna ran along the pavement to join them. 'It could get unpleasant.'

'It probably will, but unpleasant I can deal with. I grew up in Avon Street, remember?'

Beatrix nodded reluctantly. 'We'll stay right here in case you need us. Just wave from one of the windows and we'll come rushing straight in.'

Nancy pressed her lips together, biting back a smile. Touching as the offer was, it was hard not to laugh at the image of her three best friends bursting into the Robinsons' drawing room like a horde of avenging furies.

'Thank you, but I'm sure I can manage.' She stepped up to the front door and knocked. 'But be ready to lie down in front of their carriage if you need to. Don't let it leave.'

'May I help you?' An aged-looking butler appeared almost instantly, looking from her to her friends, now lined up behind her like a military parade, and then back again with a quizzical expression.

'I need to speak with Miss Robinson.' Nancy thrust her chin into the air. 'Please tell her it's urgent.'

'I'm afraid it's not a good time.' He started to close the door again. 'Miss Robinson has another engagement. An important one.'

'Yes, she's getting married, I know, but I need to speak with her first.'

'I'm afraid not.'

'And *I'm* afraid so. Now, I've tried asking nicely, but unless Miss Robinson wishes to discuss her engagement and everything I know about it in public, she'll see me now.'

'And if she refuses, tell her the Duchess of Howden has a few words to say to her, too!' Beatrix called out before meeting Nancy's eye and grimacing. 'Sorry.'

'Quite all right.' Nancy swallowed a laugh. The Belinda-Beatrix she'd met a few months ago wouldn't have said boo to a goose. A lot had changed in that time.

'Very well, miss.' The aged butler finally stood aside. 'You'd better come in. Please wait here.'

Nancy stepped over the threshold, smiling at her friends before the door closed behind her and the butler disappeared through another doorway. Evidently, she wasn't deemed worthy of waiting in the drawing room, which was absolutely fine with her. She didn't care where she spoke with Miss Robinson, just as long as she got an opportunity to say her piece.

'This is a surprise.' The lady in question appeared at the top of the staircase only a few seconds later, as if she'd been eavesdropping the whole time. Apparently the practice was catching. 'I thought you'd still be in Oxfordshire.'

'I'm sure you did.' Nancy folded her arms as her rival descended the stairs, dressed in a cream-coloured chiffon gown and lace shawl. 'However, as it happened, we left only a few hours after you did.'

'Indeed? Any particular reason?'

'Yes. Jem.' She looked the other woman up and down appraisingly. 'You look lovely, by the way. Beautiful actually. Everything a bride *should* look.'

'Oh.' Miss Robinson blinked, taken aback by the compliment. 'Thank you.'

'There's just one problem. You have the wrong bridegroom and you know it.'

'I beg your—'

'I know what you said to Jem the other night. I know that you're blackmailing him.'

'Perhaps we ought to discuss this in private.' The other woman's face muscles tightened. 'Although I've no idea what you're talking about.'

'Yes, you do. I overheard you in the library.' Nancy followed her into an elaborately furnished drawing room. 'That's why I'm here. Beatrix and Anna and Henrietta and all of their husbands, too. The men are at Belles right now, baking, as it happens. They're going to open the shop and serve the customers themselves. So you see, the cat's already out of the bag. In a few hours, everyone in Bath will know about Beatrix and your threat won't work any more.'

Miss Robinson's face blanched until it was almost the same shade as her dress. 'I don't believe you.'

'Then come to Belles and see. Or we could ask Beatrix to come in and tell you herself. She's waiting outside on the doorstep, just itching to speak with you. You know, some people take it personally when you stay as a guest in their house and then threaten to reveal their deepest secrets.'

There was a long, tense silence while Miss Robinson simply stared at her, panic and outrage warring on her features before she dropped down on to a sofa and promptly burst into tears. 'I didn't know what else to do!'

'Um…what are you doing?' Nancy stared at her blankly. She'd expected an argument, not crying. She wasn't entirely sure what to do with tears.

'It's not fair! I never even *wanted* to marry him!'

'Well, you're doing a pretty good job of pretending otherwise.'

'Because I have to! I can't afford not to. My dowry is minuscule.'

'I thought your father was a lawyer?'

'He is, but he made some bad investments a few years ago. He lost thousands, but my parents completely refuse to economise. They always spend more than they have. Money is a constant struggle. You have no idea how hard it is.'

'Is that so?' Nancy moved her hands to her hips, any sympathy she might have had rapidly draining away.

'Oh, you know what I mean. You've never

had money. To have had it and lost it is so much worse.'

'I'll have to take your word for it.' Nancy rolled her eyes. 'You know, you could always get a job.'

'Don't be absurd. Ladies don't work for a living. *That's* why I have to marry James. I know that I'll be safe with him. He'll support me and my family, too, if necessary.'

'Lucky him. Meanwhile, you'll try to turn him into someone he's not.'

'For his own good! I'll turn him into a gentleman!' Miss Robinson shot back to her feet, pushing her face furiously towards Nancy's. 'We could have been happy if it hadn't been for you!'

'I doubt that.' She lifted an eyebrow. 'If you're waiting for me to flinch, we're going to be here a long time.'

'I won't let him go! He's engaged to me and I won't release him!'

'Then *I'll* ask him to break off your engagement himself.' Nancy smiled nonchalantly. 'I couldn't the other night because it seemed like the wrong thing to do, but funnily enough, I don't feel even the tiniest bit guilty any more. I don't think Jem will either. Honestly, you've done us a favour. I ought to be grateful to you.'

'Grateful?' Miss Robinson's face turned from very pale to very puce.

'What on earth's going on?' Mrs Robinson came into the room at that moment, dressed in a flamboyant pink and mauve gown trimmed with vast quantities of white lace. 'Miss MacQueen, I'm surprised to see you again so soon.'

'Yes, we've already discussed that. I came to stop the wedding.'

'I beg your pardon?'

'Your daughter doesn't want to marry Jem, not really.'

'Don't be absurd. Of course she does!'

'She doesn't love him.'

'What does that have to do with anything?'

'What does it—?' Nancy looked between the pair of them in disgust. 'What's wrong with you people? Love is everything! I love Jem. I have for years, only I was too stubborn to admit it for a long time, and then I thought it was too late for us because of you, but after what I heard in the library, I'm not about to stand back and let the pair of you leech off him for the rest of his life.'

'You love me?'

They all spun around together to find Jem standing in the doorway, his expression somewhere between thunderstruck and ecstatic.

'Mr Redbourne.' Mrs Robinson recovered

first, bustling forward to greet him. 'What must you think of us? We were just about to leave for the ceremony.'

'You were late so I came to see if anything was wrong.' He didn't look at her, his gaze fixed on Nancy instead. 'You just said you love me.'

'Yes.' She caught her breath, her body trembling with anxiety and relief at the sight of him. 'I did. I do.'

'Why didn't you tell me the other night?'

'Because there seemed no point in telling you when there was no way we could be together, but now there is.' She swallowed, summoning all her nerve. She'd spent almost the entire journey from Oxfordshire trying to find the right words to persuade him, but now her mind seemed to have gone blank. All she could manage was the blunt truth. 'Jem, I love you and I want you to call off the wedding yourself. You don't need to feel dishonourable about it now, not after the way she threatened Beatrix.'

'You heard us in the library? How did you—?'

'That's not important,' she interrupted quickly. 'I'll explain later.'

'No!' There was a high-pitched screech followed by a blur of movement as Emily launched herself across the room, fingernails raised like eagles' talons. Fortunately, from Nancy's perspective anyway, the attack was entirely predictable. She waited until the last moment before stepping neatly to one side, sending Miss Robinson flying straight into her mother.

'Aaah!' The pair of them tumbled to the ground in a heap of chiffon and lace.

'You want me to end my engagement?' Jem ignored all the screaming, advancing slowly towards Nancy instead.

'Yes.' Her stomach was fluttering so fast, she felt positively sick. 'I want to accept your offer to court me.'

'No.'

'No?' She thought she might actually *be* sick…

'We've gone past courting. I want to go straight to the marriage part.'

'You do?' The sickness evaporated, replaced by elation.

'You're proposing to her while you're engaged to *me*?' Miss Robinson staggered back to her feet, her carefully pinned ringlets now hanging loose around her shoulders.

'You're right, it's bad-mannered of me.' Jem turned to face her. 'How much do you need?'

'What?'

'How much money do you need for a respectable dowry? So you can marry someone you actually like? A gentleman, this time.' He glanced towards her mother, still sitting on the floor. 'I'll put the money somewhere safe, where only you have access.'

'I don't…that is, I don't know.'

'Roughly. A thousand pounds?'

'Jem!' Nancy gasped. 'You can't give away a thousand pounds!'

'You'd do that for me?' Emily's eyes widened. 'After what I did?'

'Only if you answer in the next five seconds.'

'A thousand pounds is good.'

'What about all the money I've spent on wedding arrangements?' Mrs Robinson chimed in from the floor.

'I'll cover that, too.'

'What's happened?' Beatrix burst into the room suddenly, closely followed by Anna and Henrietta. 'We heard screaming.'

'I haven't touched anyone.' Nancy held her hands up.

'We're just working out a business arrangement.' Jem looked completely calm. 'Aren't we, Emily?'

'Yes.' Miss Robinson nodded emphatically. 'You're completely free and…' she glanced nervously towards Beatrix '…for what it's worth, I'm sorry. I would never have gone through with it.'

'Then we have a deal.' Jem stepped past her,

catching hold of Nancy's waist and drawing her towards him. 'Now say that you'll marry me and *please* don't tell me you need any longer to think about it.'

'I've thought for long enough.' She flung her arms around his neck. 'I accept.'

Chapter Twenty

Nancy stopped at the garden gate, letting go of Jem's hand at the sight of his parents' cottage. It was exquisitely pretty, with a thatched roof, gable windows and rose-covered trellises adorning every spare inch of wall. Fifteen miles in distance and a whole world away from Avon Street.

'What's the matter?' Jem reached for her hand again, lacing their fingers together this time.

'Are you *certain* this is a good idea?'

'As certain as I've ever been of anything.'

'But your mother wanted you to marry a gentleman's daughter.' Nancy retreated a step. 'She's bound to be disappointed. Both of your parents are. I don't want to make her ill again.'

'You're not going to do that. There's no use thinking that way, believe me.'

'But what if—?'

'Nancy.' Jem's smile was full of reassurance.

'They encouraged the match with Emily, yes, but I've thought about this a lot over the past few weeks and I've decided that what my parents want most is for me to be happy. And if by some chance I'm wrong about that then it's still all right. I love you. I'm going to marry you. I want to tell my parents and have them celebrate with us, but if they won't then we'll get married anyway. I've done everything else they've ever asked of me, but I'm allowed to choose my own wife. I've waited for her long enough.'

'All right.' Nancy took a deep breath, still regarding him dubiously. 'But if anything happens…'

'Then it's not your responsibility. Now, come on. I can see curtains twitching already.'

He opened the gate and drew her up a neat gravel path towards a small, ivy-clad porch. He hadn't been joking about the curtains, she realised. They were definitely twitching, which meant that it was too late to turn around and make a run for it now.

'Jem?' His father opened the front door almost immediately. Nancy recognised him from eight years before, although his hair was noticeably greyer and he was regarding her with somewhat more interest than he had back then, as well as a definite hint of panic.

'Father.' Jem dropped her hand to embrace him. 'It's good to see you.'

'It is, but what are you doing here? Why didn't you send a message ahead?'

'It was a last-minute decision. How's Mother?'

'She's well. Sitting out in the garden, enjoying the sunshine, the last time I saw her.'

'Good.' Jem cleared his throat. 'In that case, we should go and join her. There's somebody I'd like for you both to meet. Father, this is Miss Nancy MacQueen.'

'Miss MacQueen.' His father inclined his head politely. 'Are you a friend of Miss Robinson?'

'Miss Robinson and I are no longer engaged,' Jem interrupted before she could answer. '*This* is the future Mrs Redbourne.'

'You're not...this is...?' His father's jaw appeared to have detached itself.

'We have a lot to talk about.' Jem draped an arm around her shoulders. 'Let's make some tea, shall we?'

'I know it's a shock, but I hope that you can be happy for us,' Jem said gently, looking around the stone terrace at the back of the house where he, Nancy and his parents were sitting on two curved metal benches, facing each other. He had to admit, his father was certainly keeping busy in retirement. The garden was a tranquil oasis of vivid colours and heady scents, a perfect place to sit and bask in the sunshine, although at that precise moment, he couldn't have vouched for either of his parents' moods. Neither of them had spoken for several minutes. Instead, they both appeared faintly stunned. As for Nancy, she was sitting with her hands folded and knuckles clenched tight, looking as awkward and uncomfortable as he'd ever seen her. He wasn't entirely sure how he was feeling either. Nervous, apprehensive, excited and protective all at once. He wanted his parents to understand and approve of his choice, but he couldn't force them to either. He only hoped they didn't say anything to offend the woman he loved. He also hoped that his mother wasn't about to collapse.

'Forgive me, but I don't understand what went wrong with Miss Robinson…' His mother spoke at last, her voice small and tremulous sounding. 'You and she were such a good match.'

'No, we weren't.' He shook his head adamantly. 'The more I got to know her, the more obvious that became. It was a mistake from the start, but it was *my* mistake, not yours. I rushed in.'

'I'll have to write to her mother.'

'Write to whoever you like, but Miss Robinson agreed—eventually—to end our engagement. I'm not the kind of man she wants and I can't marry one woman while I'm in love with another.'

'I see…' There was another long silence while his parents exchanged glances.

'What *I* don't understand…' his father spoke haltingly '…is that if you were in love with Miss MacQueen here for so many years, as you claim, then why did you become engaged to Miss Robinson in the first place?'

'That was my fault,' Nancy interjected. They were the first words she'd spoken except for 'good afternoon', 'just milk please' and 'thank you' since their arrival. 'I made Jem think that I didn't care for him. To be honest, I thought he was too good to be true. I didn't know how to trust him and I thought I didn't want to marry anyone until, one day, I realised that if I could trust any man, then it was him. Unfortunately, that was also the day I found out he was engaged. We both tried to put our feelings aside, but in the end, we couldn't.' She sat forward on the bench. 'Mr and Mrs Redbourne, I know that I'm probably not the kind of person you wanted for your son. I'm not rich or from a good family and I have the worst temper you can possibly imagine—'

'Nancy?' Jem coughed.

'They have a right to know.' She put a hand on his knee. 'I'm just saying that I would understand if you had objections to me. I wouldn't even blame you for thinking I'm some kind of social climber out to snare your son, but I promise you, I love him and I would never hurt him. I think that he's the best person I've ever met.'

'Well, I can't disagree with you about that.' His father's expression warmed.

'And I think, if all that's true, then you might be exactly the kind of person I want for my son.' His mother put her teacup aside. 'Perhaps we've interfered too much in his life in the past. I suspected that the only reason he proposed to Emily was because I'd pushed him and he wanted to please me, but I had no idea that he was in love with you. If I had, then I would have said something. We've only ever wanted him to be happy.'

'He will be.' Nancy nodded firmly. 'I intend to make sure of it.'

'In that case, perhaps we need something stronger than tea.' His father stood up. 'We ought to make a toast. You'll both stay for dinner, I hope?'

'I'm afraid we have to get back to Bath tonight.' Nancy shook her head regretfully. 'I need an early night so that I can get up and do the baking tomorrow.'

'Actually, Beatrix and Anna are going to do it.' Jem smiled. 'They're staying at Belles tonight with Quin and Samuel. It's going to be just like old times, apparently.'

'Then you can stay here...' his mother beamed with delight '...and we can get to know each other properly.'

'I'd like that. And maybe...' Nancy lifted a shoulder, her expression uncharacteristically shy. 'Maybe you'll help me to plan the wedding?'

'I'd be honoured. Between you and me, the Robinsons didn't really want me involved at all.'

'Well, I do. I don't know the first thing about weddings.'

'Are you sure you're feeling all right?' Jem regarded his mother anxiously. 'You don't feel unwell?'

'Oh, Jem.' His mother's face softened. 'You worry too much. I'm not as fragile as you and your father seem to think.'

'Still, maybe you should have a lie down?'

'For goodness' sake. I know what I can and can't cope with. There's a difference between good surprises and bad ones and, trust me, Nancy here is an *extremely* good one.'

Two weeks later

'What do you think?' Nancy caught Beatrix's eye in the mirror. 'Tell me honestly. Don't be nice just for the sake of it.'

'Just because it's your wedding day, you mean?' Beatrix laughed and stepped forward, tucking a stray curl behind Nancy's ear before pressing a kiss to her cheek. 'As if I would dare. For what it's worth, however, you look beautiful. Honestly, hand on heart, beautiful.'

'That's right, you do,' her mother agreed, sitting on the bed behind them, looking somewhat overwhelmed by all the activity on the upper floor of Belles, not to mention the presence of an actual duchess in the room.

Nancy smiled sheepishly and looked back at her reflection in the mirror. She had to admit, she was pleased with the way Anna's lady's maid had styled her hair, twisting her curls into some kind of intricately coiled plait over one shoulder, leaving just a couple of tendrils loose to frame her face. Her blue dress was lovely, too. Simple, but with a lacy white trim that made her think of snowflakes. Maybe she was just a *little* bit beautiful, after all. Jem seemed to think so and that was all that mattered.

'Are you feeling nervous?' Beatrix handed her a pair of white silk gloves.

'No, not at all.' She frowned. 'Is that a bad sign?'

'No. It proves that you're doing the right thing.' Anna's face appeared in the doorway. 'Now it's time to go. Your bridegroom will be waiting.'

'Right.' Nancy picked up her bouquet of red roses and swept to the door. A bride ought to be a little late, or so she'd been told, but after all their to-ing and fro-ing over the years, she didn't want to keep Jem waiting for as much as a minute. The sooner she was Mrs Redbourne, the better.

'Come on, Mama.' She held a hand out. 'The mother of the bride gets the best seat, apparently.'

'It all feels so strange,' her mother whispered as they descended the staircase together. 'I still can't believe you have a duchess and a countess as your matrons of honour.'

'Don't forget Henrietta. All the women of Belles are my matrons.'

'There must be something in the water here.'

'Maybe there is. Maybe I should have waited for a marquess to come along and sweep me off my feet.'

'I think you've done better than a marquess.'

'So do I.' Nancy smiled. 'It's funny, but I met Jem long before Anna or Henrietta or Beatrix met their husbands, and yet we're the last to marry.'

'Then you've been saving the best until last. And you really do look lovely. At least no one will be looking at me and your stepfather.' Her mother tapped her arm reassuringly. 'Don't worry, he's going to be on his best behaviour today. I've made it clear that he'll be sleeping on the street otherwise.'

'Really?' Nancy twisted her face towards her mother curiously.

'Yes. I decided to take a leaf out of my daughter's book and stand up for myself again. It's working so well, I wish I'd done it years ago. Your old mother is back and not before time.'

'Then I don't want any other wedding presents. That's the best one I could have asked for.'

'You're a vision, Miss MacQueen.' Sebastian met them at the bottom of the staircase, a broad grin on his face. In the absence of her actual father, and with only some minor grumbling from her stepfather, he was going to give her away, relinquishing the role of groomsmen to Samuel and Quin. 'Jem's a lucky man.'

'Yes, he is.' For once, she didn't argue with him. 'And I'm a very lucky woman.'

* * *

'A toast!' Sebastian stood up from his seat at the high table and lifted his glass. 'To Mr and Mrs James Redbourne! And might I personally add, it's about time!'

A cheer of approval rose up from room as the collected guests all joined in the toast. Quin had arranged a special licence and offered to hire the Assembly Rooms for the wedding breakfast, but Jem had insisted upon taking a room in the Grand Hotel instead. It was, he and Nancy had decided, more 'them'.

'Happy?' Jem asked, nudging his chair closer towards Nancy's.

'Very.' She lifted a hand to his cheek. 'If I'd ever dreamed of getting married, this is exactly what I would have wanted.'

'You never even imagined it?'

'No. I was very determined *not* to get married, until you came along and ruined everything.'

'Ah. My sincerest apologies.'

'Since you apologise so nicely, you're forgiven.'

'Seb's right about one thing, though. It's been almost a decade since we first met.'

'Some people are worth waiting for.' She smiled coyly.

'True.' He leaned closer, pressing his face into her neck. 'However, there are some things I don't want to wait any longer for.'

'What kind of—? Oh.' She flushed as the warmth of his breath skimmed her throat. 'But we can't leave now. It's *our* wedding breakfast.'

'Also true, but just so you know, our carriage will be leaving in an hour.'

'Carriage? Where are we going?'

'To the coast. Quin and Beatrix offered to lend us some kind of hunting lodge for the week.'

'Why do I get the feeling a "lodge" is a lot bigger than it sounds?'

'That's exactly what I thought. So I declined and requested a smaller property. Now we'll be staying in an empty gamekeeper's cottage instead. It'll be just the two of us. No staff at all. I insisted.' He nuzzled closer, pressing his lips to the space just behind her ear. 'How does that sound, Mrs Redbourne?'

'Much better. One hour, did you say?' She turned her head, her whole body trembling with desire, to catch his lips with her own. 'I can't wait.'

Chapter Twenty-One

They arrived at the cottage at dusk, after, in Nancy's opinion, the longest and most frustrating journey in the world. Having spent the majority of it on Jem's lap, exploring his mouth and neck and any other accessible areas, she was extremely aware of just how keen he was to reach their honeymoon destination. She felt the same way, but neither of them had wanted their first time to be in a carriage. The result was that she'd never been so hot and bothered in her entire life.

'It should be unlocked,' Jem announced when they finally descended from the carriage.

'It looks lovely.' Nancy smiled as she looked around. There was smoke coming from two of the chimneys. 'Like somebody's home.'

'I expect Beatrix arranged for it to be made ready.' Jem glanced over his shoulder and waved as the carriage rolled away.

'Wait!' Nancy spun around in alarm. 'What about our luggage?'

'Someone from the lodge will bring it over tomorrow. I've got everything we need for to-night in here.' He held up a brown leather bag.

'But why don't we just bring it in now? It won't be completely dark for a little while yet.'

'Nancy.' Jem pushed the front door open, tossed the bag inside and put his hands on her waist. 'How long have we known each other?'

'That depends on what you mean by knowing each other. We met eight years ago.'

'And how long since the first time we kissed?'

'Six years?'

'And how long since I made you that offer?'

'About three months?'

'Exactly. And I've been wanting to take you to bed ever since. The luggage can go to hell, as far I'm concerned.'

'Oh.' She batted her eyelashes coquettishly. 'So are you saying that you *don't* want a cup of tea first?'

He narrowed his eyes broodingly and then bent down, grasping her hips and tipping her over his shoulder.

'I thought you were supposed to carry me in your arms!' she protested, swatting at the backs of his legs with her hands. 'Not like a sack!'

'It's your fault for goading me.' He kicked the door shut behind them and started up the main staircase. 'Besides, I'm used to carrying sacks.'

'You wouldn't do this if I were a duchess.'

'I might if I wanted to take a duchess to bed. Fortunately, I've never been tempted.'

'Good! Considering who my friends are, that's a huge relief.'

He swung her back to the ground as they reached the landing upstairs. 'I never had eyes for anyone else, not really. There was only ever you.'

'You must be crazy.' She lifted her arms up and looped them around his neck.

'I've wondered about that a few times myself.'

'I'm glad that you are. Not to mention patient.' She pushed herself up on her tiptoes, letting her gaze roam all over his face, taking in every beloved detail. 'There was only ever you for me, too. It's hard to believe that we're finally together.'

'Speaking of which...?'

He opened another door and led her into one of the upstairs chambers. It was large and lit up with a roaring fire, in front of which was the bed, a plain wooden frame with a deep mattress covered in a white linen counterpane and sprinkled with hundreds upon hundreds of white and red rose petals.

'Beatrix really has thought of everything.' Nancy took a step towards it, trailing her fingers across the frame.

'Nancy.' Jem's voice sounded rough. 'I know I said that it's been a long time, but I can wait longer if you're not ready. I don't want you to feel as if you can't say no.'

'I'm ready.' She spun around, unfastening her bonnet and tossing it across the room.

'Are you certain?'

She unbuttoned her pelisse and pulled it down over her shoulders. 'Completely.'

He didn't ask a third time, tearing his cravat, jacket and waistcoat away and wrenching his shirt over his head in one swift, surprisingly fluid movement. By her calculations, the whole process took less than twenty seconds.

'Oh.' She felt her lips part at the sight of his bare chest. She'd imagined it enough times, but her imagination hadn't done him justice. He seemed to be all muscle and sinew, with just a faint dusting of hair, tapering downwards in a kind of arrow towards his trousers.

'Now what?' She had to force herself to breathe evenly.

'Now we get you out of that dress.' He took

a step forward and reached behind her, close enough so that their bodies were almost, but not quite touching, drawing at the laces at the back of her gown.

'And now?' She wiggled her shoulders, then her hips, letting the fabric drop to the floor.

'Your chemise.'

'What about your trousers?'

'They're next.'

'How about we do both together?'

He inhaled sharply as she unfastened the falls on his trousers, then heard herself echo the sound as he caught at the hem of her chemise, drawing it over her head.

'Now we get into bed?' She was faintly alarmed by the strangled sound of her own voice. They were both naked now, standing face to face, still not quite touching.

'Now we get into bed,' he agreed. And then they *were* touching and then somehow they were in bed, under the covers, and she couldn't have articulated any more questions if she'd tried. All she wanted to do was revel in the feeling of his skin against hers, in the weight of his body pressing her down into the mattress, in the soft sweep and caress of his lips and tongue as they explored her mouth.

'Nancy.' He broke the kiss finally, his voice deep and husky. 'I can't wait any longer.'

'Me neither.' She nodded as he nudged her legs apart and positioned himself over her, his dark eyes gazing down into hers with an expression so fierce and tender that she couldn't resist taking his face in her hands and pressing her lips to his with a whisper. 'I'm certain.'

He gave a guttural groan and then thrust forward, pushing inside her with a slow, steady pressure. She cried out as her body tightened around him, then clamped her arms around his waist, pulling him deeper when it seemed as if he was about to withdraw.

'Nancy?' He moaned her name as he filled her.

'Yes.' She sucked in a breath, taking a few moments to get used to the sensation. The immediate pain was easing already, replaced by a hot, wet sensation, one that made her want to move against him. So she did, and then they were both moving, rolling and writhing around the bed in perfect accord, the movements coming so naturally that she felt as though they'd been made for each other.

She kissed him and he kissed her and then they were lying on their sides and then she was on top of him, rolling herself back and forth and arching her back as the friction between them built to a fever pitch. And then something inside her seemed to burst, sending hot pulses shooting out through her body, all building towards a feeling that was half pleasure, half pain, deep in her core, more intense than anything she'd ever felt before.

She cried out, collapsing on top of him at the same moment as he gave one last thrust and shuddered inside her.

'If I'd known it was like that, I would have accepted your offer years ago.' She laid her cheek against his chest, panting and limp. 'I would never have waited so long.'

'Now she tells me.'

'Was it worth it?'

'What do you think?' He lifted his head with a lopsided grin. 'Every single moment.'

'We have a problem.' Nancy shook Jem's shoulder gently.

'What is it?' He lurched upright, sending her sprawling across the bed.

'Ow!'

'Sorry.' He leaned over, scooping her back into his arms. 'I was asleep.'

'I know. You were smiling.'

'I was having a dream. A good one.' He grinned

sheepishly before rubbing a hand over his face. 'What time is it?'

'I've no idea. That's the problem.' She gestured towards the window. The curtains were still open, letting in enough moonlight for her to make out the lines of his face, but that was all. 'The fire's gone out, we're in a strange house and we have no idea where the tinderbox is.'

'We don't need another fire.' He tightened his arms around her, using his body as a blanket. 'We can keep each other warm.'

'But I'm hungry.'

'All right.' He chuckled. 'Wait here and I'll see what I can do.'

'I'll come with you.'

'Oh, no, you won't.' He tucked the bedcovers back in around her shoulders as she started to get up. 'Believe it or not, I came prepared. Just wait here and you'll see.'

'Be careful on the stairs!' she called out as he pulled his trousers on and made for the door, snuggling back against her pillows to wait. Fortunately, it wasn't long before he returned, the brown leather bag slung over one shoulder.

'Champagne? I don't have glasses, but we can drink from the bottle.'

'That sounds like fun.' She patted the space on

the bed beside her, smiling lazily as he popped the cork.

'We're just lucky the bottle didn't break when I hurled the bag inside earlier. I was too distracted to worry about it at the time.'

'You *were* rather enthusiastic. Not that I'm complaining.'

'Good. Ladies first.' He passed her the bottle. 'Now, as for something to eat. I brought a small present for you. Just promise me you won't be offended.'

'Why would I be offended by a present?'

'Because…' He reached into the bag and then tossed something small and round into her lap. 'I thought it was appropriate. For us.'

'What is it? A ball?' She stared down at the mystery object for a few seconds before erupting into peals of laughter. 'An orange!'

'That's a relief.' Jem sat down on the bed beside her.

'Did you think I might lose my temper?'

'It's been known to happen.'

'Not any more. I'm being calm and ladylike these days, remember? I'm going to be the most docile wife you could possibly imagine.'

'Don't you dare. I want you just the way you are. Now, what else do we have…?' He rummaged inside the bag again and drew out a box.

'Ah, here we are. Belle's finest biscuits, baked only yesterday by the distinguished hands of the Duke of Howden and the Earl of Staunton.'

'That still sounds bizarre.'

'I know.' He took a swig of champagne before offering the box to her. 'Here. Call it a midnight feast.'

'Mmm.' She took a bite and then froze, midchew. 'I'm afraid we might need to call off the honeymoon.'

'Why?'

'Because they've forgotten the sugar. We need to get back to Bath before they start selling these.'

'Too late.'

'Oh, dear.' Nancy shook her head regretfully. 'At this rate, I might not have a shop to go back to.'

'Actually, about that…we haven't really discussed the future.' He snuggled up beside her. 'Do you still want to keep on running *Belles*? Now that we're married, I mean?'

'Of course. What else would I do?'

'You could always come and work with me?'

Nancy pursed her lips, considering. It might be nice, spending each day together. On the other hand, she liked managing her own shop… 'Maybe one day, but for now, I still love working at Belles. It was the first place where I really felt happy being me. I'm not ready to leave yet.'

'Then don't. You don't even have to move out if you don't want to. I'll move in.'

She looked at him in surprise. 'You wouldn't mind?'

'Nancy, I've lived above a shop my entire life. Why on earth would I mind?'

'I thought you might prefer your own rooms. Or a house.'

'Not if it means dragging you away from a place where you're happy. We'll just be happy there together. The only condition is that you get a new assistant. You work far too hard and I want you to have energy left for the evenings.'

'Any particular reason?'

'I'll show you again in a minute.'

She laughed and curled her legs across his lap, tipping her head against his shoulder as he wrapped an arm around her. 'Actually, it's already taken care of. I offered Kitty Palmer a job last week.'

'So Belles has a new shopgirl?'

'It does and I think she's going to fit in perfectly.' She reached for the bottle of champagne and raised it. 'To our new home. To Belles.'

Epilogue

~~~~~~~~~~~~~~~~~~~~

Belles Biscuit Shop, Bath—eight years later,
1815

'No, no, no! You need to mix the butter and sugar first!'

Nancy stacked some boxes under the counter and smiled as the strident tones of her seven-year-old daughter Matilda drifted through from the kitchen.

'Don't tell me she's scolding them again?' Jem came in the front door of Belles at that moment. 'We're raising a harridan.'

'I'm afraid she might actually be worse than I am.' Nancy grinned, walking into his arms and folding hers around him. 'Only I get the funny impression they're both enjoying it.'

'You might be right.' Jem twisted sideways, peering through the hallway to where young

William Delaney and Charles Roxbury, the future Earl of Staunton and Duke of Howden respectively, were busy doing exactly what they were told. 'They both look besotted. I think our daughter could join the aristocracy some day if she wants to.'

'Stranger things have happened, although I think she might be more interested in becoming Mrs Antonio Fortini.' Nancy rolled her eyes. 'Have you noticed that she never gives him orders?'

'Only because they know each other too well. He's learned how to ignore her. *And* he has a twin sister to keep him in line. Chloe's almost a match for Matilda. Whereas those two are only here on a visit.'

'We'll see. Is everything ready at Henrietta's?'

'Yes, that's why I'm here. The others are all waiting, only we should probably let our little apprentices finish what they're doing first. The birthday party can wait.'

'You don't know Samuel's grandmother very well, do you? She was belligerent and outspoken long before she turned eighty-eight.' Nancy laughed and then sighed dreamily. 'I want to be just like her some day.'

'The title of Dowager Baroness aside, I'm sure

you will be.' Jem placed a hand on her stomach. 'Are we going to tell everyone our news tonight?'

'No. I don't want to steal Lady Jarrow's thunder. Besides, we should probably tell Matilda first.'

'In which case, everyone else will find out five minutes later.' He lowered his head, rubbing his nose against hers. 'All right, if that's what you want.'

'It is.' She rubbed his nose back. 'By the way, I think this one's a boy. It feels different from last time.'

'I don't mind either way.'

'Really? You don't want a son to carry on the family business?'

'Why would I need one when I already have a perfectly competent daughter? I don't care if I'm overwhelmed with fierce, redheaded women. The more, the better, as far as I'm concerned.'

'Be careful what you wish for.' Nancy leaned forward and kissed him. 'I love you, Jem Redbourne. Now let's go and save those poor boys from our daughter.'

* * * * *

COMING SOON!

We really hope you enjoyed reading this book.
If you're looking for more romance, be sure to
head to the shops when new books are
available on

Thursday 21ˢᵗ July

To see which titles are coming soon, please visit
millsandboon.co.uk/nextmonth

MILLS & BOON

MILLS & BOON®

Coming next month

THE EARL'S MYSTERIOUS LADY
Louise Allen

Cressida was sitting up and wearing a loose gown that Guy recognised as a *robe de chambre*.

'Mrs Grainger sent one of the maids to collect some clothes for me,' she said with a smile. Guy suspected it was forced. 'Will you sit down?'

'No. Thank you. I came to apologise and that is best done standing at a distance.'

'In case I throw something at you?' There was an acid tinge to the smile now.

'In case I succumb to temptation again,' Guy said frankly. 'I should not have kissed you the other day.'

'I kissed you back.' Cressida sounded angry, although whether at him or herself, or both, he could not tell. 'I was not so weak that I was unable to say no. I wanted you to kiss me, but we know perfectly well it can go no further.'

'We do?' Guy sat down on the nearest chair and tried to read Cressida's expression. 'You have every reason to expect consequences.'

'An improper proposal?'

'A respectable one,' Guy said stiffly. 'You are a lady.'

'You are the heir to a marquess. I would have to be deluded if I thought your intentions towards me included marriage, Lord Easton.'

'I had no *intentions*,' he retorted. 'I acted on instinct

and attraction and I should have thought first. For which I apologise.'

'Accepted.' She looked away from him, out across the front lawn.

'Perhaps it would be best, to avoid any further misunderstandings, if I assure you that I have no intention of marrying anyone. Neither would I accept an irregular relationship from you or any other man.'

'But why? I mean, I am not so arrogant that I imagine you would want to marry me for myself and I acquit you entirely of scheming for a title, let alone envisaging an *affaire*, but why are you set on remaining single?'

'For an independently-minded woman of comfortable means spinsterhood seems to me to be a perfectly reasonable state.'

'Should a woman of means find herself without offers of marriage, I can see that it is. But why assume that you will never encounter a man you would wish to marry?'

'What I wish has nothing to do with it. We must all live according to the situation we find ourselves in.' She looked back at him at last and smiled faintly.

Guy found himself staring at the twist of those soft lips. He knew now how they tasted, how they felt beneath the pressure of his.

Continue reading
THE EARL'S MYSTERIOUS LADY
Louise Allen

Available next month
www.millsandboon.co.uk

MILLS & BOON

THE HEART OF ROMANCE

A ROMANCE FOR EVERY READER

MODERN

Prepare to be swept off your feet by sophisticated, sexy and seductive heroes, in some of the world's most glamourous and romantic locations, where power and passion collide.

HISTORICAL

Escape with historical heroes from time gone by. Whether your passion is for wicked Regency Rakes, muscled Vikings or rugged Highlanders, awaken the romance of the past.

MEDICAL

Set your pulse racing with dedicated, delectable doctors in the high-pressure world of medicine, where emotions run high and passion, comfort and love are the best medicine.

True Love

Celebrate true love with tender stories of heartfelt romance, from the rush of falling in love to the joy a new baby can bring, and a focus on the emotional heart of a relationship.

Desire

Indulge in secrets and scandal, intense drama and plenty of sizzling hot action with powerful and passionate heroes who have it all: wealth, status, good looks…everything but the right woman.

HEROES

Experience all the excitement of a gripping thriller, with an intense romance at its heart. Resourceful, true-to-life women and strong, fearless men face danger and desire - a killer combination!

To see which titles are coming soon, please visit

millsandboon.co.uk/nextmonth

JOIN US ON SOCIAL MEDIA!

Stay up to date with our latest releases, author
news and gossip, special offers and discounts, and
all the behind-the-scenes action
from Mills & Boon...

 millsandboon

 millsandboonuk

 millsandboon

It might just be true love...